WONDERLAND

a novel

MAX EIDELMAN

PART ONE

PERSEPHONE

THE FLOWER SHOP

Pangaea's purple hair seems an extension of the flowers around her. She holds a bundle of pinks and yellows, trimming the stems.

The yellow: Good day for a haircut.

The pink: As good as any, I guess.

Pangaea: Stay still. You don't want me decapitating you by accident.

Pink: Wouldn't want that now.

Yellow: I'd prefer not.

Flowers cover the walls of the shop and line the aisles that are set up lattice-like within.

There's no apparent ordering to the placement, other than where some flowers fit here and some there. The flowers tend to talk more freely when the shop is empty, though they're always happy to chat with Pan.

Pink: Ouch! Is that a guillotine in your hand, Jacques, or are you just being careless? Last time you gave me a trim, you—

Pink stifles as its attention is arrested by a mother and daughter who've entered the flower shop.

"Remember, sweetie, when we get to the hospital, you tell Aunty, 'Congratulations! He's beautiful!'"

"But, Mommy, what if the baby's ugly?"

"He won't be. Now, let's pick out some flowers."

Mom strokes her daughter's hair, guiding her into the chaos of color that constitutes the shop.

Pan postpones the barbershop treatment and approaches the woman. "Hi there, can I help you find anything?"

"Well, we're on our way to Brigham's. My sister just had a baby and—"

"Oh, I'm so sorry to hear that." She covers her mouth once she realizes her words. "I'm sorry. I mean, that's wonderful. Really." *Some people, in fact, want kids*, she reminds herself.

She looks at Pan dubiously as the girl giggles. "Right...thank you. So, we're on our way to see her, and I'm here to pick up some flowers."

"Of course, of course. There anything you have in mind?" *Since, after all, not every mom is like you.*

"Well, I'm just looking for a colorful bouquet." She surveys the shop, letting her MyAIs analyze the flowers and blurb descriptions behind the lenses. "They're all so beautiful. Anything in particular you like?"

"If it were me," Pan leads them through the aisles, "I'd probably go for some apple blossoms and irises." *I wonder, if you saw me through those, would the description say 'daughter'?* "I think these would be nice to have if I were yanked afresh from the womb." She again covers her mouth after hearing her thoughts vocalized.

The girl giggles, and the mom looks at Pan quizzically. "Excuse me?"

And even if it did, would that be anything more to you than just a word?

"I'm sorry. Here," she says, trying to mute her thoughts. She holds some samples, gesturing them toward the mom to hold and sniff for herself. "They really are beautiful flowers."

But it's not the same woman in front of her anymore. It's Pangaea's mother. Lena takes the flowers.

Mmmmmm. She sniffs them. *Oh, great choice, Pan. Something about these flowers always smells like...like April, you know? That time of year when—*

"When birth and death are the same." Pan sees her reflection in her mother's eyes, wondering just how much of her is still in there behind the irises.

"Excuse me?"

Pan startles as the vision of her mother vanishes only to bring the woman back into focus.

No, the truth is, there's probably nothing in you that you ever saw in me.

"I'm so sorry." Pan regains her composure. "I was just thinking about, uh." She can feel the blush crimsoning her cheeks, then sees the girl holding her mother's hand. "I'm sorry. It's just, something about these flowers always reminds me that birth is the other end of death. One flower dies only for another generation to grow from the decay. I think they're perfect for a newborn."

"Right...," the mom replies, staring at Pan uneasily and clutching her daughter a bit closer. "You know, I think I'll just go with the tulips and roses."

Pan watches them leave once the transaction is complete and holds the door for Isaac, who's just now coming back from lunch.

"What a bouquet! They getting those for any special occasion?" he asks and checks on some azaleas.

"Birthday party." Pan heads back to the apple blossoms.

"Ah," he makes his way through the aisles, "love to hear it."

Isaac continues to talk, but Pan's attention falls into the center of the flowers she's just picked back up. *Where were we.* She stares at the stem as a green flicker pulses within. The density of the surrounding flora thickens, and a forest musk, damp with vegetative decay and birth, silhouettes itself into her nostrils as the shop becomes a jungle, Issacs's voice nothing more than an echo from a future unstamped on this world's dirt. *There you are.* Pan sees her mother's face in the bouquet, the face she's seen in photos and dreams for twenty-seven years. She hears her mother's voice: *I used to sleep on the floor of the shop,* Lena says from the center of the flower, *and stare up at the sky, the wild stars galloping in the night.*

What happened? The vision of a night sky, her mother's vision some night so many years ago, paints its way across Pan's eyes as she's transported into the memory the flowers have held: vines zigzag over the floor of the shop; the only luminescence borrowed from the citylight and the swan song shimmer of starlight over Boston. Ancient breath of plants in the dark. *What happened,* she asks again, *that made you go?*

Lena reaches through the flower and strokes her daughter's hair. The grip is mere shadow, but Pan smells April in her nostrils as her mother says, *Go?* She twirls Pan's hair, now wistaria and hyacinth, scarlet runner bean. *The seeds of a plant never go away. They just grow. Is any life that begets another ever separate from it?* Pan tries not to dwell on the words, but only hear the voice. *I'm still with you here, aren't I?* The vines blossom and sprout, obscuring Lena's face as her words become nothing more than a murmur behind mountains.

Pangaea sinks deeper into the plants' history, feeling the tectonic shift of eons crash and divide the soil, the beehive hum of human voices learning to shout. *So you would have me believe I'm somehow you?* She loosens her grip, and the reality of the shop returns to Pan's sight as the jungle wilts. *That you and me are just fractals of the same body?* She looks down from the petals to the stem. *That the way life spreads through plants is the same for us? That's all life is?* Then, despite herself, Pan wonders, *But is that all life is? Some endless iteration of flesh doomed to wilt and rot, only to leave behind a seed for another flesh to do the same? Is life just the creation of anything that ends?* She looks for Lena in the flowers but just sees colors. The smell of water and dirt and the tenacious pulse of life that ripples through the plants around her as the memory fades. *Or is the truth just the simple fact that you're not here? That life is just as simple as being here and then not being here?*

"Pan?" Isaac asks, standing next to his daughter, who's staring trance-like into the flower. She looks at her dad but neither speaks. They let the gaze between their eyes talk instead:

Isaac: *Bury her from your mind. She's not out there.*

Pan: *Did she choose to leave? Or could she not've done anything else?*

"Listen," he begins the schmaltz she's heard before, could probably recite, "I don't know what I can tell you. If you keep her in your thoughts, if you keep hoping to find a mom who isn't there, then she'll just keep haunting you."

And that's what I want her to do, she wants to say, *that way, if all she'll ever be to me is a ghost, dead, then she might as well have never been alive at all. Which means I've never needed her.* But what she tells him instead is, "I don't think we choose our ghosts. I think it's the other way around," and she hands him the flowers, the memory drained dry.

He can only stare at Pan and wish he knew what to say, twirling the flower in a fidget. "How about you go home. I'll close up, all right? You've been here all day."

She's surprised for a moment, then remembers, *Well, not like he can ever maintain a serious conversation beyond a few sentences anyway.* "All right. I'll see you back home."

Pan steps outside, her senses acclimating to the concrete gray of Government Center. The buildings' windows cycle through advertisements, sunsetting the sky in a synthetic sepia spectrum. Pan walks toward the station to hop on the Blue Line back to Wonderland. She's so accustomed to the noise of people's MyAIs that she doesn't hear the ads speaking through the glasses perched atop nearly everyone's face. She distracts herself by tuning into the chorus of Government Center's concrete eye pollution, which Alvin once pointed out is best heard through a Yiddish filter:

Boston City Hall: *Veyzmeer, you'd think they'd renovate my plumbing, if nothing else.*

The intersection of State and Congress: *What're you kvetching about? My roads are still built for horse and buggy.*

The JFK Federal: *Both of you be quiet. I look like I've been transplanted from the Soviet Bloc.*

And to think, some shmucks see these buildings and don't hear them, Pan remembers Alvin saying on one of their earlier dates. *And to think,* she had replied, *some people can hold a flower and only hear silence.* She pulls out her phone, about to call him.

"Oh, excuse me." A man bumps into her, his glasses falling to the ground.

"No worries." Pan bends to pick them up and inadvertently sees the advertisement playing across the interior of the lens. She can't make out what's displayed but hears: "Opening soon, a place where, truly, you can live any fantasy you desire. A place where you can bring anything you want—to life."

Hey, that's the same ad that was—

"Thank you." The man takes back his glasses, hastily putting them back on as if blind without them.

That's the same ad that's been peppering me. Oy, speaking of, I wonder if Ellis was finally able to put that ad blocker in. She had given him her glasses a few weeks ago.

You know they make life so much easier, right? Like, you have the power of all search engines right on your head. And you don't have to take out your phone and press anything. It's just linked to Human Solutions' algorithm of your search habits. She remembers Ellis breaking his own rule and venturing out of his house the day the glasses were made available.

And you know, Pan had replied, *that those things are literally a way for them to paint their own world over your eyes, right? They can put anything they want into your head.*

That's how the world's always been, Pan. It's just a different "they."

Look, I get that it's the future, but I think we're moving in the wrong direction. Instead of trying to bottle our idea of life into some screen, we should be trying to listen to the life that breathes in the world around us. The thing about plants is they never die, and there's no such thing as parent or child. It's just...life. Spreading from root to root.

Lena: *But you don't really believe that, do you?*

Pan tries to mute Lena as she steps onto the train. *Her voice is no more real than the electric chatter of everything else.*

"Next stop: Government Center," the bus's automated voice reminds her.

After a long breath, Pan begins to stare at reflections trapped in the windows, waiting to hear what they have to say. With discretion, she looks at the reflection of a woman sitting a few seats to her left. She notices exhaustion in the woman's cheeks, the dumbbell weight of the bags beneath her eyes and the cloudy look of makeup that's been pummeled by the day. Pan hears the woman's reflection ask, *Of all the whys that have brought me to this moment, is there anywhere it's all going? Is there a destination? Or is it just a continuation of the same Here, simply erasing the future in the portrait of Now?*

"Government Center. Next stop, State Street."

The train halts, and the woman departs, taking her reflection with her.

How much different can a reflection be from the body it shares? Pan wonders. *Or is it actually—*

Lena: *Is there anywhere you're going, though? Is there any Why that brings you wherever you are?*

Pangaea: *Yeah, home. Since where else can I go to mute all the noise?*

She stares at her reflection but doesn't hear Lena, only silence.

Pangaea: *Right. That's always been your specialty—silence. Since whenever I've actually needed to hear you, I've only heard myself.*

Dad, I'm telling you! Hold them and you'll see. The flowers are alive. They talk to me. Sometimes it's Mom's voice I hear in them.

Sweetie, what've I told you before about letting your imagination run away with you? Even all these years later, Pan can still hear how he had said *if you're not careful with it, you'll lose the world.*

Lena: *All I can tell you is it's easier to find direction when you're moving. Like this train. You know where it's going to take you.*

The T resumes its movement, and Pan closes her eyes, telling herself, *All we have to do is carry ourselves through the day until the moment at night when the sun closes its lid and promises that, if we do the same, somehow being awake tomorrow is better than the dream of tonight.*

A federal bulletin plays through the T's speaker: "Five years into the Maternity Pact's enrollment, we've seen nearly a fifty percent reduction in infant mortality among the indigent population. We've even begun to curb our previously declining birth rates. Just like we took manufacturing back from China and perfected it here, soon we'll take back pride in having the healthiest, most productive population too."

She tries to mute the voice by staring out the window, looking at the familiar trainscape as it approaches Wonderland Station.

Is that how we lost Mom? She can see Isaac's face just as clearly now as she had as a child. *Did she lose the world?*

Lena: *Is that why you ride the same train every day? Walk the same streets and sleep in the same bed? Because you're afraid you'll lose your bearings if you take even one step outside of what you know?*

Pan, Isaac had told her, *there's nothing in those plants other than the cells that build them. Mom isn't in there. And if you keep indulging these fantasies—*

They're not fantasies, trying so hard not to cry that nausea percolated bile in her throat, the acid burn of elementary school pride, *I'm telling you, she's in the plants. Nothing feels more alive than when I hold these. No. It's more like, like everything feels alive when I hold them.*

She stares through her reflection out the window as the T begins to slow. *What the hell is that place gonna be?* She looks at the construction across the street, where the dog track used to be as the train stops.

"Last stop: Wonderland."

She gets off and walks toward the parking garage. Electric billboards covering the walls filter through different landscapes every minute. As Pangaea walks up the floors she moves from the tropics to Antarctica in a matter of steps. *If you still have to commute to work*, the ads used to run, *then at least make it a journey. Travel the world without stepping on a plane.*

She heads toward her car, deciding to make a pit stop at Devorah's apartment to ease her worries. *There's no way it's registered in her head yet. That's the only explanation why she's still so calm about it. That or the weed. Or shrooms. Assuming, I guess, that she's responsible enough not to drink alcohol.* Pan takes her phone out to call Devorah but stops when she sees a woman in a Dior suit approach. *Strange. She isn't wearing a pair of MyAIs.*

"Hello, do you have a moment?"

"Look, thanks for whatever you're offering, but I'm not—"

"Believe me, I understand. I'm accosting you out of nowhere. Please, bear with me? I'd just like to ask you a few questions, and I assure you, I won't be long."

My God...her eye. Pan notices the woman's left-eye: iris-less and glass. A blank globe.

The woman speaks on, but her words are lost on Pan.

Can she see out of it? Wait, shit, shit. I'm staring.

"You know what, sure." Pan tries to look at the woman's other eye and not be rude but can only focus on trying not to stare. "Go ahead."

"Thank you. I appreciate your time. Please let me to introduce myself. My name is Persephone. May I ask you for your name?"

"Pangaea Green."

"Excellent. Let me tell you a bit about myself, Pangaea. I'm guessing you've heard of the company I work for: Human Solutions." She pauses, giving Pan a moment to admit she has, indeed, heard of the company that introduced the MyAI line of products.

"Yeah, I think I've heard of the only company that gives Apple a run for it."

"Well, that's not how we like to think of ourselves." She does a terrible job hiding her smug smile. "But I notice you don't seem to be wearing one of our products?"

"Well, I've been getting peppered by ads that I've specifically indicated I'm not interested in. And, don't take it personally, but sometimes it's nice to see the world through my own eyes, rather than something else's filter. I like to tell myself I'm still in touch with reality."

Persephone grins. "One thing at a time, I suppose. But we'll get to that in a moment. What I'd like to speak with you about is actually the building across the street. Surely, you've noticed the construction that's been going on over there." She nudges to the decrepit Wonderland Greyhound Park sign that's remained standing in the decades since the track was demolished. "That, too, is one of our projects. A new line. The name shouldn't surprise you. We're calling it Wonderland. What we're designing is a product that allows customers to immerse themselves in a virtual experience of their own design. And we'd like for you to participate in the test run. There's no danger, and we're seeking people to test its performance. The AI obviously—"

"Whoa, whoa, whoa. Slow down. What are you talking about?"

"There's only so much I can say until you formally accept this proposition. Excuse me, *unless* you formally accept. What I can tell you is this: we have successfully created a product that allows you to experience an immersive simulation of your own design. We, of course, must test this out before opening to the public."

"What do you mean, 'an experience'?"

"Well, you're getting into semantics here, but another way to phrase it is: a digitally designed simulation."

"Like…on a computer screen?"

"More like *in* a computer screen. For lack of a better phrase."

"And what, um," she can sense Lena's about to speak, "what exactly do you want from me?" but mutes the voice.

"It's quite simple, really. We're curious to see how people use our product and how they react to it. Like anything made for consumption, it's important to see how a sample population responds before we introduce it to the general populace. It's a privilege to be among the first people to experience what we've worked so hard to create. Should you accept the proposition, that is. I do, however, understand why some people might hesitate. There are some who still tremble at the advancements we make in engineered intelligence."

Whatever you say, Pan. Call this all movement.

"Like I said, I try to keep the chatter away. Maintain my own filter. So, again, with all respect, this isn't my kind of thing."

Pan is about to walk past the woman, but she holds her ground. But somehow it's not entirely obstructive, this stubborn proximity between the two.

"I understand. But if I may, I don't think you're seeing the whole picture. You say you want to maintain control of your perception of the world. That you don't want it filtered."

Pan tries to smother the seed of curiosity growing in her. "Let's just say I don't like the idea of rendering the world I see into an advertising board."

"All the more to my point then. This product doesn't distort reality. It *creates* one. *You* create one. Wouldn't you like to create your own world? Wouldn't you like to design something exactly how you see fit? Not just some image on your computer or even some landscape in a headset. Not some world that corporations are funneling into your head or propaganda that the government wants to grip your brain with but a whole world where you can do and be anything *you* imagine."

Because this is my world, Pan is back in the flower shop, *where the death of one flower is only the birth of another, and so, really, where's the difference.* She blinks her own voice out of her head.

Persephone continues. "Wouldn't you like a chance to do that? To truly live in your own world?"

For a moment, the two simply look at each other.

"And I guess the last thing I'll say in my little pitch here is this. Change always happens. That's a fact. People have always had to choose, and always will, if they want to embrace what is destined or cling to what is obsolete. The past is just a fantasy for people afraid to embrace the present, and the future isn't made by looking behind. It's made by those who see ahead and work to bring the present to that vision. Now, you don't have to say yes or no just yet, but a week from today, we'll need your answer. You must understand, we're operating on a schedule and plan to begin the beta run this month." Persephone hands her a business card with *Wonderland* in curving pink and green font, along with contact information. "It was wonderful speaking with you, and I hope to hear from you soon."

DEVORAH'S IMAGINARY STOMACH

"You all right? You look a bit pinched." Devorah opens the door for Pan.

"Yeah." She makes her way to Devorah's frayed couch, tufts of white fuzz foaming out. Dried food crumbles off it as she situates herself in the solidified miasma of leather. She doesn't even notice the smell. *A week from today.* She hears Persephone's voice but can only picture the glass eye when she tries to recall the face. *Why am I even thinking about it? It's not like I'll say yes.*

"I'm fine. Isaac let me loose early today, and I just don't wanna head straight home."

"Fine by me. Not like I'm gonna be going anywhere the next nine months." Dev's vacant gaze is directed at the TV as she sucks on her Juul. Pan looks over the coffee table littered with stems, spliff tobacco, crumbs, crumpled soda cans, a little flowerpot filled to the brim with cigarette butts, some of which have lipstick kissed on the filters.

Lena: *You're right, why would you say yes? Why would you say yes to a chance to step out of this bubble of yours?*

Pangaea: *Is that how you justified leaving me and Dad? That it was a just a matter of stepping outside some bubble? That there weren't any lives your choices would affect?*

And at the thought, Pan looks at Devorah's stomach. Over the weeks since Dev had told her she was pregnant, Pan's eyes have been magnetically pulled toward her stomach, which looks no different now than before but is simultaneously more pronounced than ever.

"You know," Dev notices Pan's glance, "I think I already have a name in mind."

"Yeah?" Pan welcomes the distraction. "You're due in, like, November. It's only April."

"Yeah, I know, but I have to start getting my head around it. I'm leaning toward Page."

"Page?"

"Yeah."

"I mean, that's a nice name and all, but why?"

"From Phish. You know?"

Pangaea snort-chuckles and is about to embark upon the debate she and Dev have carried on since high school, whether '94 was in fact the better year for the band than '97, but her thoughts are pulled by the commercial on the screen:

"…a place where, truly, you can live any fantasy you desire. A place where you can bring anything you want to life. Easy access on the Blue Line. Whether it's your last stop or first—your destination can always be Wonderland."

"Holy shit. I was just…"

"Huh?"

It's not like I'm going to do it. It's just, that's not me. I wouldn't do that. "Nothing. Nothing. I was just coming back from Wonderland is all."

Lena: *Right. That goes against your whole luddite persona. Letting her know you might just be interested.*

"Oh. Well, finally they're opening something there. It's been an abandoned lot for what, like, twenty years? Only that sign's stayed up. I'd be interested in going whenever this place opens, but I don't think with this," she pats her tummy, "that's going to happen any time soon. It's funny: the biggest thing I haven't planned for has taken care of any plans I may've had."

Pan can feel the doubt spread across her face as she watches Devorah suck down her Juul, the smell of weed perpetually in the air; Trulys and Claws overflowing the trash can. She remembers the call:

Pan, Pan!

Jesus, Dev. You're screaming. What?

I'm fucking pregnant.

No.

That call was only two weeks ago, but *she won't really understand what it means until the end. Maybe not even then. Even if somehow she does bring this thing to term and holds it, I don't know if she'll really understand it's a life in her hands.*

"At least I have this delightful shit to fill my time with." Devorah uses her foot to scooch a little pamphlet on the coffee table to Pangaea. "They gave me the code for the MyAI's program last week at the Maternity Center. The first of many visits."

Pan picks it up and flips through it. "What the hell is this?" She sees images of women at various stages of pregnancy.

"It's supposed to be a simulated guide through your term. You basically queue the program up to your guestimate conception date, and you have to go through a simulation once a week or so. They call it 'Therapeutic Instruction.' It's supposed mirror whatever you may be going through at that given time. Tough to feel that therapeutic about it when there're mandatory tests at the end of each simulation."

"What if you skip one?"

"You get a few strikes, and your credit score takes a beating. Even though mine's pretty much nonexistent. But I think, first, the Maternity Centers will refuse to give you free medical aid—just little things, antinausea shit and stuff like that—and then another strike after that, and your funding is cut off. So, no more monthly stipend checks. Which kind of spits in the face of the whole 'The Only way to Keep the American Dream Alive Is Life' campaign you see all over the place. And I guess eventually they force you to check in to one of the centers for the remainder of your term if you fuck up too many times. Whatever. The simulations aren't that bad. I did one a few days ago. I can just get high and let it play. It's not like I have to worry about the real thing yet."

Pan finds herself staring at Devorah's stomach again. Her mind's eye fast-forwards to the months when it will indeed appear as a mountain under which life is molding itself into form.

"When do you think that'll change?"

"Huh?" Dev stares at the TV.

"When do you think it'll start to feel like the real thing?"

"I don't know." She pretends to look like what's on the TV demands her attention and speaks with a clear intent to change the subject. "That's just not my world, being a mom. That's not exactly how I envision my life."

Wouldn't you like to design something exactly how you see fit?

"But it is your world." Pan doesn't notice the scorn in her tone. "It's not like you really have a choice. You're pregnant. You're responsible for a life. Even if you didn't want it, it found its way to you. What more do you need to hear?"

"Hey! Don't come at me like that. I know all that. You see me drinking? I haven't had booze since I first did the piss test. Lay off. It's not like I planned this thing. Pretty soon I'm gonna start puking every day, just wait. We'll see how accurate those simulations are then."

"Just saying."

Lena: *Is it her you're talking to you right now?*

"You shouldn't need to wait for anything else to sink in here."

Pan: *Yes. She's the only one actually here.*

"It's your choice when to believe it's alive."

Devorah switches out the Juul for a bowl that's been sitting on the table. "I hear you. Look, let's change the subject, all right? You my fucking therapist or what? If I could abort it, I would. But I can't. That's the Maternity Pact for you. And it looks like I can't give him up for adoption either."

"What? Why not?"

Dev hands her a piece of paper from the rubble on the coffee table. Pangaea reads another pamphlet from the Maternity Center:

"As part of your application for enrolling in the Maternity Pact Adoption Program, you must sign the following terms of agreement, one of which stipulates that Maternity Centers will require conferences and home visits at random checkpoints, with given notice. Prospective adoptive parents are entitled to request, with notice up to twenty-four hours prior, a conference with you at a conveniently located Maternity Center. Urine and blood analyses are expected to be…" Pan crumples up the already crumpled letter and throws it back on the table.

"Fucking Big Brother."

"More like Big Mother." Devorah sighs, patting her stomach and staring into nothing. "How am I gonna do it? How am I gonna *love* it, you know? Like…forever. How can I make myself love someone who doesn't exist yet?"

Lena: *Would you love me if you actually met me? Would seeing me in the flesh be any more meaningful than just seeing me in your head? What if all I could do is disappoint?*

What we're designing is a product that allows customers to immerse themselves in a virtual experience of their own design.

There's only one way to find out. Pan surprises herself with the thought. *Maybe there, maybe in whatever these simulations are, I could find you.*

Lena: *I would still just be in your head. How would a program make me any more alive than I am behind your eyes?*

Dev's phone rings on the coffee table; she uses to her feet to accept the call on speaker.

"Dev. I need you to pick me up," Ivan says, harried.

"How about a 'Hi, baby. How are you doing,' first?"

"I'm not kidding. I need a ride. I'm in Brockton."

"What? You usually just pick weed up in Everett."

"I'm in Brockton. And I need a ride."

"You know I'm pregnant, right? You're the father. Not sure if you've gotten the memo."

"Dev, quit playing around. I'll text you the address. Thanks."

"You really can be a dick, you know that? I'm with Pan, so she's coming too."

"Brockton?" Pan asks. "That's South Shore; there be dragons. What the hell's he doing there?"

"No clue." Dev gets up. "You can drive, though, right?"

Pan tries focusing on the road as she drives them to Ivan. She watches the blur of the pavement, immobile beneath her, noticing how *the mirage of the road always seems so close, up ahead* she stares at the lane partitions, watching them approach and then fall behind *right there then right there and then right there again but never here. Like the shimmer of a horizon that always seems so close.*

Lena: *Are you so sure it's me you want to find? Or maybe I'm just some excuse.*

Pangaea: *For what?*

Lena: *For moving in a direction where there's nothing to find.*

"Up here, that's it." Dev points at a crooked, gray-brick building, an infrastructural relic from the nineteenth century that New England hasn't decided to renovate. "All right, I texted him. Should be coming down in a sec. God. What an ugly fucking place."

Pan takes the moment to survey the environs, but it's not the colorless concrete bloc she sees, the warzone potholes pimpling the pavement as memory brings her elsewhere:

"Pull over here," Dev told the Uber driver.

"But, miss, we're not even close to your destination. Amherst is still twenty minutes away."

"I don't care. Right now, buildings are the last thing on Earth I want to see. We'll still pay for the full trip. Pan, come on. Ivan, don't forget the water. I could drink it all right now."

Which made Pan tongue the roof of her dry mouth, the Sahara within somehow dry only as a thought, not a physical reality to feel, the sandpaper sensation just an idea manifesting through her mouth. "I guess I should have some too."

Then the three stepped out of the car, walking into the forest abutting the highway.

"Whoa," Pan looking at the leaves open and close their benevolent fists, fairies eyeing new visitors, "imagine what the shop would be like," she said, Devorah and Ivan a football field away from her, not realizing that she'd been standing still for two minutes without blinking, watching the trees breathe.

"Do you have any more acid I can bring back?" she asked Ivan later as the three sat around a pond, shoes off and bare feet skating atop the late-September water.

"Sure. When we get back to the dorm I can give you a few tabs."

"You just gotta visit more often, Panny. Or fucking apply. I mean, you'd get in. You scored like a twenty-two hundred on your SAT. They'd probably give you a full ride. Not sure how you're not boring yourself to death in the shop all day with your dad. No offense to the guy, I love him, but you're nineteen; you gotta be here. You can't be daddy's little girl forever."

She watched her reflection in the water, opening her mouth and closing it, wondering if the face in the water had words of her own to utter. "If I left him, he'd have no one," which she knew wasn't true, knowing Isaac would love nothing more for her to leave the nest he'd spent nineteen years weaving alone. "I'd just be another woman who came into his life only to leave it." Hearing the maudlin nature of her narrative but allowing herself a rare moment of self-pity, finding this fragmentation-of-identity stage of the trip cathartic.

"I don't think I've ever heard you mention her," Ivan said.

Pan peered a moment longer at her reflection before looking up at him, wondering if her eyes appeared as engulfed in pupil as his.

"Try as I might not to think about my mom, somehow it feels like she's always with me. You know," looking at her palms to see if they were as soaked in sweat as her nerves suggested, "she and Isaac went to college together too. I bet they were even a bit like you both. Only she liked computers and he studied plants." Pan could only see the top of Dev's head as she gazed at the water, maybe interrogating her own reflection. "Strange as it may sound, sometimes when I see you two, I can't help but wonder if I'm seeing an iteration of them." She blushed as she let words slip out. Pan looked up to the sky to forget she had even said it, the clouds swimming through the blue, the sun molting. She cupped her hand around it, testing if the light spilling over her hand could seep into her flesh. If the heat of the sun was within her too.

"Hey." Ivan gets in the car, his voice bringing Pan back there, too. "Didn't know you were with Pan." Frustration in his voice.

"Hey, Ivan," Pan says, the world concreting back to equilibrium as she stares at him in the rearview mirror, noticing the evasiveness of his gaze.

"Didn't mean to rope you into this," he says as he looks through his backpack and then out the window, still not having glanced at either of them.

"You mind telling me just why the fuck we're picking you up here?" Dev asks, which does capture his attention.

"Can we talk about it once we're back in the apartment? I told you I was probably coming here. Or somewhere like here, at least."

Pan can feel the chain reaction bubbling in Dev before she even shouts at Ivan.

"Are you fucking kidding me?! We talked about this! I said, no! I told you no, Ivan!"

"And I told you it wasn't your fucking decision! We talked about it, I gave you a heads-up, and then I went. Don't pretend to be surprised."

"Heroin. You think that's the solution to our problems? You're gonna sell heroin?"

"How the fuck else are we supposed to make enough money for a kid, huh? You think selling weed is gonna cut it?"

"You could get a goddamned job. Ever think of that? What if you got robbed in there? What if you got fucking shot?"

"Well, at least I wouldn't have to worry about your situation anymore."

Pangaea drives as the argument avalanches between Dev and Ivan, but she doesn't hear it, listening instead to:

Isaac: *We both have to commit to the shop is all. Full-time. We can make it work.*

Lena: *Are we going to be able to raise a kid off the shop, Isaac? Do you really think that?*

Isaac: *Honey, I know you love your startup idea, but with this... with a baby on the way, don't you want to make sure we're in a situation to raise her right?*

Lena: *So you want me to give up my life for it? Is what you're saying? To completely give up what makes me happy for a collection of cells that's renting my stomach?*

Isaac: *For 'it'? For 'it'? I'm talking about our baby here, Lena. Not some thing. And you know I'm not saying that you need to put your life on hold. You can still work on your coding as a hobby. I just think we need put all our chips in the shop. I mean, you and I have grown it from the ground up.*

Lena: *Pun intended?* (then, after the tension-breaking kiss) *I just wish—I just wish I could rewrite it, is all. These last few years. Sometimes that's what coding a program feels like. Like a chance to write a new world.*

Isaac: *I know, but having a baby is kind of like that too. You know? A chance for something new. Or maybe it's a way for the world to be new. Through her eyes.*

But who knows if they even had that conversation. If she even gave him that much room to predict she'd leave once I came. Then Pan hears it again in her head: *Wouldn't you like to create your own world?*

Lena: *You already do, don't you?*

Pan tries not to listen to the argument, tries not to let the millwright apocalypse of South Shore architecture blot out the vestiges of greenery gasping outside Boston.

It's not the same. Once a thought is in a screen it's no longer imagination. It's bits of code and electric chatter.

Pan, she remembers Ellis once saying, *why can't it be that all this technology is the realization of human creation? That it's what ingenuity has been leading up to? A chance not to just paint a world or write it out but to fully create it.*

Lena: *You just have to let yourself admit it. That escaping this world is all you ever want to do.*

"It doesn't even matter, Ivan. The reality is that the little fucker doesn't even need to be alive and I'm already its mother."

But it wouldn't be real, Pan tells herself, again wondering if she just might say yes to Persephone after all, *it would just be some delusion.*

Lena: *Just because something's only in your head, does that mean it matters less than anything outside it?*

"You know why?" Devorah tells Ivan, "'cause now his life owns my body more than I ever can. Even though he isn't even real yet. Now all I am is some thing for people to look at and see the idea of life that's otherwise stuck in their head. Since the idea of life is always easier to swallow than the real thing."

ROUTINE VITAMIN

Ellis is sitting in his car, waiting for Lauren.

"Does she ever walk home, or do you always pick her up?" Pangaea asks, sitting shotgun as she adjusts her MyAIs.

The numbers in front of his retina blink 2:45 once they register Pan's question and then fade away.

"Usually, I get her."

Why do I drag her along? he asks himself. *She doesn't want to be here.* He casts a discrete glance at Pan.

You know what she's thinking right now, don't you?

Stop.

She's thinking you have nowhere to go other than home and nothing to do there other than jack off and stare at the TV or your computer. And stuff your gluttonous face. The only reason she's even here is because she needed the glasses back.

Stop.

Ellis's virtual therapist had recently suggested he try to incorporate at least one routine that would get him out of the house. It was his mom's idea for him to take up service as Lauren's elementary-era chauffer.

Pan doesn't like spending time with you. She never has. You're just that pathetic, sad loser she's grown up next to. That three-

hundred-pound monster with ten contacts on his phone who she can hear and smell from a mile away.

Ellis scrunches his eyes to stifle the voices.

You're wrong. And, if Ellis could hear Pan's thoughts, they'd sound like this:

Lena: *Two days left. What's it gonna be?*

Pangaea: *I don't know. It's nothing other than AI make believe. Does the world need any more of it?*

Lena: *Is the make believe of me any more real just because it's not on some screen and only in your head?*

"Hey, guys." Lauren gets in the car.

"Hey, you. Here, two squirts each hand." He passes his sister a bottle of hand sanitizer.

"What took you so long?"

Lauren hands back the bottle.

Ellis rubs his own hands together after an application to each palm. Pan doesn't even have to be asked; she knows that she, too, is expected to apply sanitizer whenever a person comes in contact with Ellis.

"You came just in the nick of time, Laur'. We were about to drive off without you, but then we remembered we need you for the ransom money," Pan says via the rearview mirror.

Lauren sticks out her tongue. "I had some questions for Eva, is all."

"Eva," Ellis says with some awe, checking his blind spot before pulling out. "Imagine if they had those things when we were her age."

"We're not supposed to call them that," Lauren says.

"What, 'Things'?" Pangaea says.

"On the first day of school, Principle Neely said that Adam and Eva were no different from our other teachers. That they have the same feelings as we do. Adam teaches the sixth-graders though so maybe I'll have him in two years."

"Isn't it amazing?" Ellis says.

"You say *amazing*, I say *shameless*."

"Pan..."

As they leave the school's cul-de-sac, Pangaea notices Eva waving goodbye to a few other students leaving with their parents, the mechanical elbow joint buckling like a clock hand.

"It's sick, Ellis. That's the only word. We'll see twenty years from now just how bad this first generation of synthetic teachers are."

"I mean, sure, it's strange. But you had to know it would happen. Teachers have been using MyAI the last five years anyway. These are just...I don't know the word. These things cut out the middleman, so to speak."

"They cut out the middleman? By *middleman*, don't you mean *human*? That these things just replace the need for a teacher to explain information to kids, and some android with network access can do it."

They stop at a red light, and Ellis begins to sweat. *She hates you. Don't you know it? Everything you say is poison in her ears.* He worries that people in the intersection will stare at him. *Let's not forget them either. They see you and think you belong in the zoo.* His palms cultivate the salt mire of sweat as he fidgets his hands over the shrink-wrapped steering wheel.

Meanwhile, Pangaea:

Lena: *Are they really all that bad? If they can educate you better than a person, what're you losing? Other than the person.*

Pangaea: *It makes sense you'd think that, since you don't know what it is I've lost without you here all these years.*

The light turns green.

Lena: *You've only lost me if you let yourself believe you once had me. That I had any obligation to you just because you were once part of my body.*

What if she's right? What if it's just the feeling of a relationship that matters, not the flesh?

Pan hears Lauren chatting but doesn't dwell on the words, seeing her in the rearview mirror and travelling ten years back as the car moves forward:

"Oh my goodness, look at her little hands." Pangaea dolloped her index finger between the tiny fist, letting the infant limbs squeeze. "Ellis, you tell your parents they better never hire a babysitter, cause I'm gonna be here watching her twenty-four seven."

"Haha, okay, I'll pass along the message." He hoped his blush wouldn't reveal the intoxicating notion of Pan spending even more time with him.

"Hi, queen. Oh, aren't you just the most adorable little bundle of pudge on the planet," she cooed at Lauren, whose large eyes stared back with an impenetrable wisdom. "How could your mom wait so long before having another kid? I mean, look at her." Pan was unable to move her eyes from Lauren, asking a question without even hearing the words.

"You'll have to ask her. She's cute and all, but there's a lot of work to do between birth and eighteen years."

Pangaea sees the infant face clearly before her as she continues to watch Lauren talk in the rearview.

"True," Pan replied, "but maybe it's all worth it just for these first few years. Maybe even days. When Lauren is simply and purely and entirely alive. Just that. Alive. And so all the sorrow that follows in being a mother is just an effort to recapture the feeling."

Pan looked at Lauren, imagining what Lena might have once seen when she looked at her.

The reality is that the little fucker doesn't even need to be alive, and I'm already its mother. Pan remembers the last thing Dev had said to her the other night. "I dunno, Pan. Maybe I'll love him once he's here, once he's actually *him*. But right now, all his life is is a bad idea. Nothing more than an idea."

The sound of Dev's voice and image of the oval canopy that was once Lauren's infant face fades as the present moment returns.

"And I thought she helped, like, design them, right?" Ellis has been talking to her, trying to pave out their disagreements on the subject of Eva.

"Huh? Sorry, zoned out for a sec."

"Didn't your dad tell you that your mom worked on early coding for machine learning?"

Pan rolls her eyes. "No. Not quite. She just worked for some company that helped write code for machines that were to have a bit of autonomy. Self-driving vacuums and stuff like that. It was more a hobby of hers than anything else."

"Oh, I thought it was more."

"Well," she hesitates, "her claim to fame was that she tried to apply the same coding to digital photographs. She thought she could create this world of 'living' photographs that behaved just like the people they were of."

Ellis pulls onto their street. "Oh, right. I thought it was something like that. I mean, it is pretty cool. Did she—"

"So what's on deck for the rest of the day, Laur'?"

See, she hates you. You know it. She doesn't want to hear anything you have to say. He pulls into the driveway, conscious of the crimson spreading over his cheeks.

"Are you gonna come in for a snack?" Lauren asks, trying to

sound nonchalant, as if nothing in the world could mean less than her de facto sister partaking in the ritual three o'clock (whole grain) Chef Boyardee.

Pan can't resist teasing. "I dunno. Ellis and I do have big plans in store once we drop you off." Happy for the change of subject.

"You're just being silly." Lauren tries to eat her smile before Pan can glimpse it in the rearview.

"No, I'm serious. We," she winks at him, "were just waiting for you to get out of the car. You see," she turns around and faces Lauren, "this car is magic. When there's just grown-ups in it, it turns into a spaceship, and we go flying. We've been every-where. The moon. Pluto. Andromeda. Everywhere. And… " She continues her make believe, but Ellis can't hear it; he's too busy mapping out the next phase of his day.

All right, first: wash hands in the sink. Next: wash face and comb hair. After that: midday floss. Then—

Nothing you do can make you less repulsive. He winces. *No matter how meticulous of a routine you maintain for your body, it will always just disgust the world.*

He replays the events of the morning, trying by the routine of memory to silence himself:

Wake up at six. One hour of yoga. Then, forty-minutes on the treadmill. Half hour of free weights; targeted the back today. Another half hour of stretching. Then—

That doesn't matter either. You can sculpt your flesh all you want, but you still look like an ogre to the rest of the world.

Discreetly, such that Pan won't notice, Ellis presses his hand against his stomach and flexes, hoping the firmness of his abs might silence this voice.

That won't work either. You know what you see when you look in the mirror.

And behind closed lids, Ellis envisions the end of his morning routine:

He stands nude in front of his mirror after showering, flexing each muscle group to see if there's a portion that's been neglected. He combs his hair and presses his hands down to maintain the symmetry. And all the while, he tries to deceive his eyes by thinking, *You're a monster. Revolting and vile, every obese, rotting inch. People see through this shell of your body at the gluttonous, vile catastrophe of what you really are. Of what your real life is. Since, after all, there is nothing worse on this planet than the body that houses the waste of life that is you.*

"—but, you know what?" Pangaea continues to Lauren. "Ellis and I can rain check it for today."

"So you'll stay?"

Pangaea's doesn't even realize her own blush at seeing Lauren's unrestrained delight. "You got it."

Lena: *You know, you sure do have a taste for it.*

Pangaea: *For what?*

Lena: *Make believe.*

Pangaea: *She's a kid. Maybe if you'd stuck around, you'd know that a dose of fantasy is one of their vitamins.*

Lena: *Is it her who needs this mommy-daughter game you play?*

Ellis heads to the bathroom once they're in the house. He runs his hand through the scalding water, savoring the peculiar way the water's so hot that the burn feels cold on his skin, then watches the steam evaporate before drying his hands. *Maybe one day I can fade away in a puff too. Maybe one day I can leave this disgusting mess of skin and bone and be—*

Be what? You think you're something beautiful beneath this shell? No matter what form your life takes, it will always be a mistake.

Ellis finishes drying his hands and walks into the living room, noticing Pan rub her temples until she sees him.

What's it all for, Ellis, she notices how his shirt is molded to his painstakingly accented body geometry, *if you don't ever want anyone to see you?*

"So, what's new with Dev?" he asks, cycling through one of the handful of subjects he's able to talk about.

"I don't know, man. I kinda think that child is doomed."

"Isn't there, like, child services or social services? There's gotta be something out there for people—well…in her situation. That has to be built into the Maternity Pact."

"Right. And there are. But she's totally unwilling to change her lifestyle. And her Unity score is way too low to qualify for some of the perks. I don't know if the reality of the whole thing has set in yet. To her, it might still feel like, I dunno, like—"

Lena: *Like make believe?*

"Like it's not real?" Ellis tries to help Pan find her words.

"Something like that. I don't get it, though. Like, if I were her, I'd—I'd try to think of having a baby as a fresh start or something. Some chance to make a new world. But—" *What we're designing is a product that allows customers to immerse themselves in a virtual experience of their own design.* "Then again," Pan doesn't bother trying to determine if she's talking to Ellis or Lena, "can you really just think of a child as some means to an end to better your own life? Rather than think of it as a life of its own? To think of a baby not as its own person but just some extension of you? To really only look it as *her* baby… you know what I mean? To not consider the future human being with his own consciousness. As something separate from her. But," Pangaea watches Lauren walk into the room with her red cup of Chef B, "where's the line between where a fetus is part of its mom and where it's its own being? Maybe we really do never truly leave the home of the womb."

Which means maybe you are somehow always with me, Mom. And I with you.

"What're you two talking about?" Lauren asks.

"Nothing. Just grown-up nonsense," Pangea responds.

"But you're not a grown-up. My parents are grown-ups, and they're older than you. You're still a kid if you're younger than them."

Pangaea laughs, looking at Ellis. "Maybe you're right. Maybe that's just it." He smiles, but it's only a mask to muffle what's between his own ears:

Sure, laugh now. This brief fantasy of normalcy you're allowed to indulge in. Before the reality of your life settles back in. You sit in this house and see only what your computer shows you. Is that living? And do you think you'll ever change? Do you think you'll ever really see the world? Where both the filth and allure of other human bodies will just remind you of your vile existence. That all the bodily joys everyone else experiences aren't for you to take part in? You're better off fantasizing to the pixelation of other human beings, since you know you barely even qualify as one. He lets his thoughts dagger him. *You know what you're going to do the second she leaves. You're going to go up to your room to watch videos of women telling you they hate you, women who can't even see you, women talking to a screen, and you're gonna get off on it. The anonymous other end of that screen. But just remember: you're not the screen. You're you. The putrescent waste of a human body that is every cell that makes you. So, go ahead, stare at those pixels. Keep hoping one day you can become them.*

"No, it was because of some of my answers on a test she gave last week."

Ellis has missed the beginning of the conversation. "What?" he asks.

"Lauren was just telling me why she was late today. Why she had talk to that *thing*."

"Eva."

"Right. 'Her.'"

"You get in trouble?" Ellis asks.

"No, not really. Eva just wanted to ask me about my answers to a stupid test we had to take."

"Well, what'd you say?" Pangea asks.

"I dunno."

"Lauren, don't be a dope. What'd you say?" Ellis says.

"The test wasn't fair. It was one of those marketing-response tests. Usually, we just have to watch some video in class and talk about it, but this test was written. It was asking me all these questions about something called 'screen time' and how much time I spend talking to screens. And I don't even know what that means. So I just…"

"You just what?" Ellis asks.

"I just thought of…you. And how you always look at your phone or your computer or play video games downstairs, unless you're doing your sweaty stuff in the gym room. I don't know. I didn't know how to answer for me, so I thought of you."

Ellis looks down to try to conceal his blush from Pangaea, who sees it but pretends not to. And while he keeps his head down and Lauren babbles on, Pangaea wonders: *It feels like everything is just through a screen. Every waking moment. If anything, our bodies are just getting in the way.*

Lena: *Tell that to Devorah. Her body defines her whole life for the next nine months.*

Pangaea: *You're one to talk about the definition of motherhood.*

She may be more of a mother than you could ever say you were, even if it's forced on her.

Lena: *Why? Because anatomy makes it so? Tell me, do you think it's right that the potential for life molding itself in Devorah's womb makes her a mother? When is it that life enters a body? If the potential for life suffices to define it, then it's just an idea. And it can live in anything, not just a body.*

They said their typical, cordial goodbyes. Back home next door, Pan lies awake in bed trying to reconcile the curiosity compelling her to accept Persephone's offer.

Ellis sits in his bedroom with the lights off. Illuminated only in the glow of his computer screen. "You revolting piece of shit," the woman in the video says to the camera, simulating a point-of-view experience for him. "I want to throw up just thinking about the sight of you."

Pan looks at her phone:

Alvin: *u sure you don't wanna come over*

Pan: *not tonight, loves. u said you haven't been sleeping and you never sleep well when when im over*

Alvin: *i'll take cuddling over sleeping any night, you know that*

Pan rolls her eyes, envisioning him grinning at his own nauseating affection.

Pan: *talk tomorrow bb, gn*

"If I saw you on the street, I'd fucking spit on you. Do the world a favor and find a bridge." Ellis pauses the video and opens a new tab to a website, his dick throbbing with sildenafil. A blindfolded, emaciated woman is tied to a mattress on a concrete floor with a plastic funnel in her mouth.

Pangaea scrolls through photos of her and Alvin on her phone, wondering if the sight of each memory can recall the feeling. *Is that all we try to do with these?* She zooms in on one of her sitting behind Alvin's drums, clumsily holding the sticks while he stood next to her, failing at teaching her a beat. *Is the visual stamp of a moment supposed to hold the emotion in it? Is it supposed to be some tangible preservation of a feeling that we can open up just by staring at?* She remembers how they had both laughed to the point of tears at how bad she was at keeping time, but looking at their faces now on the screen, she feels nothing. *Or is the photo just supposed to be proof that we once felt something that we never can again?*

Ellis came two minutes ago. In the brief shuddering aftermath, he closed his eyes, trying to slow and quiet his breathing. When he opens them, he stares at the idling screen, seeing only the outline of his reflection.

EYE CRUST

"**C**an you pull the shade down?" Pangaea asks as if it's not a question.

Alvin heaves a dramatic sigh as he gets out of bed to pull the shade two inches lower, thus obscuring the room in a mostly brown light, the morning sun weaving its light through the minute openings.

"Much better." She exhales and closes her eyes, curling under the blankets. Her head sinks into the pillow.

Alvin returns to bed, thinking he has some morning delight coming his way.

She swats his arm as he pinches her butt. "No, none of that, you pest."

"But I closed the shades. No one can see us."

"D'you pause to think that maybe I wanted the shades closed because I wanted to go back to sleep?"

He flicks his hand dismissively and resigns to lie back down in a slumbered position as well, albeit with his arm draped over Pan. Which she welcomes.

Despite her current lack of interest in all things phallic, Pan can't help but appreciate the half-chub bulge she feels against her butt and the slight tickle Alvin's quiet exhales produce on her neck as her hair ebbs and flows with his breathing.

"What time do you wanna get up?" She can hear that his eyes are closed.

"Let's call it eleven."

He doesn't respond. And here they both are. Cocooned in a blanket that's molded in the shape of one flesh with a warmth in it that can't be duplicated by any thermostat or April sunshine. She turns over to look at him, noticing the crust still painting the periphery of his eyes but not pausing to reflect on that; instead, she sees the bags under his eyes and the tiny corpuscles that rise out of the purpled skin. But she doesn't recoil. Instead, "You haven't been sleeping well."

He opens his eyes and rubs them, dislodging some of the afore-mentioned crust, then props himself up on his pillow. "You're not wrong. I haven't slept well lately. But it's no big deal. Work's just shitty. You know how it goes. I didn't get out of the office before eight any day this week and had to keep working from home till eleven each night. They're not even sugarcoating it anymore that that's what you have to do if you wanna keep the job."

And now she's up too, both of them closer to ninety degrees in relation to their pillows. "Alvin, it's always shitty. What's new."

"Hey, you're the one who's prodding me here."

And despite her residual sleepiness, she wants a bit of a fight. Lena: *Are you sure there isn't something else bugging you?*

"All right, first of all: I'm not prodding, Al. I'm just saying. You look a bit shittier than usual."

"Why, thank you."

She gives him a look letting him know she's not going to let him joke this away. *Just like Isaac; they never want to confront an issue.*

"I know, I know," he continues, "it's just work, Pan. That's all. I need to hit the billables or else they'll automate the job to the PAIralegal. You know I hate feeling like the sum total of my worth is some six-digit number of hours logged in a program."

She rolls her eyes and lies back down, facing the other direction.

And here we go again.

"It's just…I could be doing something special, you know? I could…"

Pan tunes him out, knowing he's talking more to hear himself than to say anything to her. *Do we even really speak to each other anymore?*

She pretends a conversation:

Pangaea: *Then just quit, Alvin. It's simple. Or suck it up. Or, you know what: pull off your "special something" if you have so much talent.*

Alvin: *That's your life advice? Just suck it up?*

Pangaea: *Alvin, half of our conversations are about what you don't want to do, rather than what you do.*

Alvin: *No. Half of our conversations are me talking to you. The other half is you talking to you.*

Lena: *Then what good is he to you, if that's how you feel?*

Pangaea: *Shut up, will you?*

Lena: *Maybe Ellis is the smart one. Even though the relationships he has are through a computer screen, at least he dictates them.*

Pangaea: *Those aren't relationships. They're delusions. For all his faults, at least Al's real.*

Pan begins to wonder what her mom would think of Alvin, this fellow who still lives with his folks and breathes through a job that's ready to be automated, waiting for The Call; what would her mom think of him? Ask him at dinner? Say behind his back? Talk to Pan about in confidence? If she were here.

But you're not here, she says to the phantom of her imagination.

She turns over and puts her hand over Alvin's mouth. "Shush. That's enough."

He gently removes her hand. They snuggle in close enough not to know whose breath is whose and grateful they both practice meticulous dental hygiene.

To change the subject, he says, "Oh, so we've got a gig lined up next weekend. That bar at the end of the Bell in Hand strip."

"Isn't that where all the college students go?"

"Yeah, but a gig's a gig. You know we'd play a set anywhere."

She sees his eyes light up and can't help but feel vicariously elated.

"Yeah? So where's it at?"

"The Green Dragon. Like from the *Lord of the Rings*. They usually just get cover bands who, without exception, play 'Mr. Brightside' horribly, so I think we'll be a good change of pace."

"Right."

But even this is beginning to feel like a chore. I've heard all their songs before. She looks at him as he closes his eyes.

Lena: *Maybe something real isn't what you're looking for anymore. Maybe it's the opposite you crave.*

Pangaea closes her eyes too.

One day. One day left to let Persephone know. She imagines her reflection trapped in the glass eye.

Lena: *It may not be real, but remember: neither am I. Yet you've needed me all these years. Is that something that should so easily be discarded?*

Behind closed eyes, Pangaea sees Devorah, rubbing her stomach. Inches away from the budding life within her, telling herself through the illusion of talking to the fetus, *I will love you. I will.*

Lena: *Wouldn't you say that lies are what let us accept the realities we can't choose? Like Alvin, here. Despite everything you two may say, isn't the truth that you don't—*

Pangea doesn't let the thought finish. She pulls Alvin to her, his eyes opening with surprise at the kiss suddenly renting his lips.

"Change of heart?"

Alvin helps Pan take off his oversized T-shirt and angles his nose into her armpit once it's off. She rolls her eyes and dislodges his face after ten seconds of letting him indulge his affinity for sniffing her morning musk, then begins to enwrap her limbs around him. She doesn't let herself think, and neither does he. They simply allow the gravity of their groins to unite in orbit.

An hour and a postcoital shower later, they're walking along the trail, hand in hand. Alvin savors how the smells of the shower still cling to Pan, almost in desperation to hold on to her. "Oy," he kvetches as he watches Farfel release his bowels.

"Fertilizer." Pan smirks at the brown puddle Alvin's dog has just made.

"Good boy." Alvin leans down and pets Farfel's back.

"I'm almost seven times older than you," he growls in reply.

The three are on a leisurely stroll through Lynn Woods.

"That's gotta be the only one today; I only brought one bag."

"We'll see, boychik. Susan gave me Shabbos chicken last night. You know it's always up in the air how that's gonna come out."

"Good ol' Susan."

"That's 'mom' to you, young man," Pangaea chimes.

Pan remembers how their first date was a walk with Farfel through Lynn Woods. She had never known about the trails prior to that, despite growing up on the north shore.

It's not Mount Mansfield, Alvin had said, *but it's about as lovely as it gets.*

"Take a left here, boychik. We went right last week." Farfel gestures his head.

"All right, but don't forget about the hill we'll have to deal with if we go left here."

"Veyzmeer! Just take the turn, biped."

The trees are on the verge of their most verdant hue of green. Warm wind meanders through the branches and occasionally dances with the leaves. Somehow there's a sensation of wakefulness in the day. Usually, the end of August brings with it a nostalgia for a summer that never really happened, and the gasp of September initiates an Alzheimer's for the year to come, the year where It All Happens. Around this time of year there's only the sensation of promise, though, as the sighing light of the sun's photons weaves its way through the leaves and branches of the trees overhead.

Farfel sniffs the dirt beneath his paws. *Must have been a poodle, the last dog to walk here.* He drags Alvin over to a tree to piss on.

"Am I gonna need to fill your water bowl after this?" Alvin always brings a backpack with Farfel's food and water bowls. He brings a Ziploc stuffed with food and two Nalgenes filled to the brim. Along with Tums and Band-Aids, in case of human malaise.

"Should be all right, but I'll probably take a swig just before we get back in the car."

Alvin nods and stares ahead as Farfel pisses.

Pangaea is overcome with a wave of déjà vu before realizing, *No, it's not some illusion. I've seen this all before because I've lived this all before. Again and again.* She looks at Alvin, replaying the morning in her mind. *They're all the same. Everything we do, it's always the same.*

Lena: *And maybe you just want—*

"Hey," she begins, trying to stifle Lena, "So I gotta decide about that thing tonight. Over at Wonderland."

They're not holding hands but walk peaceably side by side, synced beyond touch.

"Oh? I didn't even think you were considering it. Doesn't really seem like your cup of tea." He watches Farfel waddle along.

"Well, I mean, I know it's just more AI make believe." She takes the leash from Alvin and tugs at Farfel, who's been sniffing the same patch of dirt for a minute now.

"Rachmanus! What's the rush, you?!" the dog barks as Pan starts to walk ahead, pulling him along.

"Just seems like the kinda thing you'd get all doomsday-ey about."

You're telling me you won't wear them? He asked soon after they started dating.

I mean, sometimes, sure. MyAIs can be helpful, but I don't like the idea of some digital filter interfering with what my eyes actually see.

I get that, but I don't know if it's practical to avoid them completely. They're rolling out this score system with these things, kind of like what Uber has with rider scores. Or how everything needs your fingerprint to sign in. For all of Orwell's genius, he was wrong that it'd be the government out to get us. It's our own toys consuming us.

I don't know if I'd call Orwell a genius; I think it was Huxley who got it right. Soma. That was the genius.

"I mean," he begins, hesitating but then adopting a slight timbre of irony to potentially hide behind, "it wouldn't be the end of the world if you stepped into the twenty-first century."

The woods vanish from Pan's sight as they walk on, memory stealing her away:

Alvin hugged her against his chest, too bewildered to notice he was bracing for tears which, despite apparent imminence, weren't being shed.

"I'm sorry. I usually don't…" She paused to regain her breath, staying ahead of the voice crack that would betray her. "I swear, I don't usually do this. Normally, I can take care of myself. It's just…sometimes I feel like there's no one, Al. I don't know if you understand what I mean by that, but I need you to hear me say it."

It was some stale hour of morning, the two a.m. shift when you've run away from yourself.

"No one what, Pan? I'm right here. What's going on?"

She called him three times before the buzzing woke him.

"Sometimes I feel so fucking empty. Like, no matter what, whatever I do is just a mechanic movement of my limbs. And I've tried every cocktail of medicine that can be prescribed, but there's always this fucking emptiness. And I'm telling you, it's worse than pain. It's nothing."

He let the silence speak for a moment, knowing there was nothing for him to say, just hear.

"And when it gets overwhelming, when I'm up in bed and the wall crawls because I've stared at it so long, I come here."

"Alone?" what surprised him was her own look of confusion at his question.

"Alone? No, Al. I come here to be with them." She nodded at the flowers, photosynthetic dreamers of the night. "When I was a little girl, my dad would take me here when he knew I needed my mom. I think he came here because he needed her too. So we'd come here and say nothing. I'd just listen to the flowers, and eventually their voices filled her void. This place is special, Al, is what I need you to know." Again pausing before a lilt could shatter the resolution of her tone. She held his hand, spreading velvet around his heart. "But I want you to be here with me. Because this is my home. And it's the only place on this empty fucking planet that feels alive."

As the trees reoccupy Pan's focus she hears the tail end of Alvin saying, "It's not like anything would really change. At least it'd get you out of the flower shop a bit more."

"That shop isn't just where I work, Al. It's where I live. Or have you forgotten what it means to me?"

"Pan, come on. Let's not blow this out of proportion. We're talking about what sounds like a video game. And, anyway, I thought—"

"And the Earth was without form," Farfel barks for their attention.

"Oy, not now, Farf. We're in the middle of something." Alvin sighs.

"Sniffing piss getting a bit boring?" Pangaea asks.

"Always the jokes with you, eh? Ay, yai, yai. I suppose it's important to keep things light, sure. I mean, our people haven't made it this long without developing a sense of humor. Some might say we developed comedy in the first place. How else do you survive two millennia being thrown out of everyplace you call a home? Laughter is how you turn oxygen into food when you don't have a stove to cook on. Baruch Hashem."

"Farfel," Pan says, "it's always a treat when you channel your inner rabbi, but we're kind of talking about something."

"Believe me, you, I'd much rather be investigating the solid stool sample of a young spaniel my neutered nuts wouldn't know what to do with, but sometimes duty calls and Wisdom answers. As I was saying, the Earth was without form in the beginning. B'reshit. You know what the Zohar tells us? Earth was once without form. What's the key word there, bubeluch?"

"Can't you just get on with it?"

"Get on with it? Give you an answer directly? Fah! Let the goyim do that. You ever see how short the New Testament is compared to Tanakh? Eh, that's neither here nor there. As I was saying: the key word, the Zohar tells us, is 'was'. The Earth *was* without form. Which means there was a world before the world of order God created. Baruch Hashem."

A world where you can do and be anything you imagine.

Farfel looks at Pangaea, cocking a canine brow, as she recalls Persephone's words.

"Don't you see, bubeluch? God built this world from the chaos of one that existed before it. Only the mystics have a vision of what that world may have been. Or maybe they ran the best gimmick in Jewish history. But what I know, and what you need to know, is the world we have is a battle between chaos and order. The land is impermanent. That's what it is to live in exile. And when you live in exile, you can only live on hope. A lineage going back to Moses, seeing the Promised Land but never entering." He solemnly closes his eyes. "But you know what Rashe tells us? He says that what redeems this place is how we make our home. He says home is the place you create in pursuit of that promise. It's the place that brings you out of exile. Baruch Hashem." Then he resumes sniffing the dirt.

"Sorry about that, Pan."

She doesn't hear Alvin, though. *She isn't here, Pan!* Instead, she's flooded with her first memory of Isaac shouting. *She left us. She's gone. You can't keep pretending she's home with us. Living like she's at the table eating dinner with us. With you and me when we watch movies on the couch. That she's here in bed singing you a lullaby. You're a big girl now, and you can't keep living in a fantasy world with a mom you never met.* She remembers that he had stopped himself after that. How he was about to hug her but knew it was best to let her run to her room. Not before telling him, *She means more to me in my head than you ever will.*

"Pan?" She doesn't realize until Alvin takes her hand that they've reached the summit.

"And what does Rashe tell us about broken homes, Farfel?"

He looks at her with his cataract eyes, the sea-glass blue lensing his pupils.

"Rashe? Hmmm, I'm not sure it's him I'd cite or even the Talmud. Rambam might be whose wisdom you seek here, bubeluch."

She gazes at the expanse of the woods, staring to the west as the sun begins to set, unsure if it's searching for tomorrow or simply ending the day.

"He tells us that when someone betrays the trust of a home, they've broken Covenant. And to live apart from the Covenant is to be lost. Not only to be in exile but to have nowhere to call home, to belong nowhere and to no one."

"Sure," she turns back from the summit and sees only the forest ahead, "that's all said and done about someone who breaks Covenant, but what about those left in the wake? What about a family that's been abandoned?"

"Pan? Are you all right?"

She ignores Alvin and waits for the sages.

"Bubeluch." Farfel comes closer and gently paws at her boots. "The only people who lose Hashem are those who turn away from him. No one can make that decision but you. Home is something within you that no one can strip away. And even those who leave it, those who leave you; if there was ever any love in them, that's always with you. After that, the person who has run away is prodigal, a stranger to all and lost. Only they can make the decision to come back home. But if you keep them in your heart, if the living stranger means more to you than a loved memory, then it's only a ghost you're welcoming in your home."

MIRROR

Pangaea sees the familiar Wonderland Greyhound Park sign as she pulls into the parking lot. She notices a line of a dozen cars parked close to the shining, glass-paned, gleaming face of the new building. Which is behemoth in size. The windows don't seem to reflect sunlight but rather consume it, showing only a reflection of the world outside, inhaling and exhaling the light, alive and organic and completely inanimate. She parks and hesitantly walks toward the building, the sensation of doing something simply because there is no other choice.

Lena: *Does it feel any different from any other day?*

"Pangaea." A voice beckons her about twenty yards away.

She looks over and sees Persephone. *How the hell did I actually say yes to this?* She's surprised by the lack of discomfort in seeing the glass eye up close.

"Please, come in." Persephone holds open the glass door. Pan tears her gaze away from herself in the eye and feels a sense of uncertainty. *I could still turn around.* She hesitates before walking in.

The first thing Pan notices is the odd color scheme of the interior. The floor is carpeted in a mauve tone; all the surfaces are glass and chrome; the walls are alternatingly green and black, swirling together in some areas and zigzagged in others. More than anything, the effect is disorienting. She hears no sounds.

"So, this is going to be, like, the main lobby, right?"

"That's correct." Persephone walks ahead of Pangaea down the hallway. Doors line either side of the wall every twenty feet or so. "We have three floors, each with forty rooms. We anticipate high volume once we're operational."

Persephone opens one of the doors and ushers Pan in ahead of her. She walks into a relatively small room that's completely black, only lit by the light of the computer screens lining the left wall. There are two men seated at the computers; they pause their typing to look over at Pan and Persephone.

"These are two of our programmers."

They nod at Pan, who nods in turn.

"This is the control room where our techs will monitor you while you're under the anesthesia."

"Can they see...into my head when I'm in there?" She notices one of the screens displaying her preliminary design form.

Persephone smiles. "Not exactly. Though this one here," she points to a screen, "functions like an MRI to monitor your neural activity in real time. But this is all very technical. Let's go to the next room so you can see exactly what we're working with." Persephone walks to the other end of the small, computer-lit room and opens the door to another. "This is where you'll actually have the experience."

The floor is carpeted a deep blue, and the walls are some mixture of dark red and purple. Four lamps are in each corner, a queen-size bed with red pillows and brown sheets. *It's like a furnished doctor's office*, Pan thinks. *Or...no, not that...it's like...* She loses her thought when she notices the rolling table of medical devices and a display for vitals next to the bed. Then she sees—"Is that," Pangaea points at an apparatus next to the medical monitor, "is that *it*?"

It's an ovular object about four feet high, balanced into a groove in the ground. There are no indentations, dimples, or markings. It's black, opaque, pulses intermittently with a red glow. At the top, coming from the center, are two wires. One runs along the wall back into the control room. The other is connected to the medical monitor as an input cable. Pan notices an output cable that resembles an amplifier cord with a syringe where the jack plug would normally be.

Persephone notices her perplexed expression. "Yes. That's the machine, The Human Connection. It fuses together the anesthetic that puts you under and the interneural connection to the control room for the simulation. It's why we want this room to be as conducive to sleep as possible. Now, please, have a seat." Persephone signals Pan to sit on the bed while she rests on a swivel chair. "Before we get to the simulation, we're going to go over some things, and you'll sign some paperwork. Something I must say, though," Persephone pauses and crosses one of her legs over the other to rest her hands atop, smoothing imaginary folds from her pants, "at any point you may end your involvement with us in this test study. But, if you sign on to this, you agree to our terms, one of which is: any data we collect from you is our property. Meaning, your biometrics, your oral and written responses and feedback, and anything else we collect with regards to your activities here belongs to us. Do you understand?"

"Listen," Pan starts, distractedly answering Persephone as her gaze roams around the room. *Maybe it's like a cave, but why does it feel so...familiar?* "I've grown up in the twenty-first century. We all know our information is up for sale, and the notion of consenting to this is nothing more than a phrase. I'm here, aren't

I? So, let's cut to the chase—what do you want from me?" When she looks at Persephone, her gaze is again drawn magnetically toward her reflection in the eye.

"Fair enough. Here's what you'll be doing. Over the next nine months into December, you're going to be coming here to design what we're calling 'experiences,' as I've told you so far. You're going to be anaesthetized in one of these rooms. After each session, when you awake, you're going to answer a series of questions about your experience. We'll also be reading your biometrics. I can assure you that the anesthetic compound and everything else have already been tested for safety and regulation compliance. What we haven't tested, though, is the actual product itself, the experience. That's what you're going to be doing."

Pan looks around the room. *It's like somewhere from when I was a kid. Or, no. Almost before that even. Almost like the shadow of a memory. Someplace on the edge between where memory begins and an abyss.*

"I guess my only question is still what I asked you before," now her gaze is back on Persephone, "why me?" though she just sees her reflection.

Persephone smiles. "Pangaea, why you're here shouldn't matter. You should simply be proud and excited to participate. This is the beginning of a new phase in human engagement with technology. For our purposes, we're only interested in the entertainment and perhaps catharsis this product can provide. But this technology can be expanded so much further."

"Well, if it works, right?"

Persephone seems to relish the taunt. "Yes, of course. *If* it works. You know," she pauses and looks away from Pan, deliberating, "I think it's worth mentioning that, in our research, we studied people's habits and psychology as they relate to technology available at present. You know what we noticed?"

"They go blind sooner than they used to?"

Persephone doesn't smile at this one. "What we noticed was a tendency among people to view the actual world, the one we live awake through, as a 'sketch'," she air quotes, "of the virtual one. The one they ultimately spend more time with. In other words, they would see people in the flesh, events in the waking world, as some preliminary step in the process of seeing and experiencing the same, virtually through the screen. What we're curious to see, as an analogue, is if our clientele—whom you represent in this test study—will come to see the world outside of Wonderland, the 'real world,' as a secondary experience to the world you create in here."

"And what if you do?"

"I'm sorry?" She seems to have expected more sarcasm from Pan.

"What if you find that that's true here? That people will see reality as—what'd you call it?—as the sketch of the experience you can have in Wonderland? Which is really just in your head."

Pan can't read Persephone's expression. "Well, then I suppose we'd have to ask what's more important: your sense of being at home in the world around you or the one within you? Now. Shall we begin the paperwork? It's all rather straightforward."

A half hour later, the last thing Pangaea sees before wincing at the anesthetic needle is her own reflection, trapped in Persephone's eye. Then:

She's outside. Snow slips through the sky, down from the clouds. It sprinkles the air's black with white specks that shimmer like glitter, and above her in the sky: a purple shade below the starlight, a luminescent silver from the moon in the night. The snow falls on the ground, forming a canopy, white and silent. Pan can see her silhouette sigh a vaporous puff in the wind.

Certainly looks like the memory, she thinks. Then pauses. *But in here I'm all alone.* And she attempts to grasp the infinity of it, being stranded in her own mind, as if she's trapping herself. *But I don't have to be.*

"Why are we out here, Pan? It's freezing."

Pangaea turns to the voice and sees Lena standing next to her.

"Mom," she says before even thinking it. Pan looks at her, waiting for some visceral reaction in her guts at seeing her mother in the flesh, but there's nothing. *She's not real. What did I expect?* No sensation at all. *She's just in my head, even here.* Lena is nearly identical to the body in all the photos Pan submitted through her preliminary design but somehow paler in hue, the eyes somehow one-dimensional and dry. A frailty throughout.

Lena stares at her quizzically. "You think I'm not real. But if everything I am, say, and do in here is just an extension of you, then how real are *you* in here? Everything here is still your thought."

Pan tries to maintain her composure. *I have a body. Everything in here—including her—is just synthetic. But I have a body. You— this thing I'm looking at now—don't. And that's what makes me real.* She resolves to move along and pursue the experience before any more doubt creeps in.

"Let's walk a bit." The two commence through the snow. "Do you see that?" Pan gestures ahead. In the distance: a faint pulsation of red, disembodied, beneath which blurs an underglow of green. The night drapes black behind it.

"I see it."

Pangaea thinks of the actual memory she has. Of venturing there alone all those years ago. "This is the place I've been closest to death."

Lena has no reply.

"How about you ask me how I almost died. How about you ask what I was looking for."

But Pan can't fool her own mind. So they continue in silence.

Eventually, they pass under a little forest of evergreens. Their branches finger through the air as if reaching for something.

To Pan's surprise, Lena reaches out her left hand and takes Pan's right. Tenderly squeezes. Pan feels the warmth.

"It's nice we can do this, isn't it?" Lena says.

No, don't let yourself think there's any more reality to her in here than out—

But she stops her thoughts and turns to look at the woman who's only lived in the ink of photographs and the fog of dreams in her head. She sees this woman in full flesh and body, and without waiting another moment for uncertainty, Pan hugs Lena and squeezes.

"Mom," is all she can say in the embrace as her mind empties and the sensation of this embrace fills every subatomic iota of her being. When she finally does let go, she looks up and sees aurora dancing in the sky, a tango with the stars for the moon's delight but remembers that she has a purpose here. So they walk through the forest under the quarter-crescent of the moon and the stars sprinkled beside it, the snow there too like white sparks in the dark.

"Are you going to tell me where we're going?"

"We'll be there in a moment."

"You know," Lena begins, "you look just like I did at your age. Only," she affectionately takes Pan's purple hair in hand, "you're a bit less original in style than I was. But only just a bit."

Pan smirks as she thinks of the photos she's seen of Lena. The ripped jeans. The leather jacket. The hair painstakingly styled to look like it's not styled and changing color and length every six or so months. So cliché in the aesthetic that it was astonishingly unique. Like a dare to call her an imposter. The look Pan has tried to replicate in her own right.

"Well, if you'd stuck around, you might've actually gotten to see me." But Pan only feels a sense of embarrassment as she recognizes that she can't hurt the feelings of something that can't feel. "You know something—in here, just like out there, I'll never get an answer from you about why you left. Maybe all I can do in here," she tries to stymie the heat rising in her chest, "is show you all the things you've missed." They stop in their tracks. "And I figure this is the best place to start."

The carnival's entrance is twenty feet away. A big clown head on top of the gate, mouth open and tongue sticking out. Dry. The paint chipping. Above the head, a sign, curving like an upside-down smile, flashing orange and green: Winter's Wonder.

"The carnival?" Lena's eyes reflect the myriad colors ahead of them.

"It was a weekend festival that Dad took me to when I was ten. We stayed in a motel down the road for the weekend. Let's take a look. He'll be here soon enough."

They walk under the gate into the whirlwind of color. The snow coats everything in a peach-fuzz white. "He had to drag me away from that when we were here during the day." She points to the carousel, frozen still, the lights orange-bright and illuminating the porcelain of the horses, the manic panic of their pupil-wide eyes. "And over there." She points at the Ferris wheel. "I couldn't drag him on to that. No matter how pity-me-please I could get my ten-year-old girl voice to be. He just wouldn't budge. He hates heights. But you already know that."

Lena looks at Pan with something resembling pity. "Why'd you take me here?"

They head toward a building that abuts the edge of the forest. The contrast between the black of the open door and the white of the snow outside dichotomous and real. Above the black vacancy of color is a sign: House of Mirrors. They walk in.

The pitch-darkness shocks Pan's senses, and for a moment she feels like she's falling.

"I can't see anything. Is there a light?" Lena asks.

"Wait a second. Just wait." Pan guides her along, regaining her composure. *It's just a memory. Not even that. It's just...* The subtle illumination of night outside meanders in through the zig-zag shape of the hallway. Pan turns and faces one of the mirrors, studying the dim reflection. She begins to move her arm to touch the reflection but stops midway once she sees Lena's reflection next to hers. The difference between them indistinguishable. "Okay," Pan looks at the mirror for another moment and turns around to face the door, "now watch."

They hear footsteps and then see the shadow of a little girl walk into the door. The light of her flashlight is hazy, obscuring her outline and then revealing it as she angles it across the room. The way the mirrors line the room and zigzag throughout seem to trap the light and at the same time fling it.

"Look, Mom. Just look."

The little girl points at her reflection in a mirror, which reflects an image of that reflection pointing to its reflection in another mirror down the hall. An infinity of faces moving in glass simul-taneously being one, the asymptote of zero division.

"Can she see us?" Lena asks.

Pan doesn't answer.

The girl walks slowly down the corridor, looking at her various selves in the mirror, each identical yet distorted. She passes by Pan and Lena; they notice how chapped her face is and that she's hardly bundled up. They can hear her teeth chatter.

"Shouldn't we put our coats on her?" Lena looks at Pan with a hint of worry.

"That's what a mom's instinct should be, I guess." Then Pan looks at her. "But I don't see this girl's mom anywhere."

Lena looks back at the child, watching in quiet passivity.

"The motel was just over a mile down the road from here," Pan narrates. "I had told Isaac earlier that I thought I saw you here in the crowd. He cried for a little bit and hugged me and just reminded me that photographs were the only place I'd ever see you. But that as I got older, if I look in the mirror, I might see you looking back." The girl stops in front of one of the mirrors, across which is another mirror facing it. She moves back and forth between the left and right of the one position where her reflections are blocked by her body. And then she approaches the mirror and puts her hand against her reflection, turning off the flashlight to remove the glare. "I thought maybe it'd be a way I could hold your hand." The girl's hand seems to slip a little before she sinks down to the floor, her face florid and her eyes clenched shut. "But you weren't there." And as she watches her younger self, Pan begins to feel pain, visceral pain, spreading throughout her. *That's what it felt like then. This is exactly what I felt, when This was Then.*

For a few minutes there's nothing but silence, interrupted by the girl's chattering teeth as Pan tries to breathe through the pain.

Then, faintly, "Pan! Pangaea!" becomes audible outside. Hurried footsteps. A man runs through the door.

"Pan!" He runs to her and scoops her off the ground, pressing his cheek to hers and swaddling her into him close. He rubs warmth back into her slightly frostbitten body. He wipes his tears off her face first, then wipes them from his own. His words are incoherent; there's only the primordial nonsense of vocal cords vibrating. He leans back against one of the mirrors and squats down on the floor, holding his daughter. A police officer runs into the door.

"They took me to the hospital," Pan tells Lena as they walk outside, her pain subsided. "It was only minor frostbite to my fingers, but obviously Isaac was terrified. When he woke up and saw my empty bed, his first thought was that I was abducted. So he called the police. And then thought about it a bit and realized I might've made my way back to the carnival."

They sit down on a bench.

"I'm sorry I wasn't there, Pan. I'm sorry I wasn't there to see you grow up. To be—"

"I don't need to hear it. There's nothing you can say that I haven't already told myself. You're not here, and you never have been." She's not sure if she's talking to Lena now or herself, forgetting the question can't exist. "I really don't know why I brought you here." *I mean, she's no more real in here than she is out there in my head.* "I think," she watches Isaac and the police officer leave the house of mirrors, her younger self wrapped in Isaac's coat; she watches this but envisions herself looking in the mirror, seeing...*but who is it I see in the mirror?*

Pan turns to Lena. "I think maybe I wondered if I could forget you're just a reflection."

Then the world begins to fade away, as if dissipating into fog.

Pan blinks rapidly as she comes out of the simulation. The lights in the room, dim as they are, hurt her eyes, and there's a moment of tinnitus.

"How was your first experience, Pangaea?" Persephone asks as she sits up.

Pan stares at her as sleepiness evacuates her brain. "Oh, um, well," she feels groggy, no concept of time, "it was…good, I guess? I mean, what am I supposed to say?"

Persephone smiles. "Remember, I'm here to ask you the questions." She gives Pan some water and allows a few moments to collect herself before saying: "So. Tell me about your first experience in Wonderland."

PART TWO

EVENT HORIZON

THINGNESS

P angaea deep breathes at the traffic light, closing her eyes after a glance at the Wonderland sign in the rearview. She almost forgot to put the gear in drive before pulling out of the parking spot.

"It wasn't real. It's just a computer."

Lena: *Then what's wrong?*

She looks at the passenger seat to be sure she doesn't see Lena.

Lena: *What's there to be alarmed about? Aren't you the one always saying I'm just in your head?*

How could it have felt so real? How can a computer duplicate what my memory can't even recall? What my body can't remember.

Lena: *Can you be sure what you just experienced was anything more than just something a computer created? How can you know if any of that came from your mind or was just projected into it through wires?*

She decides to call Devorah as a distraction. "Hey. Doing anything right now?"

"Hey, Pan. Um, actually..." She sniffles.

"Oy, what's going on?"

"Well, Ivan and I just ripped out our vocal cords at each other, and he's banished for the night. So, I guess it actually wouldn't be bad if you can come over for a bit."

Pan welcomes the distraction. She's at Devorah's twenty minutes later, staring at the mountain of parenting pamphlets on the kitchen table. Devorah looks at her phone through red eyes, and Pangaea adds more Enya to the soothing Spotify queue. The windows in the kitchen are open, but the air sits heavy, laden with an accumulation of particles disproportionate to the space such a quantity of loose particulates should inhabit. There's a faint smell of fish and Clorox; the perpetual buzz of flies hovering near trash that's overstayed its welcome. Devorah has tried to aerate the house the past few days. *Everything makes me nauseous*, she says.

It looked so real. Pangaea envisions the snow falling atop the trees, the carnival pulsing in the distance. Pretending not to notice the current environs. *But it was all just a program. It was all synthetic.* She looks at her hand as the skin prickles with snow falling atop it.

"So," she starts, clenching her fist, "tell me about the checkup. The little one's doing all right?"

"Yeah, he seems to be doing fine in there." She rubs her stomach. "But they gave me the whole spiel again. About clean living and how a social worker is going to start checking on me if they don't see improvements next time we meet. After the history lesson, that is."

"What do you mean?"

"Like, at these checkups, they give me a physical, but they also have us—they do it in groups, by the way; so, like on Tuesdays, there are twelve of us assigned to show up, and they give us these presentations."

"About pregnancy?"

"Sorta. And the Maternity Pact in general. It's like we're back in sex ed. They played this animation of a fetus growing in the womb, then some collage of home-movie footage of perfectly adorable little munchkins with their moms. And then the history lesson. Remember the infomercials that started to air on TV and all our apps right around the time the bill really got traction? Well, they played one and..."

Pangaea remembers it:

We're not taking away anyone's freedom. We're not oppressing anyone. All we're doing is trying to preserve the sanctity of life. What could be worse for a child than having the first person who's supposed to love it, what could be worse than having its mother betray it?

How Lena asked her then what she asks again now: *Who could want a mother who only was one because she had no choice?*

"Goddamnit!" Devorah shouts and steals back Pan's attention. "What? What do you want!" She yells at Ivan through the phone.

Pangaea can hear him. "Dev. Cut the shit and let me in. I'm outside."

"Fuck you. I told you I don't want to see you tonight."

"Dev!" Now Pan hears his voice, calling up from the street. "I can stand here all night! Do you have all night in you?!" Devorah gets up and unlocks the door.

"Dev...I thought you—"

"I don't wanna hear it. At this point, I just don't wanna be stressed out. And if he's gonna raise hell all through the night, this is easier. I just—" She stops short, beginning to heave. She mutters and rushes to the bathroom. Pan hears the familiar kerplop of vomit meeting toilet water. The dry, painful rasps in Devorah's throat between convulsions. She can almost taste the acid sting in the back of her own throat.

"I'm really asking you that," Persephone had said. "Why design a fantasy to do nothing but reflect reality?"

She's back in Wonderland, answering Persephone's questions, "I don't know. I guess I wanted to—I just wanted to revisit the memory. It was with my mom. I don't know if I mentioned that she left me soon after I was born. But, I guess that doesn't matter. You're twisting my words a bit."

"That's not what I meant to do. I guess I'm asking, why design a person you can actually hold? Why limit yourself here to an experience of someone you can't escape in reality?"

Which brought the image of Alvin into Pan's mind. "You make it sound like I'd *want* to get away from people," she could smell his lemony soap in her nostrils through the distance of memory, but soon he faded out of her head, and she could only think of photos of Lena. *When the fact is, the only way I could ever hold you, until now, is through the Polaroid's ink.*

"Oh, Jesus, Pan. Didn't know you were here." Ivan has entered the apartment.

She blinks the kitchen back into focus.

"Where's Dev? Is she—" Then he hears the bathroom sounds and nods, sitting down at the table. Pangaea notices sickly exhaustion shading his face and sees the polka dots on his forearms. "I don't know what she told you but, well, it's not like I'm some bad guy here."

Devorah comes out of the bathroom. "Not some bad guy? No. You're worse than that. You're some little, immature boy who can't accept the mess he's fucking made. Hoping for me to be your mom too."

That's what a mom's instinct should be, I guess, but I don't see this girl's mom anywhere. Pan tries to shut the simulation out of her mind, but suddenly she's back in the house of mirrors only... *Is that my memory of that night all those years ago or my memory of the simulation just an hour ago?*

Lena: *What's the difference? If they're both just in your head. If they're—*

"We have almost a year, Dev. We don't need to start babyproofing the place yet."

"We have eight months, you idiot. He's gonna be here before you know it. I know it all seems like some distant event in your head, but whether you like it or not, you're going to be a father. And, fuck, I'm going to be a mother."

Lena: *Do you ever think maybe that's why I left? Because maybe "mom" wasn't a reality that matched who I truly am? But just a fantasy I pretended to be because of some event within my body. They used to say "your body, your choice," but doesn't that also mean you choose how much you let your body define your life?*

"Well, you should have thought of that before you had a daughter. You at least had the choice."

Pan doesn't realize she spoke aloud until Devorah asks, "Is that supposed to be some sort of joke?"

Pangaea stares at her and Ivan. *Wait, wait, wait, is any of this in my head or are they—*

"I'm sorry, Dev. I think I was just—"

Lena: *Why should someone else's life determine how I own mine?*

Pan shuts her eyes. She sees herself in the infinite mirrors and scrunches her eyes harder, as if trying to dim the blackness of her closed lids even darker, and when she opens her eyes, for a fleeting moment, she still sees the mirrors. She blinks the kitchen back into focus, and the three of them heave a collective sigh in the silence.

It's Ivan who penetrates it. "It doesn't feel real. You can't even see the bump." He reaches a hand out across the kitchen table and Devorah takes it. "It's like—it's like he's just an idea. Like he's not even alive. But just on his way to thingness. You know?"

Devorah rubs her thumb over his hand. "I know. You think I have any idea when the magic moment comes and he suddenly feels—fuck—*is* alive? Cause I don't. Even if the world's telling us he's real. I don't know if I can believe it yet."

Pangaea can't hear them, though:

She looks up at the night sky, seeing snow, mountains in the distance. The blur between the blue and the black that does nothing less than purple the sky with winter. The solace and the wind and the death silence of December midnight. She inhales deeply, letting the ice of the air frost her lungs and freeze everything within her. She sees the flowers of the shop, slowly sprouting through the snow.

Lena: *You're not still there, Pan. You're here.*

The flowers wilt in the frost, and even the snow melts away the sky. Pangaea is back in Devorah's rancid kitchen.

"But when does anyone ever stop being an idea?" she asks herself, rather than cramming her voice in her head. "When is anyone not somehow just trapped in the minds of other people or even their own mind? Who's to say the body is the quality that makes a person just that—a person? When's the magic moment when a body is alive?"

Devorah and Ivan glance at each other.

"Pan, uh, what the hell are you talking about?" Ivan says.

But she doesn't hear him. She continues. "Maybe someone can be just as alive in our minds as they are in flesh." She remembers Persephone saying, *But here we can recreate just that.* "Or maybe that's the only place they're alive. Because what if there's nothing special about our bodies that gives them the premium of life?" *With this technology, there truly is no difference between what lives in your mind and what lives outside your body.* "Maybe," and now she sees Lena, surrounded by the snow, but when Pan reaches out to see if she's there, her mother's gone. She's left staring only at herself, trapped in the house of mirrors. *Here, the world* is *your mind.* "Maybe we can give life to any fantasy in our imagination." She looks at Devorah, "And so being a mother has nothing to do with what's in your stomach, Dev, but just your head."

When she's back home, Pan doesn't even try to go to sleep. She sits on the rocking chair in the screened porch, fidgeting with an iPad-like prototype that Lena had brought back some time before she was born. *You held this once. Your fingerprints are embedded in it just as much as mine.* She imagines her mother looking at it:

"I'm telling you, Isaac. These are gonna be everywhere in a decade. Just wait. This one might be junk, but someone's going to hone this."

"I hear you. Look, can you hand me that spade, dear?" He was potting a new bundle of cymbidium orchids.

She handed it to him, keeping her gaze on the machine. "Did you hear anything I just said? Or are you lost in your plants?"

He pushed his glasses back up as if they were slipping. "Of course I hear you. You know we see things differently. You like playing with your toys," he gestured to the contraption in her hands, "and I like playing with mine." He handed her one of the flowers.

Lena put down the prototype and twirled the flower, listened to the color speak through it. "You say it like I prefer to lurk in some cave while you're out frolicking in the fields."

"Lena…"

"No, no." She smiled at him, "I'm not trying to fight. I'm just letting you know what you're saying. Even if you don't hear it."

"What can I tell you? I like holding living things. I like watching life spread through them. From seed to bloom."

Still smiling, she handed him back the flower and picked up the prototype again. "And you'll never understand that I do too."

CUSTOM

"Three...four..."

You're fucking pathetic. You absolutely disgust me.

"Five." Ellis pauses longer after this squat, staring at the plum of his perspiring face in the mirror. Then focusing on the woman in the lens of his MyAIs.

You know the thing about you fat, lazy sacks of shit? You want people to feel bad for you, and you feel all sorry for yourself about being alone when the reality is: it's your own fucking fault.

"Six," he nearly shouts, then puts the weights down and collects his breath.

Reach in between those revolting, stinking rolls for some crumbs to chew on, loser.

He turns the volume louder on his headphones as he starts to do clap pushups, doing each pushup slower than the prior, focusing on the burning sensation within as he envisions the tendons stretching, ripping until he has an erection. He pauses the video and looks at the door, knowing it's locked but needing to see it. Then, he takes out his phone and looks at the video he's been listening to, the woman he paid on Clips4Sale to make a video for him, before switching to another video, another custom clip he bought.

He watches, panting and soaked in sweat, a woman whip an obese man wearing a mask who's tied upright against a pole, arms behind his back, exposing his stomach. He watches this ten-minute video twice, letting his dick throb in erection, imagining the blood pressure rise to such an extent it truly rips the flesh apart in castration. Then he resumes his workout.

He exercised for another forty minutes and showered, bringing his glasses to bed with him. He watches another custom video.

"Pass the bread, babe." A brunette stares at the camera, smiling directly at it.

Should I ask the waiter for more?

"No, ha ha, you know I'm watching carbs. Just one more piece. Then tell the waiter to take it away!" She laughs, having waited five seconds. Then, "This place is so nice, honey, but you know what I really want to do right now?" She smiles coyly, taking a sip of wine and then moving the vase to the left, making her face more visible on the screen. She reaches her hands across the table, closer to the camera, and squeezes an imaginary pair. "I just want to cozy up next to you in bed and hear you moan, babe."

But that'll never happen, will it?

Stop.

"But I'm just blabbing on and on. How was your day?"

Tell her it was the same as every other. Just you alone with yourself. And these videos you buy to forget that fact. Or is this one of the nice ones you let yourself watch every now and then?

He pauses the video and takes off the MyAIs, closing his eyes and counting his breaths, hoping this time the trick will work to drift him to sleep.

But that never works, does it?

Just let me sleep, please.

I am you. You know that. You're your own executioner, victim and ghost.

He puts the glasses back on and goes to a different screen.

Oh…interesting. So you're in that kind of mood tonight.

It's a photo album he put together.

You don't want to sleep tonight, huh? Tonight, you want the pain.

Stop. Please, just be quiet.

The funny thing is, no matter how much you pay these anonymous women to look at the camera and follow a script, to go through the motions of any fantasy you can cook up, this is the only one that makes you feel anything.

Ellis lets the slideshow progress at its own pace over the course of an hour until it halts at the last photo, though he's been unable to see most of them through the tears blurring his eyes.

BACKSTAGE

"I t was raining?" Pan asks.

"Yep. Downpour, actually," Lena says.

"Of course."

"You're the one who wants to see it firsthand."

Pan is in the backseat. Nora rides shotgun with Lena at the wheel. Pan's gaze is fixated upon Nora, whose gaze is fixated upon her reflection in the flip-down visor mirror, applying purple lipstick.

"Were they at least any good?" Pangaea asks.

Nora looks away from herself to give Pan a glance in the mirror. "The Meathooks were the best band that never made it, back in our time. They played everywhere worth playing. Except the places they probably thought were worth playing."

"You have to understand, Panny," Lena keeps her eyes on the road, "we thought we were seeing them from the ground floor. Like we were seeing Heart before *Little Queen*."

Pan's heard the story from Issac before. *Your mom saw more live gigs than everyone I've ever known, combined.*

But she wants to witness this memory firsthand.

Lena pulls up to the curb, and Pan is about to open the door, but Lena stops her. "Wait. You can't go in like that."

"From what I've heard, we don't make it far anyway. What difference does it make what I wear?"

"They won't let you in. Here." Lena pivots in her seat and takes Pan's face into her hands. Pan resents the warmth she feels at the touch. *It shouldn't feel so real.* Lena puts her thumbs just beneath Pan's eyes and smears her eyeliner. "There. Now you're punk."

Pan follows Lena and Nora to the bar. She can hear the indistinct clamor of the band from around the corner, assuming it won't sound much different once she's in. Just louder.

"Christ." Pan sees the line. "We're not gonna get in until after the show."

"No," Nora begins, *"they're* not going to get in until after the show," pointing at the line. Then she looks back at Pan. "But we're not them. Just follow us."

Lena and Nora walk around to the alley in between the bar and the adjacent building. "All right, let me and Nora talk and maybe make a bit of eye contact with the door guy. Try to look like you're bored and know you have someone better to be; he'll be hooked."

Lena bangs on a door, which moves about an inch or so with each bang, barely held closed with a bolt lock. Pan hears some metal move; a guy wearing a headband opens the door. "You have passes?" he asks, giving all three of them a slow once-over. The flash of lust in his eyes reminds Pan that, in this memory, she and her mother are the same age.

Nora and Lena look at each other with superbly faked glances of "Oh, shit, did you remember them," before giving the guy similarly deceptive wide-eyed looks of surprise. "Ohhhh, no. Fuck. I think we forgot them."

A few seconds pass as he gives them another appraising look. "I'm sorry, but I can't let you in. Not my rules but the bar's."

"Oh, can you just go talk to Vince? I'm sure he'll come get us," Nora says.

Doorman hesitates. "Vince…the lead singer?"

"Yeah." Nora twirls a lock of her rain-matted hair. "I'm his girlfriend and—" she giggles, "well, *one* of his girlfriends. You know how it is." She gives him a glance through fringes of hair that she's let fall over her eyes. "Anyway, we forgot our passes, but I'm sure he'll come get us if you let him know we're here. My name's—"

"Hey, I mean the guy's in the middle of a set; I'm not just gonna interrupt him. Best I can do is tell ya to hang tight, and I'll talk to him during a set break."

"I'm sorry," Lena chimes in, her voice a timbre lower than usual, lending it a sultry breath, "but you can't seriously be telling us to wait out here in the rain, can you?" The tinge of venom in her tone adds more sting to the seduction.

Pan glances at the guy, who catches her eyes and stares. She knows they're in.

"Look," he starts but then pauses and takes in the sight of all three of them once more. "All right, all right." He begins to open the door then stops. "But you each gotta give me twenty bucks."

Lena and Nora smirk at each other before looking back at him with lethally feigned smiles of acquiescence.

"Sure thing," Lena says, giving him three twenties. "This should cover all three of us."

They walk in, then Lena pauses, fishing in her purse. "And *this* one's just. For. You." And hands him a penny.

"That's why he's a doorman, Pan," Nora says.

Pan follows them. The walls are some mixture of brown and black, almost as if the grime has been added for aesthetic. The lights are florescent but flicker and are completely dead in some spots. Everything looks sticky. The passersby all wear the same look of impatient anger. The premium of angst. Lena and Nora walk with an assurance, as if this place is their home.

"Mom," Pan starts, "just how many shows did you really see here?"

"Ever? Hundreds. I couldn't tell you. When I was your age, I was here or at another bar with music every night. Sometimes I'd see three shows in a night. That's just how it was."

But where can I find that now? Could I even find it now? Or are these simulations the closest I'll get? Forgetting momentarily all of Alvin's gigs that she's gone to.

They walk through the kitchen, where three people whom Pan guesses are cooks sit around a metal prep table smoking cigarettes, playing poker.

"I'll tell you one thing," Lena continues, "for all the shows I must've seen here, I never once ate anything out of this kitchen."

"Or drank anything that wasn't from an unopened bottle," Nora chimes in.

They exit the kitchen and head toward the green room. Pan can feel her stomach stirring. She doesn't pause to wonder if there's a difference between the reality of what the setting was and what she's always envisioned it to be. Nora opens the door and startles backward a step.

"Oh, um, are we in the wrong room?" Lena asks once they step into the green room, which is just a large closet with a few chairs lining the wall, a smudged mirror, and quite a few bags, which a man is currently rummaging through. He stops and stares at them.

"I'm, uh, just." He hesitates, searching for words. Pan notices how his pupils consume the entirety of his eyes and how frantically they flit between the three of them and the door they're blocking. Then she notices how gaunt he is. The bags beneath his eyes, the weight of them almost dragging her down too. "I'm just getting some cables for the band," he says as he continues to rummage through a bag. "Yeah, the, uh, the, um, the guitarist's cable just busted in the middle of a song, you know. And, uh, they, they sent me back here to get it and…"

Pan's focus is now on the bag next to the man's feet, which he's been moving equipment into. A lump blocks her esophagus when she sees the pistol handle protruding out of it. She looks at Nora and Lena and can see from their glances that they, too, have spied the gun.

Lena begins in a slow voice. "Okay, um, I can tell we're in the wrong room. We're just gonna head out now, all right?"

"No. Wait." He stands up a bit straighter and speaks with more assurance. From the way his glance changes, Pan discerns that he knows they've each seen the gun. "Close the door."

"Hey, listen, man, we're just gonna leave and pretend—"

"Now."

Nora looks over at Pan and nods for her to close the door. No sooner does Pan shut it than he reaches for the gun.

"Listen," his eyes dart between the three of them with frantic speed, "you three walked into the wrong room at the wrong time. That's just it. And now you're in this with me. Here's, uh, here's," he scratches the wrist of the arm that holds the gun, and now Pan sees the track marks pimpling his skin, "what's gonna happen." For a moment, Pan hears him speak in Ivan's voice before he swallows and exhales a long sigh. "I'm going to fill this bag with equipment. But I can't get all of it in here. So, you," he points the gun at Lena, "are going to take *this* bag out of the room in a minute, and you," he points the gun at Nora now, "are gonna take *this* bag out," lifting up the bag that previously stored the gun. "All right? I'll take the others. And you," now he points the gun at Pan, "are going to, uh, walk out with them next to me. My car's parked around the block. We're going to drop these bags off, I'm going to drive away, and you're going to forget any of this happened. All right?"

"All right," Lena says in a calm tone. "But what if," Pan feels her stomach drop, wondering what her mother could possibly ask this man who has no answer to anything, "someone stops us?"

"What?" his face scrunches with sudden frustration. "Why would anyone stop us? Why? Unless," he waves the gun, "unless *you*," now he points it at Lena, "do something that'll make some-one stop us. Is that what you're planning?" He moves closer to them. "Is that what you're planning on doing?"

"No, I'm just trying to be safe here. I just want to have a contingency plan."

"A what? What?" His frustration is rising.

"A backup plan," Pan says, "she just wants a backup plan, is all."

Now he scrutinizes Pan, as if he hadn't really recognized her presence until this moment.

"Yeah? How about this for a backup plan?" He gesticulates with the gun, "If anyone does anything other than walk out of here with these bags, I'll just shoot you and anyone else in the way. How does that sound? Sounds good to me." He scratches his arm again and starts nodding, surging adrenaline through his confused nervous system. "Sounds fucking good to me. You, pick up the bag. You, pick up the other bag. And you," he stares at Pan, "keep your mouth fucking shut, and walk next to me. And Be. Fucking. Calm."

Nora and Lena pick up the bags. He nods to Pan to open the door. "Lead the way."

Pan glances at Lena—*Help me, Mom*, she tries to ask with her eyes—but Lena returns an icy stare that translates to, *You're on your own*. She inhales deeply and opens the door.

"Be calm," he whispers just as she's about to leave. "We'll be out of this soon enough." She's surprised how soothing these words prove to be, forgetting this isn't really happening.

Pan starts to walk but realizes she doesn't know the interior of the place, having blindly followed Lena and Nora. "I don't know where the exit is." She looks at the junkie, hoping, blindly, that he might have a sense of where the exit is. She feels her face flush when she sees his look of fury.

"Get us. The fuck. Out of here," he mouths to her.

Pan knows she can't glance back at either Nora or Lena for guidance. And then she remembers that she's never been able to look to Lena for guidance. She's never had a mother to talk to, to ask anything. She's only had herself. *Okay*, she thinks, *I'm going to walk us out of here*. She walks with feigned confidence. The storm thundering through her nerves must be blocking her ears, because she doesn't realize that the direction she's heading is becoming louder and louder, denser with people. She opens a door and recognizes the mistake she's made, since the first thing she observes is the back of the drummer about ten feet in front of her, then the backs of the bassist and guitarist. And then the glances of the men and women dressed in all black clothing with "Crew" printed on their shirts, staring at her and the rest of the gang.

"Fuck."

"What's all this?" one of the crew asks, gesturing to the bags in their hands.

The volume of the music is brain-fuzzing.

"We're just, uh, we're just—"

"We're bringing backup cables," Lena shouts above the volume. "Jason told us that a fuse blew out a few minutes ago and that you guys needed some backup cables. We," she nods over to the junky, Pan, and Nora, who each stare dumbfounded at her, "obviously have no clue what any of this equipment is. So, we just figured we'd bring it all."

Two other crewmen walk over, glances tinged with confusion and suspicion.

"Who the fuck is Jason?" one of them asks, staring at the junkie, who's averting his eyes.

"Jason, you know. The doorman," Lena says with complete confidence. "He tracked us down in the green room and told us a fuse blew in the middle of a song and—"

"No fuse blew out here. Who'd you say you were?" the crewman asks, keeping his gaze primarily on the junkie.

"Look, obviously Jason was confused. We'll just turn around now and drop these back off. Sorry."

"Hold up," a different crewman starts, "tell us again, or for the first time, just who the fuck you are. You aren't moving a foot until we hear some names."

Pan groans as she watches the junkie reach for his gun.

"How about you shut the fuck up?" He points the gun between both crewmen; the rest of the crew's focus diverts from the stage to the scene unfolding. "Just shut. The fuck. Up." He starts to back up toward the door, keeping the gun facing the crew. He looks at the three women. "One of you better start getting us out of here. Now."

The largest of the crewmen takes this opportunity to bulrush him.

"Shit!" The junkie fires the gun. The clang of the bullet hitting the ceiling isn't much louder than the music, but it's enough to draw the bassist's attention, who stops playing as he sees the crewman tackle the junkie to the ground. And then the rest of the band follows suit.

"Pan!" Lena shouts from the hallway as she and Nora run out.

Pan, too stunned by the events of the past few seconds, stands immobile.

"Let's go!" Lena shouts again, running back to grab Pan's wrist.

"Mom?" she says, still dazed with shock as she looks at Lena's face.

"Help!" the junkie shouts as one crewman pins his legs down and another starts punching his face. "Help!" he shouts again, looking into Pan's eyes, and for a moment his face seems to look like—*that was...no, that can't*—then it resumes its anonymity. She feels nauseous with sympathy, and without realizing what she's doing, Pan grabs the man's wrist and yanks him up. It's not lack of strength that relaxes the doorman's grip but sheer shock at seeing Pan help him.

"Pangaea!" Lena shouts. "Let's go!"

They zigzag through the hallway as people move out of their way in confusion. Pan can barely discern different murmurs: "What's going on?" "Did someone shoot a gun?" "Is this part of the show?" She doesn't realize that she's holding the junkie's wrist, leading him along.

They run through the kitchen and out the door into the alley. They head toward Lena's car, the rain plummeting in torrents. Pan is abruptly halted in her tracks by the junkie's sudden cessation of movement. He proceeds to vomit in the middle of the street. She let's go of him, and he crumples onto his hands and knees. She notices the mixture of blood in his vomit, the rain swirling the contents into a nightmare collage of intestinal refuse.

"Pan! Get the fuck over here!" Lena shouts from the car. "Leave that asshole and let's go!"

But Pan can't move. She looks at him, and again his face modulates and *that's Ivan. That's Ivan's face*, and she won't leave him.

"Come on." Pan puts her arm into the crook of his elbow and heaves him up and guides him back to the car, throwing him across the back seat.

"What the fuck?" Nora says. "We're not taking this asshole with us. The cops are gonna be here in a second."

"Just drive, Mom." Pan looks at Lena. Some connection inherent in blood must find its way into the gaze they exchange because Lena nods and turns the key in the ignition.

"Where are we gonna take him?" Nora asks. "He's sure as shit not coming back to our apartment."

"I know, I know. I mean, I dunno. Should we just drop him off at the hospital?" Lena says.

Pan looks at the junkie, whose face still resembles Ivan's, then she thinks of Devorah, the myriad clinic pamphlets she's seen strewn in her apartment. But something strange starts to happen. Pan looks at the junkie, whose head rests in her lap; the gaunt face with the bagged eyes begins to change again. She sees Devorah. Devorah staring up at her, saying, "Help." Pan looks aghast at her friend's face. "Help me, Pan," Devorah says. *How?* she asks herself, forgetting where she is. *How can I help you?* She looks down at the body, at the scars on the arm, as it, too, begins to change shape into Devorah's.

"Mom." Pan looks into the rearview mirror, where Lena meets her eyes. "Take her to Harbor View Recovery. It's in Malden."

She accelerates.

"Pan, did I wait too long?"

"For what?"

"To think of him as real?" Dev cradles her stomach. Pan moves her own hand over her abdomen, feeling the rise. "How can I kill someone who's not even alive?"

Pan looks in the rearview mirror at Lena. *Would it have been kinder of you to kill me before I even knew there could be a you? Before I could be an I?*

Lena responds aloud, staring ahead at the road: "Well, ask yourself: would you rather have the reality of a mother like Devorah than the delusion of me in your head?"

The difference is that you could have aborted me. I only know your absence since you let there be the possibility of your presence. Since you chose for there to be a me.

Pan looks back down at Devorah. "You're not gonna die. I promise. For better or worse, you're gonna have this fucker. And I'm gonna help you get there. And you're going to love each other. I promise. You're going to love this child," she says as she meets Lena's eyes in the rearview mirror.

Devorah's face begins to lose form and congeal into an ovular mass of skin as she says, somehow now in Lena's voice rather than her own, "But what if I wait too long for that too?"

"Too long for what?"

"Too long for the idea of my child to actually feel alive?"

The light is bright as Pan comes out of the simulation. She feels nauseous and reaches for the pink, banana-shaped bowl placed next to her, proceeding to hurl into it. Pan hears Persephone's footsteps before she sees her.

"How'd this one go?" She offers Pan a tissue to wipe her mouth.

"Um…" Pan rubs her eyes as if waking from an interrupted sleep before collecting her thoughts. *Just let me go to sleep. All I want to do is sleep.* "It was pretty much how I wanted the design to be, I'd have to say. Except…" She pauses, still weary.

"Except what?" Persephone's eyes and attention are upon her laptop, taking notes.

Pan envisions Ivan's face melding into Devorah's, "Can we pick this up next time? I gotta admit, I'm a bit beat."

"Unfortunately, no. We need to conduct these interviews right when the simulation is fresh in your mind."

Pangaea looks at her, trying not to focus on her reflection in the glass eye but rather look at this woman.

"Remember," Persephone begins, "you've signed an agreement. This is all for research. Everything you experience in there, we have a proprietary right over. We expect your truthfulness throughout this test-study. In fact, it's legally obligated."

"But they're my experiences. How can you own an idea that's come from my head?"

"It's a bit more complicated than that. The distinction between what you're calling your own ideas and the products of our machines is blurry." Persephone pauses. "Before we continue, I feel I should remind you: you're free to stop your involvement with us at any time. But, unless or until you do so, your experiences in Wonderland are our product and our research. Per the contract, you're required to tell us about your experience. Now, please tell me about this simulation."

Pan looks at the floor. "Well, one of my friends sort of, hmm. I'm trying to think how to phrase it. But, I guess, one of my friends sort of...replaced one of the people in the simulation. One of the people I had the engineers design."

"Can you be more specific?"

"I was looking at this person in the simulation—just this random guy I sketched for the programmers to design—but, at one point, his face began to shift."

"Shift, how?"

"Into the face of someone else I know. Someone who wasn't supposed to be in there, in the simulation."

"But someone who had somehow entered your thoughts?"

"Isn't the whole thing supposed to *just* be my thoughts?"

Persephone looks up from her laptop. "To an extent, yes. Our product is designed to allow freedom and agency in the simulation but within limits. What you're describing sounds like something we encountered in an early stage of development: conscious interference."

"Right. I totally know what that is." She's caught off guard by how familiar Persephone's laugh sounds.

"Sorry. Sometimes I get a little caught up in all this. It's rather technical, but think of it this way: these experiences occur entirely within your head, with the aid of our instruments. In many ways, your head is essentially *in* our instruments when you're plugged in to the Human Connection. Your preliminary design allows us to create a shape, so to speak, for your thoughts to move in, but this shape functions as a barrier too. Conscious interference is the phenomenon of your thoughts outside our design penetrating the shape. So, while we want you to have freedom within the simulation to do what you choose, we also need to bear in mind that you've designed something specific. In this way, outside thoughts that penetrate would detract from your desire. And so, we try to limit the amount your mind can stretch while immersed in the simulation."

"Isn't that mind control?"

She's again surprised at Persephone's laugh. "We wouldn't call it that. I'd say it's more akin to cognitive sculpting."

Pan drives home, blasting a bootleg from the Japan stretch of Pink Floyd's '72 tour. Her windshield wipers are at full speed pelting away the rain.

Lena: *Am I just conscious interference? Just a voice breaking through the shape of your thoughts?*

Pan: *No, you're just a nuisance I gift to myself in my masochistic glory.*

Lena: *How come you didn't tell her about the past week? How you've seen snow where there isn't snow. Mirrors where there's only air.*

Cause it's all just in my head, she's convinced herself. *It's just my head trying to wrap around these simulations. Nothing more.*

The past two nights she's had seemingly dreamless sleep with the assistance of Alvin's trazodone, half a bottle's worth that she heisted from his room. *All I needed was some sleep.*

"Pangaea?" Persephone had asked her again. "Can you tell me why your friend might've entered the simulation unwanted?"

Because she's just as lost as that junkie. "I really don't know. I think it was just as simple as the person I designed to be in the simulation resembling someone I know."

Persephone seemed to read through this story but simply asked, "And is there anything else you'd like to report about this simulation? Or anything, really, since your first simulation?"

Lena: *You're not at all worried it could be something serious? They have you plugged into a machine, after all. Do you really want to ignore side effects?*

"Jesus Christ, it's fucking pouring," Pan says as she stops at a traffic light, hearing the pelts of precipitation percuss against the car. She continues to drive, listening to the live rendition of *Dark Side of the Moon*, how the songs were pronounceably more melancholic on tour than the studio album. She pulls into the driveway and flicks off the wipers, hesitating for a moment as she sees, for just a second, Nora and Lena sitting in the car with her. It's only once she opens the door that Pan realizes there's not a cloud in the sky.

A PROMISE

"**N**o, man. There's batshit in there."

"Guano."

"What?"

"It's called guano."

They see bushes rustling a hundred yards away and can hear the distant, excited chatter, indiscernible but palpable with energy.

"Whatever. Simon and Ben are gonna see us in a sec if we don't keep going. I'm gonna hide in there. Even if you're grossed out by bat shit." Sam got on his knees and started crawling between the boulders.

Damnit. Alvin looked around, trying to pick a direction to run. *It's almost four, though…it's gonna get dark soon.* "Sam," he whispered louder than his normal voice. "Sam! We probably need to stop soon anyway. It's gonna get dark, and Ben's mom is gonna freak out if we're not back in the parking lot."

"Shut up and get away. Don't get me caught just 'cause you're a pussy."

Alvin hasn't heard a word Pan has said as he remembers seventh grade, the forest the same in every way but different down to the atom.

"But I'm not that worried about it. I think these quick visions are only brain fog."

"What? Oh, right. The simulations. Yeah, I mean, if they don't stop soon or get worse, then you should probably mention it. But it's probably no different than MyAIs making people need contacts sooner."

He hasn't heard one word. Pan smiles, shaking her head. *Talking to him is no different than talking to you.*

Lena: *At least I listen, though.*

As Alvin lets the whimsy of memory arrest his attention, Pan visits the future:

Pangaea: *Remember how you promised we'd live on a lake? That when I step outside the door, there'll be mountains everywhere I look?*

Alvin: *Not easy to do that with an eighty-K salary.*

Pangaea: *I'm not accusing you of anything. I'm just reminding you. You used to tell me that eventually I won't even remember Lena's name. That you'd love me enough that I'd forget she could ever have existed, let alone left me.*

Alvin: *Are you saying it's my fault now that you don't have a mother?*

Pangaea: *No, I'm asking you why I was dumb enough in the first place to believe that loving someone solves anything.*

"I still have a tab if you want one, Al." Pan returns to the present, trying to reel him back with her. "Probably wouldn't kick in for an hour, though."

"I'm all set. Besides..." He's unable to prevent the inevitable blush that covers his face when he can't resist being sappy. "You're my drug."

"Aww, that might've been sweet enough to make me gag a bit." There's, of course, a requisite kiss. "Put that on my tombstone: 'Pangaea Was a Drug,' all in bold font."

As it's Wednesday, there are very few other people on the mountain with them. That and it's about ninety degrees with humidity. Pan told him she was only microdosing when, in fact, she ingested three drops of blotter acid that Devorah had given her.

I don't know old this shit is, Pan.

Does it smell weird?

Devorah sniffed. *No. I mean, it's acid.* Which was reassuring enough for Pan to take the whole bottle back home.

Lena: *You've been hallucinating quite a bit this past week.*

Pangaea: *I'm fine, Mother. Thanks for your concern.*

"I really think this is the month I'm gonna quit," Alvin says, resuming his ramble.

"Yeah? And what makes this May different from the last four?"

He glances at her, hearing the unmasked venom in her tone. "Are you all right?" He stops walking and gently grabs her wrist. "You've been sounding fatigued or something since this morning. For the past week or so, really."

"I'm fine." She disentangles the grip. "I just feel like I hear a broken record from you whenever you talk about work. And then I sound like a broken record too, either just telling you time and again to quit or to just put up with it. Stop moaning. You have a choice in the matter."

They're walking along a side trail that borders a boggy river; there's a thick smell in the air of what can best be described as earth-crotch. Gnats and mosquitos orbit their faces. For the moment, Pangaea isn't disturbed by the modulating greens, browns, and yellows the scenery paints for her chemically altered perception.

Alvin adopts a bashful tone and looks at his feet. "Well, I'm sorry if I sound so mopey, but I just, I dunno, I guess I really don't know what to do. Maybe slightly mopey is my natural state. You also have your moments when you decide to open up a bit."

The part of the trail they're on now is muddy, splaying their ankles with goop.

"I think I'm just," she stops herself, stifling the urge to vent about the simulations. *Why bother telling him anything important?* "I'm just worried about Dev. I can't stop thinking about her having to carry this thing to term."

"Well, what about *it*? Do you think of that at all?"

"Huh? What 'it?'"

"Her fucking baby."

Did I wait too long? Pangaea feels the weight of Devorah in her arms again and hears her ask, *How can I kill someone who's not even alive?*

"Of course I'm thinking of it too. I mean both of them whenever I say 'Dev.' Even though I suppose you could say right now there's still only Dev." She tries to focus on the fractal modulations of scenery, hoping the acid can supersede the vestiges of the simulation creeping into her head.

Lena: *That's not what the Maternity Pact says. As soon as there can be a him, there is a him.*

"I was over at her apartment the other day. She has to do these weekly programs from the Maternity Center. She let me do one. This program's supposed to recreate the experience of the fetus from within the womb as it develops over the next months. As if anyone can possibly know what that is. So you put the glasses on, then watch from a first-person point of view. Your limbs begin to take shape, and the womb begins to take on contours as your eyes start to function. And then, get this, you know how it ends?"

"Hmm. It cuts to the ending of *Space Odyssey*?"

"Close. With a bright, white light that conveniently spreads out in a cross. Welcoming you to the world. And then the screen goes blank." She halts, feeling the same nausea she had felt coming out of the last simulation.

"Oy, you all right? Here, let's sit down."

Alvin guides her to a rock, and Pan feels rain plummet atop her, despite the glaring sun. *It's just the acid.* Again, the imagery of the last simulation begins to take shape around her as she looks at the forest, intermittently pulsing with shimmers and darkening with an overcast sky, obscuring the reality of its clear-blue state. She sits on the rock next to Alvin, looking down at her hands like the weight of Devorah is in them, splayed across her lap in the back seat of the car.

"You just take a bit too much today?" he asks. "I feel like you never know where Dev gets her drugs."

"No, no, it's not that. I'm fine. Maybe I just need," she looks at him, wondering if the lip-glue of a kiss is what she wants right now or *Maybe I just want* She feels a foreign sense of yearning, almost an itch, for the anesthetic needle *to be back in Wonderland.*

Alvin does indeed start to bring her face to his but before their lips entangle—

"Don't be indecent, you." The ghost of his great-great-great-grandmother, Yetta, oy veys herself into form in front of them.

"Hey there, bubby," Alvin says with resignation as she interrupts what he thought might otherwise be a pleasant exchange of saliva.

Pan waves. "Good to see ya, bubs. How's paradise treating you?"

"Eh." Yetta bats her wrist. "What can I say? Even though we had to sleep with one eye open in the Shtetl, at least it kept our nerves active. Our minds moving." She gesticulates in frustration. "But up there, you might as well be sleep-walking, everything's so blissful. You know, Moses saw the Holy Land from afar. He knew better than to step in it."

"Sounds terrible." Alvin smirks at Pan.

"You think I'm joking, eh?"

"Well, I think most people would rather have a day up in heaven than one down here."

"Feh!" Yetta exclaims. "Most people aren't Jews; that's what it is. I mean, what other people have had God turn His back on them only to return to them as much as we have? Eh? You tell me that. One moment, He loves us for a generation or two. The next? A pogrom here and a ritual-murder riot there. I'm not just talking about the Krouts—you ever hear of the Romans? Don't get me started on the Spanish. The Polish...then again..." She halts her speech and pulls her shawl closer to her body, despite the heat. "God is a very lonely man. Who else could've created free will? Who else could've needed a love so strong that people can only feel it in belief? The choice to love Him, only if you can believe He's there. Without any assurance He can love you back. Without any reason to think it. But maybe that's why we're here. To suffer with him. To be the people who suffer for the promise of love." She sits on the rock next to Alvin and takes his cheeks in her hands, staring at his face and seeing those of his fathers before him. "Or maybe *suffer* isn't the word. Maybe it's *survive*. To be the people who survive on the promise of love. And don't be so quick to count yourself out." She looks at Pan. "I know you and your father don't practice, but it's in you. Our faith is in your blood, bubeleh. You can't run away from the past. Baruch Hashem."

And it can't run away from me. Pangaea's back in the house of mirrors as the forest around her vanishes; she's her younger self, looking into the carnival mirror as the reflections blur together and snow falls atop her.

"Just remember, you two." The sound of Yetta's voice yanks her back into the forest. "We all had to die our way here. Every one of us." She lightly jabs her own chest. "Everyone who's died before you lives in you. Breathes in you. *Is* you. To be Jewish is not just to inherit the past. It's to keep it alive. Because what else can make you *you* more than the blood you come from? In fact, that's all you are. The soup of the blood before you." And then she's gone.

Pan and Alvin are quiet. She scootches closer to him, and both their breaths deepen, as happens when two hearts feel the other's pulse. They can't see it, but from afar they appear immersed in a green fluid that is the phenomenon of the sun's photons mingling with those of the leaves above and around them and, in fact, mingling with those emitted from their own bodies. This union of light. Pan and Alvin choose to unite even closer, the marriage of light now becoming one of touch and taste and smell as they kiss and hold each other, oblivious to the way the beaded sweat of their brows sticks together just as closely as their tongues.

When their lips part, their eyes remain closed. The blackness behind Pan's lids seems to percuss and swell and, this close to Alvin, her own minute movements of breath and pulse appear in her hallucination unified with his. When he speaks, it's almost as if his voice is within her.

"There's something you're not telling me, Pan. I can feel it."

Pangaea: *I was eleven, but I remember it like it just happened. It's not something you'd forget.*

Alvin: *No, it sounds spooky. I've had a few times where I thought I saw a ghost too.*

Pangaea: *I don't think I saw a ghost. I'm telling you I felt her hand. Just like this. Are you even listening?*

Alvin: *Okay, okay. Of course. I promise, I'm always listening.*

Pangaea: *Prove it.*

Alvin: *You were eleven, and you had a dream that you still remember like it happened last night. And in this dream, you were lost in a forest. But it was scary. Normally there's nowhere you love being more than a place that's surrounded by trees and flowers.*

Pangaea: *Remind me why.*

Alvin: *Because plants are the purest form of life. They never die. Life simply moves from one form to another.*

Pangaea: *Good boy.*

Alvin: *You were lost in a forest and felt like something was chasing you. You couldn't hear anything, but you knew if you stopped and turned around, something terrible would happen. Worse than dying. It would be like your life had completely vanished. So you kept running, but the forest just kept getting denser and denser. You couldn't even see the sky between the trees, and the branches were reaching out like hands.*

Pangaea: *Claws. They weren't hands.*

Alvin: *Reaching out like claws trying to grab you. You couldn't even shout. When you tried opening your mouth, it felt like there was a weight pressing around you, crushing. You could barely even breathe, and then, suddenly, without warning, the forest was gone, and you were standing on a cliff. Still need me to prove that I'm listening?*

"Alvin," Pan says, holding his clammy palms, "I need you to tell me something. Do you remember when I told you I felt Lena hold my hand?"

"Of course."

"I'm being serious. Do you remember?"

"Pan, I just told you I do."

"Promise me."

"I promise."

"Then prove it."

Alvin: *And when you were on the cliff, you had nowhere to run, so all you could do was turn around. And even though you dreaded doing it, it was all that could be done.*

"…and then you turned around and saw—this is the part you were never clear about," Alvin reminds Pan, "you never said exactly what you saw when you turned around from the cliff."

"I know what I saw, but that's not the important thing. Finish the story."

"You woke up, and you couldn't move. It was your first episode of sleep paralysis. But in your hand—"

"Which hand?"

"Your right hand. You woke up, and you felt someone holding your right hand. But it didn't frighten you. It was the opposite of what you felt in that dream. It was—okay, now don't hold it against me if I can't remember verbatim what you said, but it was—"

"Home. It felt like home."

"You felt someone hold your hand, and you knew it was Lena when she said, 'I promise you, I'm always here.'"

She looks at Alvin now as he says this, but *why can't I feel anything? Looking at him here before me. I can reach out and hold him, feel his body. But I feel nothing.*

Pangaea: *She said, 'I promise you, I'm always here,' and then I jolted up. The sleep paralysis was gone, and I turned around and saw no one. I looked at my hand and felt nothing. And then I started weeping.*

"Let's get back to the car, Al. We've been out here long enough." She gets up without waiting for him to hold her hand.

Alvin: *Hey, listen, I'd probably cry too if I had a dream that frightening.*

Pangaea: *You already broke your promise. If you'd been listening, you'd know that's not why I was crying.*

Alvin: *Then why?*

Pangaea: *Because an imaginary promise, holding an imaginary hand that might as well have been a fantasy, felt better than anything real ever had.*

HERE TO THERE

Pangaea sits crisscross on the floor of her living room, her purple hair dangling over her face as she stares at photographs. There are shoeboxes full of them encircling her, orbiting her sedentary body in a drone of indistinct chatter. Lena's with her.

"This is a good one," she says as Pan glances at a photo of her mother holding her as an infant, Isaac smiling down over his wife's shoulder. She looks intently at it, staring into her own eyes (which, in the photo, lock on to her mother's gaze), then Pan is within the photo, inside her infant self, looking up at her mother:

"Mom." She reaches her chubby hands toward the dangling locks of Lena's hair.

Lena leans closer and lets Pan clutch her. Pan lets the squish of her hands speak affection, until she asks, "How is this not enough for you to stay?"

Lena's smile doesn't leave as she says, "Forget I exist. The only way I could have left you is if I was able to forget you exist."

It's like he's just an idea. Like, like he's not even alive. But just on his way to thingness.

Pan blinks at the barging memory of Ivan and leaves the photograph, landing back in her living room. "But I still do exist, mom. Even if you can pretend I don't." She puts the photo in a pile of other "Don't Use" Polaroids; the past month now, she's been doing this to help fill out the preliminary design forms.

She stops on a blurry one taken in a dimly lit bar. Lena is standing next to a gruffy fellow with a close-lipped smile and cowboy hat. Her left arm hangs over his shoulder while the other extends a drink toward the camera. She stares at her mother's face in the photo. "You were younger then than I am now." Gazing at her eyes, trying to inject herself behind them so she can stare back at herself through the prisoned ink of the photo. *But I can't. I can't. There I am, in you, and you don't even know it yet, and I guess I don't either, but maybe behind the ink you do know it, and so maybe I'm in there behind the ink too.* And now Pangaea is in the photo, gazing through her mother's eyes:

Fuck, I didn't bring a raincoat. I stepped out of the highway gas station, not bothering to cover my head from the rain. Nora had ridden off with her ride and told me to call whenever I got somewhere with a phone. Neither of us doubted that we'd each hitch a ride. We didn't take the variable of rain into account, though. I saw there was a truck lodging down at the end of the gas station and started heading that way. *One of them is bound not to look too fatal a mistake.* The first door I knocked on, I was greeted by an old man who looked at me like I was dripping in shit. I knew he'd say no but still asked. He just stared a few more seconds before saying I was dumb as bricks if I asked any of the other truckers there for a lift. I smiled and flipped him off. At least he laughed at that and threw me a week-old newspaper for raincover before shutting the door. The next truck I tried, I didn't like the look of the guy. His smile seemed too friendly, and the interior of his truck smelled strongly of bleach. The sort of smell that's always stronger than whatever it's supposed mask.

So instead of asking for a lift I just asked for a light. Halfway to the next truck I tossed the cigarette on the pavement and had to spit the taste out. Then I knocked on another door.

"Hi there," he said as he rolled down the window.

"Hi, honey." I was trying to gauge within a few seconds if he'd be more attracted to timid or bold. He looked like he was in the tail end of his thirties and had acquired enough weight to consider himself past his first youth, and my nose suggested he had showered at least within the past two days. "I'm wondering if I can get a lift. Think you can help me out?"

He smiled benignly enough, and I glanced at his hands. I sighed with relief to see there was a ring. "Maybe. Depends where you're looking to go. I'm heading south."

"Anywhere in Mass'll work." I didn't know how far up in New Hampshire we were, but I figured getting to Mass would be good enough. He studied me a moment, unabashedly and unapologetically sizing me up, gauging the firmness of my ass, the curvature of my tits, which I only just then considered the effect the rain had on them, determining if he could discover, in the matter of the seconds in a glance, whether we might share a bed. "All right," he eventually said. "I can take you down Route One and drop you off near Kowloon. You know the place?"

"Of course." I envisioned the triangular structure of the restaurant that was more of an asylum than dining establishment. "And thanks, by the way." I made my way around the truck to the passenger seat and, on a whim, told him my real name.

"Nice to meet you, Lena. I'm Paul."

Then we headed down 95 South. We didn't speak much at first. He asked where I was coming from, and I told him Quebec, which was somewhat true. He asked where I was living these days, and I lied about that one, telling him Quincy. Then he asked what I do, and after I gave a smart-ass answer, he asked again, amused enough at this portrait of myself I was painting as a carefree, bank-rolled suburban girl out getting her kicks in her twenties, which was true enough, even if I pretended to be more naive and trustfunded than I actually was. I told him I was a travelling saleswoman, and he laughed at that one.

"You don't strike me as the saleswoman type, not having anything you seem to be selling."

I laughed the commensurate immature-girl giggle and told him I sold software and didn't need to carry a product. I said that that was the way of the future: being thingless. He seemed to like that one, the word *thingless*.

"That'll be the day I'm out of a job, when there are no 'things' anymore. There'll be nothing to take from here to there."

And I liked the sound of that, I really did: "from here to there." So I started asking him about himself as I stared at the endless rows of pine trees corridoring the highway.

"I've been driving trucks since I was eighteen. Speaking of which, how old might you be?"

To which I flirtatiously batted my eyes.

He chuckled. "Yeah, that's pretty much all there is to say. I started driving trucks when I had to start doing something, and I've just been doing it ever since. I'll probably drive myself into the grave. Which I suppose won't be the worst way to take the last exit."

"How'd you meet your wife?" I asked.

He seemed a bit caught off guard, then glanced at his ring.

"I've hitchhiked a bit before, you know," I said in a more honest tone. "I know what to look for."

He looked over at me, appraising me more thoroughly.

"Not much of a story there, really, how I met Dahlia."

I could hear the change of tone in his voice when he said his wife's name and at that moment felt truly at ease. I stopped paying attention to the little Swiss Army knife in my pocket.

"I had a contract job for about a year in eastern Washington. That's pretty country over there, let me tell you. You can drive for hours, and you'll see mountains that don't stop. The way the clouds sit on them sometimes just like they were thrones. That'll get you thinking. Even if you're not the thinking type. But anyway. I had a contract job and was put up at a little motel. She—Dahlia—she worked the front desk, and we just started flirting. You know how it is. I fell in love with her black hair and the way she seemed so at home in her own skin, you know what I mean? Almost like there was someone in her looking through those eyes at me. I don't know if I'm making any sense, but most people don't have that, I can tell you. Even I wonder if I know anything about who I am. But not Dahlia. That's a woman who knows who she is. *What* she is. And she must've seen something in me, I don't know. Maybe it was just the fact I was the only guy within an hour's drive any direction of that place that wasn't twenty years older than her or somehow related."

He chuckled a bit, easing the tension of hearing himself.

"And so, over those months we just got to know each other. I'd be gone for a stretch of a few weeks, then come back to restock at the warehouse nearby and spend a few days in the motel; she'd just stay with me. This little twin bed that wasn't even big enough for me. And the worst—I mean *worst*—blankets your skin could touch. Like those metal coils you scrub dishes with. But eventually the contract was up, and I said, 'I'm going. Are you coming with me?' Wouldn't you know it, she did. She loved the road. She'd just sit passenger with me, which most employers don't let you do, but I kept it under the radar. And we just drove around the country for years. Sometimes we'd go a whole day without a word. We'd just stare at the world in front of us and feel like we were in a palace in that truck cabin. I'll tell you, some places we drove, we might as well have been on the moon they looked so foreign. Sometimes you see mountains that're endless, and sometimes you see flat stretches of field that are even more endless. And it makes you really wonder how big the world is. And you have to wonder what's going through the hearts and minds of everyone else out there. If there's as much going on in them as there is in you; which, sure enough, there is."

He stopped talking for a moment. I said nothing, waiting for him to continue.

"So we were really just driving. Then, after a few years, we were stopped at some roadside diner, and she said, out of the blue and perfectly ordinary, 'Either propose to me right now or take me back home.' I choked on the eggs I was eating but knew better than to ask her to repeat that; I heard her clear enough. That's not something a woman mumbles. So, in a roadside diner in the middle of the day in the middle of the week, I honestly can't even tell you what state we were in, I got out of the little booth and got on one knee and asked her to marry me. Didn't even have a ring but got one later that month. That was eight years ago."

The whole time he was telling me this, I was trying to imagine who she might be, what she might be thinking that very moment. Was she home? Was she in some anonymous office doing anonymous work that meant nothing more than an anonymous paycheck? Was she daydreaming of the times when she was on the road with her love, going nowhere but being everywhere?

"That's something special. I hope you know that."

He nodded, and I could see through the blush that he wasn't used to talking this much, maybe to anyone.

"Well, if nothing else, it's my life, and I certainly wouldn't change it. That's something that'll keep people up at night. Wondering if they could change the bed they sleep in. The day they wake to. What would you say if I asked you that, Lena?"

"Go on and ask me."

"Would you change your life right now if you could?"

"We can't just pack our bags and leave, Pan," Alvin said.

"Why not? Neither of us have rent or anything we gotta pay."

"Pan..."

"No, seriously, give me one reason why not." She lies in bed, revisiting tonight's argument.

"For starters, we both have jobs."

"Okay. I work for my dad, who would probably think it'd be the best decision of my life if I just packed my bags and left home. And you, you fucking hate your job. You're always talking about how much you wanna quit. So, let's do it."

"It's not that easy."

"But it is!"

She was still looking at the photo of Paul and Lena, pacing around her backyard with it in one hand as she held her phone in the other.

"Where would we even go? Huh? Would we just get in my car and start driving? Where would we sleep?"

We'd be with each other, Al, that's all that matters. But she didn't feel convinced that that'd be enough, even for her, let alone him. "We could just start driving down the pike. Who fucking knows, we'd end up somewhere eventually."

"Where's this coming from? What do you wanna see all the sudden? I've known you four years, and you've never wanted to move so much as to a different city. Now this?"

Would you change your life right now if you could?

Pangaea looked over at Paul, sitting there in the truck with him.

"Alvin, I just…" She put the photo in her pocket and sat down. "We don't even know what it is we're not seeing. It's like—" *What we noticed was a tendency among most people to view the actual world, the one we live awake through, as a sketch.*

"Pan? You still there?"

I don't think so, she told Paul, *if anything…*

"I'm here, Al." *What's more important: your sense of being at home in the world around you…* "Maybe you're right," she said, not thinking of Alvin's face but Persephone's as the questions began to flood her memory.

"Huh?"

She looked at the photo again, staring at her mother's face.

Lena: *You've always let your imagination be the world, Pan. or the one within you*

"I said, maybe you're right. We don't need to pack up and suddenly change our lives."

"You're talking weird, Pan. Do you want to come over? Or I can come to you."

"No, I'm fine. Let's just go to sleep, and in the morning everything will be fine. We'll be right where we are, like always. Something just got in me, I don't know."

She hung up.

As she lies awake in bed, she's still looking at Paul.

If anything, what, Lena? he asks her.

If anything Pan tries to imagine the sensation of the leather in the truck, but she can't; she can only wonder what the leather felt like in the seat her mother sat in—*I wouldn't live my life at all.*

MATCH

Would you wanna go to the aquarium? There aren't any sharks, but it's still fun, haha, Ellis types to Maria, who matched with him on the dating app last week.

No, she'll think the 'haha' is forced. And it probably smells like seawater in there anyway. He clears the message and looks at his other matches, which are beyond count at this point.

It's not like she'd reply to you anyway. And even if she did, you wouldn't go.

He looks at Bethany's profile, staring at her practiced smile that appears the same in all five photos, imagining, *If only she could tie me to burning pavement and pour scalding water on my eyes, my whole face. Burning the skin so deep the bones char. Keeping that smile fixed on my irises as they liquify into yogurt.*

He swipes away from her profile and looks at his, which he changes almost daily.

I look like a faggot in this photo. He clenches his teeth as he looks at a selfie he took after yesterday's workout, the sweat filming his entire body like Saran wrap. Ellis scrolls up and looks at a photo of him and Lauren, captioned, "Me and My best friend." *Girls think that's kinda cute.*

Maybe when they see most guys. He sighs, unable to keep the voice out. *But with you, they see that and wonder if they should call the police. Who knows what sick shit you do with her.*

Stop it. Not Lauren. Keep her out of my head.

I'm not putting her there. It's only you.

He goes back to the main page and begins to swipe indiscriminately, then stops as he knows what he's about to do.

Your favorite part.

He scrolls through the main page, swiping on girls he's grimly certain no guy ever looks twice at, and within minutes he has three matches.

Hey Ellis! omg, ur so fit! What's your routine, haha!

He looks with pity at Hannah's pocked face, the baggy clothes she wears in the only photo that shows anything below the neck.

Thanks! It's really just running and pushups and diet, haha. Um, so I don't mean to be too forward but...mind if we skip the small talk and get right to it? Are you free to meet up for drinks anytime soon?

He watches the text bubble appear and disappear three times before she replies. *Love it when I'm actually talking with an adult. Do you want to meet up for coffee?*

He feels sick as he types. *Of course! How about that shop, Drip, by the Common? You free tomorrow at like 2?*

Omg yes! Ohh I can't wait, haha. But let's keep messaging to get to know each other a bit, ok? You seem soooo nice.

Ellis will message her sporadically through the day and lie tomorrow about being on his way. He'll block her profile once she confirms she's there.

He goes back to another match, Isabelle, whose photos he's masturbated to the past three nights. He looks at the last message she sent, which he's yet to reply to: *Most guys on this app are trolls, it's such a breath of fresh air to see a guy who actually looks after himself.* Ellis looks at her main photo: she's in professional attire, heels, staring confidentially at the camera with the assurance of a woman who knows she doesn't need to try.

Thanks! Hey, listen...I know it might be kinda strange, but are you alright with video chatting? I feel like it's a good way to get to know each other before we actually meet.

She replies about an hour later. *Hey, ummm ya it's kinda weird, haha, but honestly I love it when a guy cares about making sure we're comfortable with each other. So sure!*

Oh great! Um...how about tonight?

Sure! I stay up late, haha. What time are ya thinking?

At 11:30 he FaceTime's her, distorting his features with an application. Five minutes earlier, he previewed it in a loading screen, staring at his reflection.

Your true reflection. What you really look like, beneath this façade that your body lies to the world.

He sees a face that's blotched with liver spots and scabs, a nose that hooks almost down to his lips. Wispy hair, seaweed grease. When he practices a smile, he sees crooked, brown teeth, missing most of the front. He enhances the brightness to see the cracked, dry skin, the pimples that look like they've been scratched at with nails. "Ellis," he says, the voice filter distorting his voice to a rasp of thirty packyears. The stink of his breath almost palpable in the sound.

That's right. Let her see the real Ellis.

At 11:30 he FaceTime's her, turning off his camera so that her face is the first one visible.

"Oh?" she starts, confused at seeing the blank screen, "Ellis? You there?"

"Hey, Isabelle."

Her eyes boggle at the unexpected hoarseness.

"Sorry, one sec. My computer is being weird." He savors the thrill in his stomach, the euphoric rush of adrenaline. *The closest thing you have to an interaction with women, you pathetic fucking loser.* Then he turns on his camera. "There we go." He watches her mouth drop.

"Oh...um. Hi...Ellis? I, uh..."

"Something wrong?"

"No, um. It's just. I...your profile, looks, um..."

"Is something wrong with the way I look?" His dick throbs in his boxers, the only clothes he's wearing. He starts to touch the head, playing with the skin between his fingers.

"In your photos, um, you look different. I gotta be honest. Wait... is this some joke?" She smiles with the hope that she's figured it out.

"Why the fuck would any of this be a joke, you cunt?" He starts to jerk his dick more vigorously, staring at himself to make sure it's not obvious. *You've already gotten two moderator warnings this year. One more, and you'll be locked out.*

"Whoa, chill out, dude. Look, obviously your profile is a total load of shit. I'm just gonna end the chat, and we can leave it at that, all right?" But she waits a moment.

Since all humans are sick. She wants to see this too.

"I have a disease, you judgmental, superficial bitch. Sorry we don't all start our day with makeup."

"Look, sorry to hear it, but you're taking this way too far. I'm gonna hang up now. I can report all this, you know."

He bares his rotten teeth and brings the laptop closer. She recoils at the sight but doesn't leave.

"You're the definition of gross dude. You're a fucking monster. Enjoy your disgusting, lonely life."

And then she hangs up, letting the entirety of the screen show only his distorted face.

FOREVER IN MEMORY

"You know," Pan says after taking thirty seconds to walk through the room and scan the walls, briefly scrutinizing the sheets. Sniffing the general air quality. "I gotta say, it's exactly what I figured it'd be."

The walls are lined with various maps: one of the globe, one of the known universe, one of Saturn's moons, a giant one of Middle Earth, and one of Vermont mountain ranges; there are three band posters: a candid of Led Zeppelin from a concert in Seattle in 1973; a candid of Pink Floyd playing at the Boston Garden in 1975; and one of the Red Hot Chili Peppers in Boston in 2006; there are a few frayed photocopied posters of Le Douanier paintings, one of which Pangaea recognizes as the famous self-portrait from 1890. Behind these unframed posters, she can see the wall is dark green. The carpet is a light beige, almost pink. She lets her socked feet sink slightly within it.

"And...is that a good thing?" Alvin asks, still standing in the doorway, trying to read her body language. He melts when he sees her eyes as she turns around to look at him. He's only just begun to notice how her eyes smile before her lips.

"Yeah, it's good. This place is literally, like, you, if you were a room. Which makes sense, I guess."

By now he's walked closer to her. She can read that he wants to kiss her but that he's unsure if he should go in for it; they've only been seeing each other a month. This is the first time she's been to his home, the two of them deciding it better to split hotel rooms for their trysts. By now, she knows him well enough to know how many different thoughts are punching each other in his head. She can almost hear them:

Just lean in for it, you dolt! She's in your room!

Yeah, but it'd be so robotic, wouldn't it?

Only if you keep standing here staring at her like a gelded ass clown!

Perhaps it's pity, or perhaps it's a means of keeping the voices she hears in Alvin's head out of her own, but Pangaea takes the liberty of stepping a bit closer and folding her arms around him, which does indeed prompt him to lean into her and unite their lips.

"Happy to be here, Al," she says as they keep their foreheads pressed together in the moments of the after-kiss.

Alvin steers them to his bed, which is loosely made, the sheets and blanket still folded and clumped like ocean waves. Pangaea rests against the pillow and squeezes him as he presses down upon her.

"Wait," she says.

Pan scooches the blanket down and pulls it over her and Alvin's bodies, leaving only their faces above it. As they squirm and squiggle their clothes off, heat builds within the covers, and soon enough they're both nude, cocooned within the pelt of the bed. It's impossible to know who'll be on top by (or if) the time both have cum, but this time Pangaea decides enough is enough and pretends to orgasm atop him eight minutes after he asked for a minute break once he came (a quick two minutes after the romp began). She stays atop him for a few timeless moments as his arms, coiled around her, rub up and down and around her damp back. The weakness of his breath. The way not only their skin has become embedded in each other's, but now the moisture of their sweat and groins has coalesced as well, fermenting the raw, untampered scent of them within the covers.

Pan eventually rolls off, letting her fingernails drag over his chest, thus tickling him and getting the unfortunately childish laugh that she's still wondering if she adores or is repulsed by. *Eh, this time it was kinda cute, I guess*. Whereas, after their last coitus bout, Pan had to put her hand over his mouth to stifle the laugh: *then don't fucking tickle me!*

They stare with their dulled vision up at the ceiling, hearing but not listening to each other's haggard, slow breathing. Alvin's right leg entangles Pangaea's left as they let their calf and thigh nerves play with each other. Their sweat evaporates and coats their skin in a common denominator of benign stink. Pangaea's left hand glides up and down Alvin's right arm as she teases the nerves of his forearm.

"You ready to go again?" he asks when she begins to open and close her nails, like a pulsing circle, in the crook of his elbow. "The little guy's up again."

"No." She sighs, keeping her eyes on the ceiling. "But I can hold it."

She drags her hand down Alvin and finds his cock and begins to caress. He closes his eyes and leans his head against her damp shoulder, nudging his head a bit so that her purple hair drapes his eyes, matting his head with her sweat. They don't speak words as their bodies' duet chants through the room.

After about a minute and thirty seconds, "Oy...Alvin, you could've given me a heads-up." Pan pulls her stickied hands out from the covers and looks at them with minor revulsion. "Egh, look, it's like a web," she says as she spreads her fingers wide with his cum and bugs her eyes at him.

"Ew, get that shit away from me."

Pangaea cocks her eyebrow and wipes her hand over his chest. "That shit, Alvin, *is* you."

"Hey!" He pushes her hand off him and scooches up as she starts to laugh.

"Oh, don't be such a pussy. We both gotta shower anyway. Speaking of which," she gets out of bed and starts to walk to his bathroom, "I haven't inspected your facilities yet."

She flicks on the light switch and stands in the doorway. Alvin stays in the bed, staring at Pangaea's back, her sweating ass, wanting to—but still not sure if they're intimate enough yet—kiss it and bite it and lick it and crawl into it face-first and never dream of being elsewhere. If only it were possible to truly live in her rectum. To stand guard at the waste gate and shout triumphantly at the refuse of Pan as it's forcibly evacuated: *I'm still here!*

Meanwhile, Pangaea gives the bathroom a long once-over: *All right, he's a Crest guy, which is good, even if I'm a Colgate gal. Toothbrush bristles are splayed, which means, like me, he scrubs his teeth, much to his gums' chagrin. Two of the three lightbulbs are dead, which I guess isn't the worst thing to neglect in the maintenance department. Toilet seat is* down, *which maybe he just did 'cause he knew I was coming, but the real test is...* She goes over to the toilet and lifts the lid. *Whoa! No scum circle in there. All right, I'm impressed. But, let's not get hasty. There's still...* She pulls the shower curtain and inspects the tub. *Okay, no hair clumped in here, which I guess makes sense, but there is definitely residue that could use a scrubbing. Let's see his products. All right, Dove shampoo, which is better than Head and Shoulders, but still, not great. And no conditioner? Oy. Huh, he's a bar-soap guy, interesting. Thought only seventy-year-old men still used that. Cerave face wash? Okay, could be better but that's pretty good. No Febreze, though, or candle, which is a pretty crippling blow. And no conditioner, which is a* very *crippling blow.*

She turns and walks out of the bathroom and back to the bed, bending down to kiss him. "You get a B-plus. Which, all things considered, isn't all that bad. Although, an A-minus would've been nice."

"Well, wait."

Pangaea sees the angular grin on his face, a quality she still finds surprising in him: the latent mischief in his head.

"You still have to test out the shower."

He leads her into the bathroom and turns on the water. "You a cold-shower person, per chance?" He keeps one hand in the water spray to gauge the Fahrenheit.

"Um, no. I'm not a psychopath."

"You know, they're actually really good for you. But whatever. All right, feels pretty good now." He steps in and holds her hands as she steps in too, her back facing the showerhead and Alvin's chest facing her.

"So...like, this is romantic and all, Al, but, it *is* a bit tight."

"Yeah, I didn't really think it through, but..."

He reaches over her to redirect the showerhead, unfortunately placing his armpit in front of Pan's nose, which doesn't quite wrinkle but does work overtime for a moment. *Eh, mine can't be much fresher right now*, she reflects. The water now sprays over them as if they're standing under a small waterfall, and Pangaea is pleasantly surprised at the liquid cave created by being under the same stream of water as Alvin.

"That's a bit better," he says, grabbing the bar of soap and suddsing it in his hands. He gives it to Pangaea, and she knows to do the same, then they embrace, scrubbing the other's body with lemon-scented soap. Alvin resolves to take the risk and lets his soapy index finger glide deeply up her crack. She doesn't enjoy it but doesn't quite hate it, and so, to return commensurate touch, she squeezes Alvin's balls, which makes him wince and gets him hard again. She presses her stomach into him, letting the hollow of their soapy bellybuttons form a tunnel between their bodies.

"You have one more in you?" she asks into his right ear, letting her nerves focus on the sensation of the water raining atop her head and trickling over her body, which steals and shares the warmth of Alvin's.

They try to fuck, but the positioning is taxing and surprisingly physically demanding. They laugh at the mutual recognition that neither of them is an athlete, and Pangaea resolves to make the next move; she turns and faces the showerhead and changes the faucet such that now the water is coming out the bath spout. She faces Alvin and flicks her eyebrows up and down in a *how about that?* fashion, and then, once a few inches of water accumulate in the tub, she sits down, prompting Alvin to do the same. After a few moments of trying but failing to achieve some Kamasutra, Tantra-esque position of sitting, face-to-face fucking, Pangaea settles for turning her back to Alvin to sit atop his half-chub and lean back against him as the water rises to their necks, spilling over the edge, at which point she uses her toes to turn off the faucet. Then they sit there, in soapy, wet, sloshing silence.

"Could we stay here forever, Pan?" Alvin eventually asks. "Could we just hold each other right here, forever?"

For a moment she does nothing but focus on the sensation of Alvin's heartbeat, faintly percussing against her back. She slides down him a bit and tilts her head up as he congruently tilts his down, maintaining the glue of their gaze. "Only in memory, Alvin."

"Pangaea?" Persephone asked once she awoke. "What can you tell me about the simulation?"

Only in memory. She still felt immersed in the tub, held in Alvin's arms. "Pan?" She looked at Persephone, unsure if it was her that she had just heard or... *Am I still in there with Alvin? Or is it my memory I hear?* Throughout Persephone's questioning, Pan clung to the lingering sensations of the simulation, feeling a foreign urge to not let them go. Terrified she might lose it forever.

And now, lying awake next to Alvin in his bed, she stares at him as he sleeps, mouth closed, only the centimeter rise and fall of the blanket atop him to give sign of life. *But this feels no better, no different.* She looks at him, waiting for the simulation of being in bed with him that first time to overtake her senses.

She called him on her way home from Wonderland.

"Hey, you."

"What's up?"

"I'm just driving back. What're you doing?"

"Uh, right now I'm helping my mom fold laundry."

She heard Susan through the phone. "Hi, Pan!"

"She says hi, Pan."

"And Pan says hi, Su."

Then the pause. Neither speaking nor feeling the need. Pangaea wondering if she was telling Persephone the truth:

Persephone: *Did it feel any different in there, being with him in the simulation?*

Pangaea: *Different from where?*

Persephone: *Here, out in the world.*

"How about I come over tonight, all right?" she asked, hearing Alvin folding laundry.

"Um, yeah, of course. Head on over. Just, uh, I didn't clean the sheets this wash cycle—"

"So, there'll be your drool and jizz stains on them, I gather?"

"Uh, well, yeah. Those. Plus…," she could hear the smirk on his face through the phone, "whatever stains we make tonight."

"Yeah, yeah. You'll be lucky if you get more than a French kiss."

Pangaea: *Of course it doesn't feel the same. I mean, I love him.*

Persephone: *Then please tell me—and remember, this is all for our research—how does being in love with him here in the world feel any different than being with him there in the simulation?*

She pulled up to the curb in front of Alvin's house, seeing him through the living room window sitting next to Farfel, reading *Portnoy's Complaint* for at least the fourth time.

Pangaea: *Because—*

"Hey," Alvin said as he opened the door, "I was thinking we could start watching that new—" but was silenced when Pangaea leaned into his lips with hers and pulled him to her, trying to convince herself the sensation of him in the flesh would feel different from the memory of being in his room for the first time *but—*

Pangaea: *Because here in the world, it's him I love. Whereas anything I feel in these simulations is just a reflection of my thoughts. In these simulations, it's just myself.*

She rests her head atop his chest in bed now and waits to feel the beat of his somnambulant heart. When Pan looks at his closed eyes, she's back on his doorstep, caught in the shadowed memory of their kiss. *But it doesn't feel any different.* And now she's back in the tub, feeling the pulse of his heart against her back, and when she wonders if this is memory or the simulation in her head, she whispers aloud, but not to Alvin, whom she knows can't hear her, "You feel just the same. But, it's not you. It's not you." She can't feel his heart through the blanket but can feel the memory. "It's only me. I feel just the same."

PHOTOCOPY

Isaac would always fidget when he was in the office. Dr. Robinson told him not to be embarrassed about using the toys.

Believe me, parents use these things more often than the kids do. What do they fidget with?

Nothing. They're happy enough with the chance to complain about their parents.

This afternoon, he was passing a Planet Earth stress ball between his hands. "Did you bring any pages with you today?" Dr. Robinson asked. He squeezed it in his left hand.

"Yes."

"Would you like to talk about them?" None of her questions were ever intoned as an inquiry.

"Maybe in a bit. You know I hate reading them aloud."

"We don't have to talk about them. It's your choice, Isaac. How about your own journal log? Would you like to read any of those pages?"

"Sure." He pretends to rummage through his bag, as if he doesn't know where he placed his diary, even though that's the only thing in there besides two paper-clipped pages, an orange-Tic-Tac container, his car keys, some floral detritus, and his wallet.

"Ah, here we are." He flips to the page that's ribboned and looks at the therapist, waiting for her to expressly nod as a prompt to read.

> June 5, Pangaea went to Devorah's house after school. It's Friday, so she'll sleep over there. It's great when she does this, but I wish she would branch out a bit. Her circle is so small. But whenever I try to encourage her to make new friends, she looks so hurt, like somehow she's doing something wrong. The last thing I want is to make it even _more_ difficult for her to have people she trusts.

"That's the end of the entry. Do you want me to read the next?"

"Let's first visit something you said in there. That whenever you try to encourage her, she looks hurt. Can you speak more to that?"

"What's there to say? If I suggest something to her, she thinks it's because she's doing something wrong. And then she thinks I'm judging her. It's her life, you know? If she wants to have only a few very strong relationships, then who am I to interfere?"

"Isaac," she smiled the rare, but requisite, smile she occasionally would that anticipated a moment of counseling, rather than inquiring, "you're her father. We've discussed this. It's okay, in fact it's important, that you sometimes put yourself in a position that's going to lead to her being upset with you. She's nine. She needs a parent's guidance, and you're perfectly capable of doing that. You have to let yourself be okay with her, _momentarily_, not liking you. She loves you, Isaac."

He was unaware how tightly he was squeezing the stress ball. "I get that, but I'm afraid," stopping himself when he heard his voice shake, then, "I'm afraid of pushing her away. She's already lost her mother. I don't want her to feel like she's going to lose me."

121

"Would you like to talk about Lena?"

"She's starting to look more like her. Every day there's some new detail in her face or even the way she walks."

"Do you think this makes you resent her?"

"Excuse me?" He stopped squeezing the stress ball, now covered in palm sweat.

"Do you think that Pangaea's resemblance to Lena makes you resent her?"

"I love Pan more than anything."

"I don't doubt that, Isaac. But, it's perfectly natural if she makes you think about the way her mother treated you. If seeing her reminds you of Lena."

"You want to know something terrible?" He switched to a different fidget toy, a ball with about a hundred flimsy rubber strings popping out of the center, allowing him to yo-yo it. "I keep just about all electronics out of the house. Lena loved everything that ran on programming. She thought it was a miracle of life. The fucking irony of that. She thought it was amazing you could make bits of plastic and metal move and talk but felt nothing for the human life we actually created. When Pan gets older, I'll get her a phone, of course. And she'll need a laptop for school. Soon enough, she'll find her way to all these things anyway. But for now, while I still can, I keep them away. It terrifies me to think she'll fall in love with them like Lena did. That she'll become attached to these things that pretend to be alive and forget about people who actually are."

He didn't meet Dr. Robinson's gaze, but she waited, trained to endure the silence longer than him.

"She's able to help me more in the shop now. And she loves it there. She really does. So that's encouraging. She's perfectly happy to work with the flowers. Sometimes she mutters to them. I wonder if I should stop her but…it seems perfectly harmless, right?"

"We have ten minutes left, Isaac. Would you like to read the other pages you brought?"

He put down the toy. "Sure." And took out the stapled papers, not bothering with the act of rummaging. He looked at them, the photocopied pages. "She does have beautiful handwriting. She gets that from me. Whenever Lena wrote, it looked like hiero-glyphics." Though he knew no amount of chatter would ever wipe away the guilt he felt whenever he looked at Pan's diary. "She likes to draw flowers on the edges of the page. Here, let me—"

"Eight minutes, Isaac."

"Oh, right. Um." He swallowed, then began:

Devorah's mom makes the best mac en cheese. I wish dad could. Wenever he makes it its like soup and thats grose. She crumbles chips in it and the crunch makes it taste so good. Mom can you take cooking lessons with dev's mom. You tell the best lullaby stories but how come you cant cook. Dad tries to do good. Or maybe we cood go to a resteraunt but dad wud stay home. He always worries when we go out to eat and spends most of the time looking at other familys eating but wen I ask him why he wont look at me his eyes get wet.

He stopped reading to get a tissue. "That's the end of that entry. Do I have enough time to read the next?"

She nodded.

Ellis came to the shop today. Dad drove us both after school. It was funny when we got there because Ellis was afraid to touch the flowers but I told him they don't bite. Dad looked at me like when I say something I shouldn't but I wasn't trying to be meen. It was fun bringing him there. We played hide and seek and dad even let us go in the greenhouse but usually I only go in there when you tell me to. Sometimes it's lonely in the shop when its only you me and dad. That's why it was fun bringing Ellis but I don't think he'll come back. Dad told me not to tell anybody about Ellis's accident and I wont. But maybe when I dream tonight I'll be back in the shop and all of us will be there. Remember when I brought Katie to the shop and she was so bored and I asked her what was wrong and she said there was nothing to do. Or when Rachel asked if she could go home after a half hour. No one else likes it there but I don't like them. Dad told me to forget he ever said it but im going to be like you mom im going to be the only person I want to be with.

PART THREE

PLATE TECTONICS

BIOLOGY

Devorah laments through her tears: "She's a fucking bitch! That's all she is."

They're in the flower shop. Pan put the Closed sign up once Devorah arrived. She gave her a few dying flowers to fidget with, thinking it prudent not to give her more vivacious florals (lest Dev bring them to a premature wilt). The other flowers sigh with despair as they spectate the unfortunate florae whose fates are in Devorah's twisting hands.

"It's like she doesn't think it's my life I'm living," Dev continues, "but that I'm still some piece of her body she can control and twist into her idea of the daughter she wishes she had. But she chose to have me, and this is what she gets."

"Well, just back up a bit. I know you were with your mom earlier, but what happened?" Pan tries to listen but struggles to stay focused. *This is so old. It's the same conversation with her every day. Why do I even bother picking up the phone?* She's spent most of her time outside of the shop working on preliminary design forms for Wonderland the past few weeks, ignoring texts and only answering repeat calls.

Pan, are you all right?

I'm fine, what do you want, Al?

Well, at this point, I'll settle for a pulse. It's been two days, and you haven't responded to me.

Sorry. I've just been super busy at Wo—at the shop.

"So she called me two days ago and was checking in. I told her I was fine and that I was doing what the doctors said: staying away from alcohol and going to sleep early most nights. And then, she was like, 'That's what the doctors told you to *not* do, but what about what they told you *to* do?' Only, she said it in this, like, hostile tone, coming at me and insinuating that I don't know what to do. Which, I do, by the way." Pan tries not to imagine Lena's face as she looks at Dev. "So, anyway. We…"

Lena: *What do you think it was that happened during the last simulation?*

Pangaea: *It wasn't anything. Just some glitch. It's a computer program, after all. It's bound to happen.*

It was weird Pan told Persephone during their recent interview. *One second I was in the desert. The sand was exactly how I'd designed it: red and warm beneath my feet but not scorching. The sun, too, exactly how I'd designed it to pulse blue with a white center, rumbling a low baritone so deep I could feel it under my skin. And Alvin with me. Just exploring an endless desert with dunes and oases wherever we wanted them. But then he vanished right when I wanted to hold him. And there was just this…this shimmering glow in the distance that I somehow needed to get to. But what was it?*

Devorah starts to choke over her words as tears begin to torrent, arresting Pan's attention. "She said if I don't come home, she's going to call social services and have me put in one of those Maternity Centers." She stops speaking for a moment as the tears overcome her, dropping the scraps of flowers she's decimated onto the ground and burying her face in her palms. "Can you believe that? My own mother would put me in one of those? You know those places are fucking prisons. Only you're there because of a choice you can't make, not one you've made."

Pan's heard the stories about Maternity Centers. She envisions the infomercials: *Our Centers are intended to provide medical and emotional support to women who otherwise might struggle to nurture the life budding within them.*

"So, is she gonna call them?"

Devorah wipes her eyes. "I don't know. She hasn't yet. I think even she was a bit taken aback to see me like that. She knows what those places are like. They don't care about any of us, just what's within our stomachs. Like as if the fetus is the pinnacle of life. That the idea of a life, before it's blemished with an actual human being's choices and mistakes—shit, with a human's *body* for Christ's sake—the idea of life is more important than *actual* life. I don't know how else they see it."

Devorah leaves the shop, and Pan follows behind her. Her phone vibrates, and she glances at it: *Reminder: Please submit your preliminary design form at least 24 hours in advance of your scheduled experience.*

She waves bon voyage to Dev as they head in opposite directions of the July'd city. How the buildings' sweat shimmers the air in a thickness that's intangible yet palpable. She scratches at the scab where the anesthetic is routinely administered, then once she's on the Blue Line, she takes out her phone to continue working on the preliminary design.

The train moves, and Pan closes her eyes, envisioning a sky: a canvas exploding like lava-lamp juice let loose. Splotches of red expand, and plumes of black erupt. Bursts of orange dilate and contract. Fringes of fractal'd colors pulsing behind the mosaic: a foundation of black fog that spreads, miasma-like and slow, clawing through the clouds. She hears the pound of thunder reverberate and a whirling wind warp through a wah-wah, charged and pulsed with electric breath.

The train stops, and Pan opens her eyes, staring out window at the familiar GE factory across the marsh as the fantasy fades.

Not again. She feels her phone vibrating, expecting Alvin, but surprised to see it's her dad.

"Hey, Dad…what's going on?"

"Nothing, munchkin. I'm just wondering if you're gonna be home for dinner."

"Uh, yeah, was planning on it."

"Okay, okay. Just checking. The past few weeks…I don't know. The past few weeks you've been kind of MIA. I've even called Alvin once or twice wondering if you're with him."

"Some real independence you let me have. If I'm not home, then surely I must be with another man."

"Panny…come on. It's just…lately your routine has been a bit different, is all. Which isn't a bad thing. I'm not prying…or at least not trying to. Just as long as you stay sa—" He catches himself. "Anyway. I'll see you at dinner."

The past couple weeks, Pan has begun riding the train with no destination. She's hopped on the Blue Line at the outbound Bowdoin and taken it to Wonderland just to get back on the next inbound bus. Marveling at how she can *stare at the same desolate urban landscape I've been looking at for years and make it new. I can look at that godforsaken GE factory and see a castle in the Swiss Alps…and bring it to life.* She's completed her last three preliminary-design forms on the T.

Lena: *Whatever you say, Pan. Call this movement.*

She looks out the window and, again, the reality of Lynn's

crumbling brick warehouses, the mosaic graffiti tattooed on the walls so faded they're no more than cheap scars, the mockery of vines sprouting through fissures in the pavement. It all vanishes as she sees mountains pyramid themselves up from the ground, engulfing the concrete complete; rivers run over the road so deep that even the cars become no more than anemones wading the current. Pan is unaware that she's drawing stares from other passengers at how frenetically she itches the scab in the crook of her elbow.

"Last stop: Wonderland."

A half hour later, as she pulls onto her street, Pan sees—*What the hell is he doing out?*

"Hey, you," she says to Ellis, stopping her car behind his driveway as he gets out of his vehicle. "Where're you coming from?" She notices his sigh of frustration at being seen.

"Hey, Pan. Um...nowhere. I was just..."

"You were just taking a drive? Get real, man. You know I know that's bullshit. Hang on a sec." She pulls into her driveway and walks back over to him. Ellis looks down both sides of the street to determine if there are any passersby he'll have to begrudgingly acknowledge. He sits on the front steps of his doorway, and Pan plops down on the grass next to him.

"You know how much insect shit is probably right where you're sitting, don't you?" he asks, hoping not to get caught as his stare trails its way up her thigh until he notices the faint dew of sweat at the edge where her skin meets her shorts. *She'd vomit to think of you touching her.* He winces.

"The whole world's a dump, man; what difference is a little ant defecate? But come on—where were you? It's a rare sight to see you outside that fortress." She nods at his house.

You can get inside quicker if you tell her the truth. "I was look-ing at that new gym that opened up downtown. Apparently, all the equipment is state of the art. The stuff in there," he gestures toward the house, "is good, but it's all outdated. Anyway. I was just checking it out."

"Well, hey, at least it's something. So, you gonna join?"

"No way." He's surprised by the look of disappointment on her face.

"Why not? You know you can't stay cooped up here forever. Don't you get tired of the same routine?"

"You have any idea how gross the equipment in those places can get? How much bacteria is just floating in the air? All those people," he imagines all the sweat pooling together and rising, "just exuding their biogarbage everywhere? No thanks."

"Biogarbage?" Pan laughs. "That's a new one, even for you."

"That's what it is," he says without a trace of humor. "Our bodies are just—it's like they're just recycle centers for eukary-otes and prokaryotes to wage war. And we shed their corpses. Not to mention viruses. Fungus. Shit, think of all the chemicals that—"

"Ellis," she puts up her hand, "please, shut up. I get it. Our bodies are just..." *It's like the fetus is the pinnacle of life in their eyes. That the idea of a life, before it's blemished.* "What did you just say?"

He looks at her, confused. "Per your request, nothing."

Dev's voice rings through her head: *The idea of life is more important than actual life.* "But that can't be true. You can't let yourself believe it's true."

"Um...what?"

"Oh, um, nothing. I was just thinking that..."

Lena: *That what? Maybe they're right? Maybe there's nothing more important than nurturing life before it's polluted with the mistakes of a body so that it has a fighting chance to be something pure?*

To her surprise, Pangaea envisions the simulation room, the ovular machine pulsing with its red glow. *For now, we're calling it the "Human Connection."*

A womb, she thinks, *that's what the room feels like.*

"Ellis," she pulls at grass, "you can't live your whole life thinking the worst about our bodies—"

For the past few moments, though, Ellis hasn't heard Pan:

Biogarbage. That's clever. Couldn't think of a better way to describe yourself.

Shut up.

It's what you are. Human trash. A biological catastrophe. Try as you might to hone this body, it won't change anything about the life within it. Your life. You're stuck with it. You're stuck with it in this—

"Wait, what'd you say?" he asks her, hearing only the end of her sentence.

"I said, for all their flaws, our bodies are all we have." *But you don't believe this, do you?* "They're the only thing that lets us know we're alive."

MARTIAN

Pan would let the scent of wet leaves slip its way into her nostrils; she could imagine a green mist hug itself around her brain. How scent is always married to sight. Isaac would let her wander through the bike path on her own. She would take the dog, Martian, walking down the path and exploring the woods for hours, whole weekends. He would worry from time to time but was never too concerned. He'd already lost a wife. Losing a daughter wasn't possible.

"The flowers are starting to come out, Panny. See them?"

She glanced at the pedals as Martian tugged on the leash.

"Yeah, but they're not as pretty as the ones in the shop."

"No, I suppose not. But," he squeezed her hand, "they're beautiful nonetheless."

She let go and scampered off to an unruly patch of flowers, yanking them from their roots.

"That wasn't very gentle of you, young lady."

"Flowers can't feel pain," she said, fidgeting with the dirt and pedals.

"Well, how can you be so sure?"

"I don't know. I didn't hear them yell."

He paused, wondering which tangential direction he should

explore. "I guess they didn't." But decided it would be more prudent to talk about something else. "Pan, I want to talk to you about the other day."

"Okay." Her attention was fixated on the flowers.

"After school, you said something about Mom. Do you remember what you said?"

"No," She was still staring at the petals.

"Well, I do. Mrs. Nally dropped you off, and you asked me, 'When will I turn into Mom?' Do you remember?"

She had shredded them down to just their stems. "Kinda." Then she dropped them on the tracks and knelt to scratch Martian's ear. She looked back up at Isaac. "Yeah. You told me Mom would always be in me."

"Right, and we left it at that." He scratched behind his head, fidgeting. "But there's a bit more I have to say, okay? You know your mom left us before you could begin to remember, right? I've told you that. You understand that, don't you?"

"I guess so."

"Well, I know other girls in school must talk about their moms, and I think you're getting to the age now when you'll start to think a bit more about these things, and I...I guess I just want to give you some help trying to understand what you might start feeling."

"But how could you know what I feel if you're not me?"

"I guess I can't, but I have to try. And I want you to know, when the other kids in school talk about their moms, that you're not any...," he searched for the word, resolved upon, "*less* than them. All right? You're not any less because you don't know your mom like they know theirs. Do you understand?"

"Why would I be any different from them if I don't have a mom?"

"That's what I'm saying; you're not. You're not different."

"But why are we talking about it if I'm not different?"

"Don't *you* ever wonder about her? Don't you ever look at other kids' moms and think, 'where's mine?'"

They began walking along one of the side trails; the canopy of green above them gradually became a darker hue. Pan batted gnats away from her face and walked in the muddier area of the path. He could see she was more interested in the colorful scenery than his words.

"Pan, I want you to listen for a moment. I've told you before that your mother left when you were an infant. Where she went, I still don't know. But she left you and me. And if she was going to come back," he ripped a few leaves from a nearby bush, "then she would've done it by now. But she hasn't. And as much as it kills me each day she's not here with us, it's really you who's taking the brunt of it. Whether you realize it or not. And I'm afraid…I'm afraid you're going to start realizing this in the next few years, and I just don't," he looked down at his daughter, "I don't know if I'm going to be able to give you the help you need."

She let go of Martian's leash, and the dog chased after a bunny. Which Pan proceeded to run after as well.

"Pan!" Isaac exclaimed as she scampered off into the shrubs.

When he finally caught up to her, she was sitting in the mud, rubbing down Martian, who was coated in a veneer of muck.

"Well, the damage is done, I suppose," Isaac muttered as he plopped down in the mud with them.

"Martian doesn't know his mom, and he's happy," she said, rubbing behind the dog's ears.

It won't stay this simple. "Sweetie, I guess what I'm telling you is, when you start to wonder about Mom, you can talk to me. You can always talk to me when you don't know what to tell yourself."

"Why'd she leave?" she asked as she roughhoused Martian.

"I don't know. I wonder that most days too."

"Was it something you said?"

"I don't think so. I think your mother," he plucked at a flower and fidgeted with the petals, talking to himself aloud to her, "was running from the woman she was turning into. And I don't think there's anything you or I could've done to help her." *But I wish she would have let us try*. He tossed the mangled flower onto the dirt and gestured his hand out toward Pan; she took it as he hoisted her up.

"Why didn't she tell you where she was going?"

"I don't think even she knew. That was always your mother's thing. She loved to be on the move, hated staying in one place. It didn't matter where, as long as she was going."

"And no one knows where she is now? Not even Grandma?"

"No. Your mom cut ties with all of us. Even her own mom."

"So she isn't really my mom?"

He looked at her and took her face in his hands. "She'll always be your mom, Pan. Nothing can change that. Not even her own choices. You come from her, just like you come from me. Even if Lena isn't here with us, you're still hers. She can be a million miles away and moving farther, but she'll always be your mother."

"And you're with me here now, aren't you?"

Pangaea looks away from the simulation of her younger self and Isaac and turns to Lena, standing next to her in the forest.

"Since, really, you've been nothing more to me than a bit of DNA in my body. What's the difference between the you I create in here and the you that's somewhere out in the world?"

"What good is this doing you?" Lena sighs. "You had it better figured out then than you do now."

"What're you saying? I should've just let you out of my head when I was a kid? That I should've just thought of you as dead instead of alive and living your life without me?"

Suddenly Lena's gone. Pan scans around but doesn't see her. *That's the third time now this has happened. Maybe I should tell Persephone...but any second now Lena will be back...or wait, no. There it is.*

She heads in the direction of a dense patch of forest with rustling bushes, hazy beams of a misty light poking between the trees. The light seems to grow distant, somehow dead and sighing like the memory of yellow. She extends her right arm, and the rays of light are palpable against her skin. She closes her first, and the light bends within her grip. She cups it between her hands, and when she opens them a translucent butterfly hovers out, flapping in front of her face. She puts out her hand for it to settle onto, but as the butterfly descends it disintegrates into sand that slips through her hands. When she looks up the trees are gone. She's up in pink clouds floating atop an indigo sky, and she looks beneath her feet and sees the sky ebb like an ocean, unaware of the silence of the world.

"There it is." She sees something shimmering in the waves of the sky below her and, without a moment's thought, as if driven by instinct or craving, dives off the cloud into the ocean and begins to wade. She looks down and to her surprise can discern the ocean floor, a mossier shade of green than the teal around her. She swims down frantically, noticing a sparkle where she first saw the shimmer, diamond-like, but when she reaches out to grab it, there's only blackness and the slow blurring of her vision as she opens her eyes.

"Pangaea." She blinks Persephone into focus. "Are you awake?"

"I will be in a minute."

I was so close to it this time.

"Whenever you're ready."

There's something in there, something in there with me. She tries to recall the image of the trees rustling, the ocean waving, but can't.

"I have a question."

She waits for Persephone to look up from her laptop.

"I know you've mentioned conscious interference before and how that can alter the simulation, but...can there be any other kind of interference?"

"I'm not sure I understand."

"I was just thinking that...I guess what I'm asking is, is there any way for maybe the computer to glitch and put something in the simulation that I didn't design? If my mind can interfere with the machine, I'm sure the machine can interfere with my mind, right?"

"No. We've calibrated this technology too finely and carefully for that. The only thing that can unintentionally alter your experience here is your mind. You still haven't told me, though, what happened."

"There was this," *I might as well*, "thing in there, I don't know. I designed a memory I wanted to revisit and, in the woods, I noticed this, like, rustling. This distinct sound of something moving. When I went to follow it I, well, eventually I woke up, and now here we are."

Persephone studies her for a moment, and Pan feels like she can somehow read her thoughts.

"The only thing it can be is something you put in there, either intentionally or not. It certainly doesn't sound like a technical glitch but rather on the user end."

There's gotta be some way for me to find it. But how can I get back there? "What happens to the simulation once it's over? Like, I know I'm hooked up to this machine, so doesn't that mean that somehow what's going on in my head is also going on in a computer?"

The smile on Persephone's face is the first Pan can think of as sincere. "It sounds like you're interested in the science of this all of a sudden. Yes, to answer your question, everything that goes on within your head while you're plugged into the Human Connection is translated into code that stays in our system. Your living thoughts become tangible code. Pretty amazing, isn't it?"

"Okay, so, if that's the case, is there any way I can revisit a simulation? Is there any way I can get back to that same world? Like, can the programmers just reinput whatever output there is from my previous simulations?"

"It's not something we've considered before. I'll admit that." Persephone seems as interested by the idea as Pan. "I don't see why we couldn't recycle code from a completed simulation; however, the risk is that it'd be far more susceptible to conscious interference, since it's written according to your experience in real time, rather than by a plotted preliminary design."

"Is there any reason why that'd be a problem?"

"That depends on your outlook. Some people might be frightened by a world where nothing can be predicted. A world where you're an alien."

"I mean, it would still," *really, you've been nothing more to me than a bit of DNA within my body,* "just be in my head."

Persephone smiles at Pan's uncertainty. "And you never feel alien in there?"

RETURN TO SENDER

Lena,

I hope this finds you well and safe. Hard as it might be to believe that. But even if I want to hate you, and probably <u>should</u>, I don't. Can't. That's probably the word. I know by now that wherever you are you've seen the same news I have, the same news everyone is watching right now. The writing was on the wall, and he even said he would do it, but it's just one of those things that's so surreal it doesn't seem like it can be real. Or not even that. It's something we've watched and heard about so much that it's felt like it can only happen on TV. But the Maternity Pact is now law and, wouldn't you know it, it just makes me think about you.

Did you want to abort Pan? Was it something you wanted to ask me but never did? I don't sleep, and it's because the same questions always pull my eyelids open. The same conversations I always pretend to have with you. The words are always the same. Yours and mine.

I ask,

"Do you want to bring a life into this world together? Do you want to create something that's entirely you and me?"

And you say,

"No, isn't it enough that we have our own games of life to play? You with your flowers and me with programs. You can stare at your plants, and I can stare at my screens, and we can both marvel at the things we create. We can both stare amazed at the worlds we translate from inside our heads."

You laugh when I reply,

"But these things play at life. We can bring a living body into this world. The miracle of an actually living human being."

But now it's different. Because now I see the news and can't help but hear you say,

"What does it matter? She's something within me, and it's no longer my choice."

And I say,

"We can find a way. Some med student. There's gotta be doctors who'll still do it."

Because, knowing how it's all turned out, how even after any doubt you may have had, that the reality of Pan, her living, breathing self, wasn't enough to change your mind about her. I can't stop myself from wondering if the inevitability of her birth would have made you think of her differently after all those months she spent cocooned within you. But I know the answer is simple, even if I wish it wasn't. That if we were in the same situation now, the world would just poison the idea of her life even more within you than it already was. That her birth would be nothing more than the mockery of a life in your eyes.

Speaking of, I haven't bothered asking her how she feels about the Pact. How would I go about asking her? Sometimes, it's better to say nothing than to say the wrong the thing. Do you think she still writes to you? She used to, that much I know. She would even let me read some of the letters she wrote. I remember her asking me once,

"If we put them in the mailbox with no address then there's at least a chance Mommy will get it?"

No. No. Pan's always been a realist. I bet she stopped writing these in high school. Don't you ever wonder what she might've asked you in these letters? What she might have told you? Things I can't even imagine she's kept secret from me because my mind doesn't even know such thoughts and things can exist. Like when you taste something you never knew you hadn't tasted before. Maybe it's better that way. Being ignorant of the joys you're missing. The irony is, you probably came to that conclusion so long before me. It must be how you can manage to have lived this long without once knowing the daughter you left behind. I wonder if she's even a thought in your head anymore. Or if the idea of her life has never meant anything to you at all.

Yours forever with love,
Isaac

He drank some water to ease the cat-tongue surface of his throat, then opened his desk drawer, putting this letter atop the hundreds already there. He stared at them, the college-ruled paper, each page a template for infinity until it's filled, then he pulled one out at random. The page curled at all four corners, smudged with finger shadows. But the ink the same as the day he wrote it, the words unchanged.

Lena,

I wish you could see her. I wish you wanted to. Pan's doing so well this year. Sixth grade is when they move to the different building, she'd been at the Village School since kindergarten, so this is the first big change for her. She's always been friendly with Ellis, but this year she's taken him under her wing. She knows how nervous he gets around people, so this year is especially tough. Students coming from the other elementary schools. Lately, she's spending less time with Sandra and Jane, but she and Devorah are still so close. I'm rambling. There's just so much to say. I'm a bit worried that she's not trying to make new friends. It's November, so it's not quite the beginning of the year, and by now I expected to have heard some new names. But it's still the same cast it's always been. Maybe that's not such a bad thing. I won't press her on it.

I tried surprising her the other night. We were at Bugaboo Creek, remember that place? I used to tell you we were going to go with Pan all the time. I've stuck to that. She loves it there, the talking moose head. And you know something? The steak isn't terrible. But none of that's to the point. We were eating there, and I asked her if she wanted anything special for Chanukah this year. She mentioned some Harry Potter toys, crafts; she always wants to play with crafts. But then I asked her if she'd like to go on a trip! I said we could go anywhere. London, Antarctica, the North Pole—I was just trying to get her excited, you know? I got us tickets to spend a week in Disney and wanted to surprise her with it but wanted to get her all excited first. Which I guess is selfish of me, but I really thought she'd be so happy. But when I showed her the tickets and told her we're going to spend this school vacation in Disney, her face dropped. I couldn't believe it. You know what she asked? She said, "Can Dev and her mom come? Or we could go with Ellis's family. Or what if we just stay home?"

I was so confused. I didn't get it. What kind of eleven-year-old doesn't get excited about Disney? Is she too old? That's not even the point. She wasn't excited about the idea of travelling at all. She and I went with my parents one year to Aruba, but she was too little to really understand what was going on. This would've been her first real chance to see someplace else, somewhere new. And when I kept trying to tell her about all the fun places and sights in Disney, she only looked sadder and sadder. And she asked me, "What's wrong with home? There are lots of fun things here." Of course, I told her nothing's wrong with it but that sometimes it's fun to see other places, somewhere where every face is a stranger's. I thought she'd see the adventure in it. Which, of course, was a mistake. Yet another foolish, unretrievable mistake to come out of my mouth because she heard me say that and said, "But if we leave home then we're just like Mom." And I told her, "Sweetie, we're not leaving. We're coming back. I promise you when we come back Ellis will be the same, Devorah will be the same. Everything will look like it did the day we left. It'll almost be like we never left at all." I couldn't eat one bite of my food when it finally came because of how she asked back, "Is home just a place that makes people want to leave?"

With all my love,
Isaac

145

STUCK

"There's a fucking hole in his head! Run."

Pangaea gets out of the vehicle and watches Jeffry and Tony run in opposite directions down Draper Street. The shot-spotter blinks silently down the street, mocking the firecracker snap of the gunshot. She walks over to the passenger side of the car and looks through the shattered window at Darius. The street is silent. She watches blood drip out of his mouth and left ear, his eyes blinking. His hand is slack, but the fingers still grip the McDonald's soda. Then she hears sirens.

Earlier she was in the Heath Street apartment, watching Jeffry and Tony talk in the kitchen. Celia sat on the couch doing homework on the coffee table next to the pistol. It was an assignment in practicing cursive. Her mother, Kayenne, was asleep next to her.

"It's a four-way stop," Tony said. "When we see it, I'll text Bo to come out and then *bam*."

"What if there are other cars at the intersection?" Jeffry said.

"There won't be. It'll be midnight. Why would you even ask that shit?"

"It just seems too easy."

"It's no different from any other time we go to Ronan Park for hard. You're thinking too much."

She followed them out the door, but the next room she entered was in Portland, two years earlier, neither Jeffry nor Tony there.

At least, I think that's what Al said. That the whole group had been around for a few years before that night.

Pan watched Darius approach Kayenne and whisper into her ear, "You're the best thing to walk into this whole city." She felt nauseous at the sight of Kayenne's blush, knowing where she'd be two hours later. "Do you wanna get out of here? I got people all up and down this whole state who're having parties tonight that'll make this place seem like Chuck E. Cheese."

Pan followed them out the door and was in the car with Kayenne screaming, "Pull over! Pull over! Let me out. You didn't say this is what we'd be doing!" as she tried to open the door.

"Listen, I'll pull over and smack you so hard they won't know what color your skin is if you don't shut up." The pop-up locks had been cut off, making it impossible to unlock the back doors. "It's not that bad. You'll make three hundred fucking dollars for one hour. The guys are always clean. We don't take money from tricks whose dicks got bugs. We don't need spoiled goods." He pulled over, and Pangaea followed Kayenne out the door, stepping into the thirty-dollar motel room. Kayenne tied to a chair, blindfolded, as a nude man walked around the room stepping on balloons, masturbating as he popped them. Pan closed her eyes and opened them to find herself in the Heath Street apartment again.

"Darius is a fucking snitch, dude," Tony said. "I'm telling you. He got busted last year and has been a snitch for a year. We'll fucking do him and get out of the city."

"All right, who's gonna do it?" Jeffry asked.

"We'll call Maserati."

"He's seventeen."

"We've been pimping out bottoms since we were in high school, the fuck does it matter how old he is? He can handle it. Help me move this mattress to the dumpster, all right? Jesse had a rough john last night, and the blood's not gonna come off."

Pan followed them out the door, walking into the car.

"Take a right here," Tony tells Darius, sitting in the back seat behind him. Pan sits in the middle and sees him text Maserati: *Alright. Start walking. Throw the burner away in PARTS in different trash cans.*

"Hand me my soda, bro." Darius reaches back to Jeffry, sitting to Pan's right, watching him pass the McDonald's. "Ahhhh, fuck, man. This isn't Dr. Pepper, dude. This is Coke. How hard is it—"

Pan watches his head jerk forward and back milliseconds before hearing the firecracker pop. She looks out the front of the car as someone runs across the street, bending a flip phone in half until it snaps.

"Bro...he's still breathing. Is he dead?"

"There's a fucking hole in his head! Run."

Pangaea blinks out of the simulation, the tinnitus ringing in her ears as if she had actually just heard the gunshot—as if she had ever heard it.

"Anything you care to kick off with?" Persephone asks.

"Not without an attorney."

Persephone smiles, waiting for Pan to begin.

"I used to love listening to Al talk about his cases," she starts, "now all he does is bitch and moan, but he used to love coming back late, especially during trials. He'd take out his laptop and just read his notes to me. I loved it too. It was like story time, which I never really had. Isaac couldn't make a lullaby if his life depended on it." Pan doesn't notice how Persephone has shut her laptop, simply watching Pan speak. "Al's the first person to admit he's got an empty sack but that when he worked on criminal cases it was like he could vicariously live those lives. The terrible and the victims. The cops and the killers. The worse the case, the better, he would think. And I also loved the bad ones. I remember the lawyer he used to work for would call them 'brown bag' cases. She'd have to wear a bag over her head when leaving the courthouse. She was the defense. It was so exciting. He had hundreds of cases. He'd work so late reading everything as if the sight of the ink could change his DNA. That he could know these stories so well he'd really become the people in them, know their thoughts. I feel like when we first started dating, we spent more time talking about those stories than anything actually happening in our lives. We spent more time," she looks at the Human Connection, her voice trailing as she continues, "pretending to live the stories of other people's adventures. No matter how horrible."

"Why do you think that is?"

Later that night, Alvin sighs with exasperation as he looks at his phone. "Fuck." He glances at Pangaea. "DoorDash drone isn't just leaving it at the door."

"The end is nigh." She keeps her eyes on the TV screen, watching *Stranger Things* for the eleventh time.

"Can you get the door?" He pinches her thigh, but she bats his hand away.

"Quit being a shmuck. Go."

With a dramatic grunt, he gets up and walks downstairs.

"Someone's at the door, Alvin," his mother says from the kitchen.

"Yeah, yeah." He opens the door. "Hi there, DoorDash."

The delivery drone hovers and waits for Alvin to enter his customer code before opening the compartment.

"Thank you." He smiles and closes the door.

The "tip" screen increases brightness with various amounts.

"I don't get how hard it is," he begins once he's back in his room, putting the bag of Wings Over on the coffee table. "In all caps, my instructions say to leave it at the door and text the number on file! But they don't do it. And then I have to talk with them like it's an actual person, and then it fucking waits for me to tip it. Even though," he starts to take the contents out of the bag, "I tipped them *ahead* of time on the app. It's just ludicrous. Ludicrous stupidity. Like they can't fucking read. Or refuse to. I don't know. They're all schmucks."

"You done?"

He nudges her, then they eat, quietly munching as they look at the multicolored screen with its loud noises. They chew with their mouths closed, domesticated, and while Alvin notices nothing, Pan remembers being in this room four years ago, possibly sitting where she is now…

"Are you allowed to show me this stuff? Attorney-client privilege and all that?"

"I actually don't know. Probably not. You gonna call the cops?"

She pitied how she knew this was the closest he could ever come to actual risk, that he could only do it in words. As if that was enough to think it a full experience.

"So, this is called stippling." He points at the photo on the screen. "It's when someone's shot at close range."

"What's all that stuff on the pavement? It's like beige."

"Oh. It was wicked hot I guess when he got shot, so when they lifted him off the ground some of his skin ripped off."

"That's disgusting."

"Isn't it?"

"Show me the autopsy photos again. That thing they do with the face."

"Imagine actually being the mortician who peels the face over itself."

"Sometimes the photo is enough."

Susan knocks on the door, tearing Pan out of memory.

"Hey, you two," she says through the wood, "can I steal you for a moment? Farfel needs to go out."

"You can come in, Su," Pan says.

"Oy! It's so dark in here," Susan says upon entry. "You two'll go blind if you keep your eyes adjusted to this." She flicks on the light. "Alvin," she's begun to instinctively pick up the dishes on the coffee table, "Farfel needs to go out. Can you take him?"

"Mom, are you serious? Why can't you? Or Dad?"

"He hasn't pooped all day, and you know he always goes when he's with you."

It's like we're not even alive anymore. Pan watches Alvin bicker with his mom, a scene Pan can't help but envision playing out between them in the third person. *I can't even remember the last time it felt like we said anything exciting, let alone did something.*

"Oy gevalt," Alvin mutters and rubs his eyes. "I'm with Pan. Can't you just let him shit in the house? He's likely enough to do that anyway."

"You can take him," Pan says. "I don't care. Leave those dishes for me, though, Su."

"Oh, it's nothing. Al? Please? Just take him around the block."

He huffs and gets up to walk the dog, leaving Pan and Susan in the room.

"So...what's new? Shop winding down a bit?"

And her, too, with the whole mother act. Why bother going through the motions?

By now, Susan has collected what little mess there was; she's only pretending to keep occupied by cleaning up imaginary detritus in Alvin's room.

"Eh, March through May are our busiest months. People go flower crazy for a bit around Valentine's Day, then there's Mother's Day, then after that, there're enough flowers out there naturally to satisfy most people's appetite without them needing to spend any money. August is usually a quiet month."

"And how's Isaac?"

"If he's not in the shop, he's gardening around the house. And if he's not doing that, then his head's down in some book. Usually, something he's read five times already."

"Poor guy," Susan accidentally let's slip, looking at Pan with an "oops" face. "Sorry. Didn't mean that. I just mean, well, I guess—"

"It's all right," Pan assures her with a smile, "I think the same thing. But, you know, he's made it this long without my mom. What's another quarter or so of life without her? I'm the one going a whole life."

Susan sits down next to her, caught off guard by Pan's atypical melancholia. "I'm sorry, sweetie. I didn't mean to bring her up. You know," she pauses, but as Susan speaks, Pan tries to block out the sympathy, recalling:

Persephone: *Why do you think that is?*

Pangaea: *That's what people do, isn't it? We always fantasize about a different life because we're stuck in our lives. Everyone. No matter who we may be, we're stuck—*

Persephone: *Stuck in the life our body gives us.*

Alvin returns. "Well, no bowel movement, but he did vomit."

"It was the leftover salmon," Farfel says as he waddles into the room. He tries to jump up onto the bed next to Pan, but after a few aborted attempts, he eventually says to her, "Help an old fellow out, bubeluch, would you?"

Pan lifts him and wipes the fur around his mouth with a napkin. "You coulda wiped him down a bit, Al." She rubs his ears. "You let him get away with murder, Farf. He should be rolling out the red carpet for you."

"At my age, you learn to rest a lost without wasting energy on it. There's too much energy lost on my bowels anyway."

"You're treated just fine." Susan gets up. "You had salmon for dinner, for God's sake."

"And proceeded to vomit it up, a sheynem dank."

Susan flicks her wrist in a manner that Pan has come to recognize in Alvin's own gesticulations. "Farfel, let's go; we'll leave these two be." She pats her thigh, signaling for the dog to follow.

Pan places him on the floor after he struggles to decide whether he can venture the two-foot plunge.

Then it's just Pan and Al in the room again. He picks up the remote to put another mindless show on, and she reads his profile, unable to believe *he's the same guy he's always been. How can he be? Don't the cells of who we are shed every day, just like our skin? Is this really the same Alvin who once told me—*

I just want you to know, fidgeting with his hands, *Sometimes I still can't believe you're here, you know? I can't believe that you are actually here. And, I'm just,* he paused and swallowed, unable to calm the flush on his face, *"I'm always a bit afraid that you can find someone better than I can be for you and that I'll lose you and be left with what I had before.*

"What did you have before me?"

"Huh?" He looks away from the TV.

Pangaea: *I wouldn't say we're "stuck" in our bodies. That's a bit strong.*

Persephone: *Then why do we fantasize at all? Why do we let our minds roam to places we have never been, never can be? Ask yourself what you want more—having and holding something in your grasp or the belief and conviction that you can have anything you want.*

"What are you talking about, Pan?" Alvin asks.

"Just an idea." She replies. "That's what you once said. That before me all you had was an idea that there could be a me. And that there's nothing worse than—"

"I remember. I told you there's nothing worse than being alone and pretending not to be."

VIDEO GAMES

"**A**re you sure? Exactly the same?"

"Yes. Persephone told me you can do it."

"Of course we can, it's just not something we've done before. Recycling code."

"Well, there's a first for everything, isn't there?"

"Hey, it's your simulation. We'll see you tomorrow."

She hangs up and sits back down on the living room floor, rewinding the VHS and looking at the TV:

"No, not here. Enough." Lena pushed Isaac away as he got closer to her face with the camcorder.

"Oh, come on. Be a good a sport. You're the one who brought this thing home." He turned the camera to his own face. "This is the day your mom and I first meet you. Say hi, Lena." He turned the camcorder back on her; she supplied a dopey grin before the gynecologist walked in.

"Ah, getting the little one ready for Hollywood, are we?"

"Ever since I brought that toy back home," Lena rolled her eyes, "it hasn't left his hand. I wish my company never gave it to me in the first place."

"Oh, do you work for a camera company?"

"No. We design prototypes and usually get freebees. You should see the pile of junk piling up in our garage."

"Well, that's a headache for another day." The gynecologist sat down on the swivel chair next to Lena. "So, ten weeks in. How are you feeling?"

Lena looked at Isaac, as if for reassurance. "So far so good. Still vomiting most mornings, can't keep down any food that has an iota of taste...but that's normal. Right?"

"Believe me, if you were feeling good, then we'd be worried." She began to put the latex gloves on. "How about bowels? Normal?"

Lena nodded, again looking at Isaac for reassurance, though his gaze was on the camcorder, watching it all through the screen.

"Yup," Lena replied, "all normal there."

"Good. That's half the battle. Now then," she swiveled back over to Lena and gestured for her to lift her shirt, applying jelly to the device, "this'll be a bit cold, but bear with me."

Lena shivered at the touch.

After a few seconds of circling around, she said, "Now then. This..."

But neither Lena nor Isaac heard her. Their eyes muffled their ears as they gazed at the screen with its grays and blacks and whites, the primordial pulses.

There I am. Pan stares at the TV.

But behind the screen, locked in the footage, Lena tells herself, *That can't be you* as Isaac mutters, "There you are."

They both heard the gynecologist: "And that right there will eventually be the little one's face." She pointed to a small circle, which looked more like a sketch of a snowman's head than anything.

"That's..." Lena tried to speak. "That's...it? That's my..."

"That's our baby," Isaac said.

The screen goes blue at the conclusion of the footage, and Pan rewinds it again, pauses.

Lena: *What are you trying to see here?*

"Sshhh," Pan says, staring at herself in the ultrasound on the TV. She reaches out her left hand and touches the screen, then places her right hand over her heart. *If it's real, then shouldn't I feel it. Shouldn't—*

Her phone buzzes with a text from Ellis asking if she's en route. *Eh, I can get there a bit early.* She looks at the screen for a few more seconds before ejecting the VHS, then heads next door to Ellis, having agreed earlier in the day to hang out and do nothing.

feel like u havnt come over in forevr, he'd texted her earlier

sry, just been busy lately. The same lie she's told Alvin and Dev lately, but with Ellis it stings a bit more after the fact, knowing she's his only connection to the world outside his home. *But sure,* she'd texted, *ill come over in a bit.*

"Hey," Lauren says as she hears Pan walk down the stairs into the basement. Pan gives Lauren a wave and walks toward the L-shaped couch: Ellis sits on the horizontal portion of it, leaving Pan to sit on the vertical. Lauren sits on a beanbag, playing on an iPad while Ellis leans forward in his seat, MyAIs on and staring at the screen that projects the game for bystander enjoyment. Or mere awareness. He looks over at Pan and gives her the slightest movement of his head, which she registers as a hello. *It's fucking freezing down here,* she wants to say but knows from years of visiting this basement that Ellis maintains the temperature at sixty-two as a means of preventing unintentional sweating, which he finds unhygienic. Eventually, he sighs and takes off the headset.

"We lost."

"That's tough, man. Brutal."

"Yeah, Domination is usually my best game mode, but the rest of the players suck. They're all older dudes, probably just feeling nostalgic."

"Why'd you say that?"

"This is *Call of Duty 4*. Came out, like, before Obama was elected. Or right around then."

"That is old. You," she says to Lauren, "what're you playing over there? How come you're not pointing guns at screens?"

Lauren's engrossed in her own screen and ignores her. Ellis gives her an "it is what it is" look and is about to put the MyAIs back on, but Pan stops him. "Hey, if you're going to leave Earth and fall into the screen, let's at least do it together." She gets up and grabs two other glasses she knows are in the closet. She chucks one at Lauren, who looks up from her iPad when the headset lands next to her.

"Fine, but let me finish this first." She returns her gaze to the iPad.

"What're you playing anyway?"

"I'm not really *playing* anything. Playing is for little kids. This is called *YourWorld*."

"Yeah? And what is *YourWorld*?"

"You get to make your own places. Like, you can make cities, but I think cities are boring. You can make castles and woods and outer-space places."

"And then what?"

"I dunno. You can just...be in them. It's like playing with Google Maps, except you make your own places. And they don't have to be real. Every kid at school is playing it now."

"Did we grow up with games like that?" Pan asks Ellis.

He shrugs.

"Lauren, that's fun to you?"

"I dunno. I guess. Every other kid is doing it."

"Well, whatever. Put that down, and put the glasses on."

Lauren reluctantly puts the iPad down and puts on the headset. Pangaea puts hers on, but when she activates it, nothing happens. "I think this needs new batteries, Ellis."

"No, that one's just broken."

"Fine." Pan gets up to grab the other headset.

"No!" he shouts, surprising both Pan and Lauren, "Sorry, it's just, that one's broken too. Here, take mine." He extends his glasses to her, but she waves her hand and sits back down on the couch.

"It's fine, I'll just watch."

"But," Lauren says as she presses buttons to select which game she and Ellis are going to play, "you won't see what we're doing and be where we are."

"I'm right here with you."

Ellis and Lauren queue up a game and stand up, putting the sticky pads linked to their glasses on their hands and within the crooks of their elbows.

"All right, ready?" Ellis says.

"Yup," Lauren responds.

They begin to flap their arms and move slightly back and forth, confining their movements to a one-foot radius. Pangaea is slightly surprised by the toolbox of vulgarities Lauren employs over the next few minutes. She looks at the screen and sees they're playing *Dragon Voyage*, a game she's played with both before, wherein each person is a dragon, soaring over various landscapes, racing toward a finish line and burning everything, both living and dead, to a charred crisp.

"Yes!" Lauren takes off her glasses and sticks her tongue out at Ellis once he removes his. "Looooooooooooser," she extends in his direction before changing tone. "All right, Mom's gonna drive me to Sarah's." Then she vanishes up the stairs.

"D'you wanna play a round?" Ellis asks Pan.

"Eh, not really. Let's just watch something."

"All right, I gotta go to the bathroom. One sec." He makes his way upstairs.

Now it's just Pangaea in the basement. *He never shouts.* She approaches the closet and takes out the MyAIs he said were broken. She puts them on and activates them. *Whoa.* She sits down, taken aback by what she's looking at. Across Pangaea's vision is a row of naked women of various physiques. *Are these photos or animated?* She squints but to no avail, since it's not actually her eyes that control the sight. She notices a "Presets" heading listed above the bodies and keeps scrolling but stops abruptly. "Holy shit." She sees one of the women has purple hair down just barely past her shoulders, styled like hers. She clicks on it, and now the body is the only thing visible on the screen. *That's my height.* Her eyes work their way up. *That's...* She swallows an acidic gulp as she sees her face. Not an animation of it but an integrated photo of her face atop the likeness of her body. Without breathing, she begins to take off the headset, then notices the right corner of her vision: "Customize." She clicks a button and is taken to a customization menu. The first option she has: male or female. She selects female. The next menu is for general physique, but Pan just presses the button on the headset without altering anything, simply going through the menu. She's unaware how dry her lips are becoming, the nausea percolating bile in her guts. "Christ." The next option is age with a scroll bar next to the body. "There's no way..." She begins to lower it and exhales as the face appears younger and younger, though there are no numbers correlating to the intended age. She proceeds to press the button on the headset as she's prompted to new screens for designing *whatever this is*. Then, once complete, she hears a feminine voice say in the headset, "Enjoy me."

"Oh my God," Ellis says once he reaches the bottom of the stairs. "Oh my God." He looks at Pangaea, who's facing his direction but still has the glasses on. "Pan…"

She takes off the glasses.

After staring at each other in agape silence, Pan says, "Do you have any idea how sick this is?"

He stands rooted to the base of the stairs, uncertain what she'll do if he approaches the couch to say—*What can you say? This is the truth, you pathetic waste of space. This is you. Do you understand that? This is you, and she's seeing you for who you are.*

"Pan…" He approaches the couch. To his surprise, though not relief, she doesn't get up to leave but scooches away, recoiling. "Pan…it's…it's not. I mean…" Then he looks at her, trying to let his gaze tell her what he can't find words to say.

"It's not what? It'd be one thing," she looks at the glasses, which are now on the ground, "if it was just, I don't know. If it was just anonymous. But, Ellis…you have *me* in there. I saw it. I saw…*me*."

"But it's not you, Pan. It's just, it's just…" He looks at her, knowing it's no use to lie. "I'm alone, Pan. I don't know what else to tell you. I'm alone and I…I so fucking desperately don't want to be and I—"

"So you need to pretend to rape women through a headset? You need to pretend to screw me? Don't try to deny who that thing in there is supposed to look like. You really need to take your porn disease to the next level, Ellis? That's it? I mean, do you get how fucking violating this is?"

"You don't get it."

"What's there to get? If you're sick of living like this, then fucking don't. Go outside. Go see people. You fucking sculpt your body like a model, but you're too chicken shit to try to talk to anyone. And this," she points to the headset again, "this is fucking sick, dude. That's the only word for it."

"But, Pan." He hasn't looked at her for a minute, keeping his gaze everywhere but on her body, "I mean, it's not like it's real, you know? These aren't real women. They're...they're just projections on screens. Bits of code. This is...," he tries to find the word, "this is just...cleaner. You know? It's cleaner than the mess of actually trying to be with someone."

"*Cleaner?*" She looks at him with more disgust than he's ever seen on a human face. "*Cleaner?* Ellis. This is most revolting thing I've ever seen anyone do."

He winces, thinking he can't feel any worse.

"I mean, what if Lauren saw that shit? What if she put that on by accident?"

He stares at her in shocked silence.

"This is the worst thing I can imagine you doing. It makes you fucking disgusting. And more than that: it's pathetic."

Hearing these words, Ellis can't stop the voice from telling him, *All the years of telling yourself these same words. All the years of porn you've watched of women saying those exact words. And you know what: now it's not some fantasy; you're actually living it. You're living it because everything she's saying is true.*

Stop.

The only one lying is you.

Please stop.

You're disgusting.

Stop.

You're pathetic.

Just fucking stop.

You shouldn't be alive.

"Stop!" he shouts, which makes Pan jump in her seat in surprise, although not as much surprise as she now feels seeing him begin to weep into his hands. "Pan...goddamnit. I'm sorry. I...I don't know what else I can do. I don't know how much longer..." He looks up at her with crimson eyes. "I mean, Pan, every day hurts *so* much. Every day I'm here with...*myself*...and it hurts. I just," he looks at the MyAIs, "I need some*thing* to feel good every once in a while. I need something. If I can't have someone, then at least I need some*thing*."

"Ellis, look, you're killing yourself with this shit. You're letting a fantasy replace a reality you're not even trying to find."

"No." She's startled by what sounds like conviction in his voice, only to soon realize it's not conviction but rather a morbid submission. "I have to fantasize. I have to fantasize because the intimacy I need is one I can't find."

"You have to look for it."

But I'm looking right at it, he thinks as he stares at her face.

"Ellis!" Lauren shouts from upstairs. "Mom and Dad said they're too tired to drive and to ask if you can gimme a ride to Sarah's. Can we go?"

He's relieved to have an excuse to end this but gives Pangaea an apologetic glance. "I, um, I don't know really what—"

"Ellis." she gets up to leave, no longer angry but somehow feeling something worse—pity. "There's nothing—"

Even if the world's telling us he's real and alive, I don't know if I can believe it yet.

It's like he's just an idea.

She looks at Ellis. *There's nothing worse than being alone and pretending not to be.* And with a sickening sensation of doubt she tries to convince herself. "There's no one in there." She remembers the first simulation, looking at herself in the house of mirrors. "It's only you in your head."

"That's..." Lena tried to speak. "That's...it? That's my..."

"That's our baby," Isaac said.

When they got back home, it was Lena who had to calm down Isaac enough to sleep.

"I know, I know. It's late. I get it. It's just...I mean, has anything ever felt so good, sweetie? To actually see that our baby is there. No. Not 'there'; she's *here*."

"Isaac, you know I love you, but I'm gonna have to muzzle you if you don't let us sleep. It's exciting. So exciting I don't even know what to say."

Lena kissed him, and he turned his head on the pillow, facing the opposite direction. She closed her eyes, pressing the small polaroid against her stomach, whose increased rotund she had begun to notice. *Can you see yourself?* she wondered, imagining the nonexistent eyes of the fetus within her somehow seeing x-ray through her at the ultrasound photo. *That's you. That's you I'm holding. And, somehow, you feel more real in this photo than you do in me.* She opened her eyes to look out the window, letting her eyes flit with the branches ebbing in the breeze. She held the photo in front of her, rubbing her thumb over the circles the gynecologist told her will one day be a body. *But can you feel me now?* she asked the fetus in her as she stroked the photo. *Is there any of you in this?* She closed her eyes again. *Or is all of it just an illusion to cover the fact that maybe I'll never know you, once there is a you? Since maybe I can only ever know the idea of you. Maybe all I'll do is trap the idea of you in a body. And that's all parenthood is. Trapping life in a body you create.* She put the photo on the nightstand next to her and tried to sleep.

Thirty minutes later she was in the kitchen, watching infomercials and eating Isaac's leftover chicken marsala.

"You don't even need a ladder. With the HomeRight Paint Kit, you only need one coat!"

She watched the flashes on the screen, not hearing the words or even thinking. Simply allowing the noise and motion of the screen to fill her head with insomniac foam. Then, suddenly, Lena recognized an hour had passed as the screen no longer displayed the goateed chap painting a studio kitchen. Instead, some new shmuck in a pink polo shirt tucked into jeans.

"The hyperbolic shape allows the flame to cook the meat in three distinct heating zones. The Red Devil grill solves all your Sunday headaches!"

She muted the TV and went to the kitchen table to retrieve the camcorder, taking the little cassette out to put in the VHS port, rewinding back through the tape.

"That's...." She watched herself speak on the screen, "that's... it? That's my..."

"That's our baby."

In the blue light of the footage's conclusion, her head hung bowed, eyes closed. Hands atop her stomach as she spoke to it.

I don't know. I just don't know.

Know what, Mom?

If I can do it. If I can curse you with this. With the one thing that, once you have it, you know you'll lose it.

Love?

No. Life.

If I'm not already alive, then what am I?

Nothing. Just an idea.

But, Mom, doesn't—

No, I'm not that either. I'm not your mother yet either. That's only an idea too.

So then what are we?

There is no we. Not yet. I'm alive. I have a body. That's all I know. And you, she stood up and took the ultrasound photo off the fridge, *you can be alive. Someday. Someday you can be real and exist. Someday you can leech my body to create your own. But even then, I won't be able to say what you are.*

But what if you love me? Wouldn't that be enough? Would you have to know anything more about me than that?

She stared at the photo, lids fluttering as the insomnia began to surrender. Through her blurring vision, Lena couldn't discern the parts of the photo that she'd been told were the fetus and the parts that were simply her.

SHADOWS ON THE MOUNTAIN

The sky fluctuates between the sighing orange of dusk and the lemon yellow of sunrise as Pangaea walks through the hilly terrain.

"It's like it never ends, the green just stretching forever." Alvin points ahead at a flat stretch between two mountains, one bearded with evergreens and the other coated in a total dandruff of snow—a flat stretch that joins the sun in infinite distance.

"Except here, forever is whenever we decide it to be." And as soon as she finishes her sentence, she and Alvin are at the edge of the world, the green behind them. She takes his hand and they sit. Her legs dangle over the cliff; she can feel the faint salt spray of the ocean whisper against her feet. She stares ahead, looking at the edge of the horizon where the blue of the sky marries the water. To her left is a sunset, to her right the sunrise. The sky above a roseate marriage of orange and pink. Behind her, the world now draped in the silver light of the moon where all the shadows sprint, stretching in prayer. Alvin surprises her by stealing her attention with the motion of his hand as it glides toward her cunt.

"I was wondering when you'd make your move." She looks at him, noticing the absence of his face's typical splotchiness, how his hair, for once, looks tended to, brushed, then she feels the heat of his skin where normally there's boyish, lukewarm clamminess.

"Wait." She stops him before he moves his head to her groin. "Let me look at you." She studies his naked body as his simulated eyes rove over her own nudity. *So this is how he'd look.* She notes the symmetry of his limbs, the consistent hue of his skin, how it seems dewed. *If I can make him my own. Truly, entirely my own.* She pushes him down against the grass and notices *there's only the smell of the ocean and the wind, the sleeping grass,* where normally there's the sting of his lemony soap.

The moonlit blue black of night enshrouds them as she fucks him—and he her—in every contortion of crotch geometry she's never been able to. The grass feels mossy, as if massaging each cell of her body. The silhouette of their unity stretches over the spanning mountains. The ocean roars with the waves of Neptune. Pangaea eventually rolls their embrace over the cliff, and as they plummet toward the water, she only feels weightlessness within her and helplessness spreading over Alvin in her clutch. She senses the expanding vibration in her cunt as it radiates warmth through her womb and how the eventual splash into the water isn't cold, just wet.

She opens her eyes, and they're back atop the cliff, staring at the canvased sky, letting the grass massage their backs.

How is it that this can feel better than anything else? Even if it's just in my head?

"Because that's all you need." She's startled to hear him speak and turns over in the grass to look at him. His eyes stare up at the sky. "Maybe you really don't need anyone else. Maybe there *is* no one else who understands what you need like you do. If you have everything you need, then maybe you don't need everyone you've told yourself you do. Anyone, for that matter."

She turns his head in her hands and looks at his eyes. *But they're not his* as she looks into the irises, noticing how *it's like looking at the eyes of a photo. One dimensional and trapped.*

She shuts her lids, hearing the swelling chorus of the ocean. Then opens them to look at the mountains stretching forever, tinged at the edges with the light of the sun and umbrellaed in the middle by the mystery of the moon whose light is only stolen from the stars.

He has to be more than just a thing to me. He has to be.

"And if I'm not, then it'd only be my fault."

"Stop talking. Please. Please don't speak."

"And maybe," he continues, "maybe the same is true of Lena."

"Fuck you."

"The fault is only hers."

"Of course it is. I've always known that."

"Then why look for anything from anyone at all? If all they can do is fail you. Whereas, here." He takes her face in his hands, and Pangaea lets him massage his fingers through her hair, bring his mouth close to her, and speak such that she feels the cool wind of his artificial breath percuss against her own synthetic lips. "You only have to think about yourself."

When she opens her eyes, she and Alvin are at the edge of the forest.

"Exactly where I first saw it last time." She looks to her left as Martian sprints past her. She begins to press her way through the shrubbery, heading toward a diamond-like glow that's shrouded by the greenery.

"What is it?" Alvin asks, holding her hand.

"That's what we're trying to find out." The leaves keep changing color, a kaleidoscope. For a few seconds, all is green, and then the world is coated in a bronzed red orange of autumnal foliage.

The snow beneath Pan's feet isn't cold. "Shhhhh!" she says, gripping Alvin's hand. "Listen." A sound of water trickling over ice percolates the world. "I think it's coming from over there." More frantically, Pan pushes away the bushes and branches, which are gradually becoming more prickly, hostile. Sharp to the touch. She doesn't notice that Alvin is no longer with her.

"What if it's not what you want to find?" Lena's voice echoes through the world.

"How could I put something in my head that I wouldn't want?" She sees—*There's that shimmer.* An ovular, pulsing glow a few yards away. She sprints toward it. It becomes brighter, almost translucent, and when she swats down a branch, thinking she's about to grab it—

"Here, have some water." Pan keeps her eyes closed, coming out of the simulation, trying to retain the sight of that shimmer, *but it's gone. There's only the black behind my lids.* She sips the water and watches Persephone open her laptop, the ritual glow of the screen bathing her face. "So, what can you tell me today? The same program as before? Recycled, as we discussed?"

"Not quite."

"What went wrong?" She sounds genuinely curious.

Why look for anything from anyone at all? If all they can do is fail you.

"You didn't need to be there," she says to Alvin, who briefly flits into her vision as corporeal as Persephone.

"Excuse me?"

Before fading away.

"Oh, um, sorry. I was just thinking about…" She looks at the space where Alvin just stood. "What was the question?"

"You suggested this simulation wasn't quite what you wanted, despite us reusing the code exactly how you asked. So, tell me, what went wrong?"

"Well, I wanted to recycle the code because there was something in the last simulation that I didn't want there and, I guess…I guess I want to know what it was."

"And you're telling me you didn't?"

"I was so close." She doesn't realize the earnestness in her tone. "I could almost touch it. It was barely out of my grip. And then…"

"And then it was gone." Pan's unsure if this is a question or a statement. She sees herself speak in Persephone's glass eye.

"And then it was gone."

"Well, let me ask you—how can you create something before you know what it is? How can you forecast an idea before you have it? How can something come from nothing?"

"But if these simulations are just coming out of my head, then it means it's somewhere in there too. Since, after all, you've told me there's no way the computer can create something of its own. Everything in there is just a…" *It's not like it's real, you know? They're just…* She envisions the projection of Alvin as she hears Ellis: *They're just projections on screens. Bits of code.* "Just an extension of me." She rubs her thumb over the anesthetic's puncture, alleviating an itch that isn't there as she tries to block out the image of herself in Ellis's headset.

"But can't you say that about anything you perceive? That everything is just a projection of your conscious processing?"

"Of course not. Other people are real. The world around me is real."

"Well, even if there is a world around you—that is, in fact, separate and *not* you—you can only understand it through the lens of your perception. Which means, all you can ever know is the reality of the world as *you* filter it. Not anyone else. So, my question is: what's the difference between a computer program that you readily accept is a technological extension of your perception and a world that you hesitate to admit is nothing more than an extension of your perception?"

I can't let that be true. I can't believe that. If I do, then—

Lena: *Then what? It's so easy to let yourself pretend me into existence. Why not everyone and everything?*

Persephone continues: "More often than not, these computers prove to be all we really need. They can do exactly what we tell them to. There are, of course, people who will say what the computers lack is a *human*," she air-quotes, "touch, but that's what we're aiming to change here."

There's no one in there, Ellis. Pan's back in his basement, telling him, *It's only you in your head.*

"But what about the people in your life?" Pan asks. "I mean, there have to be people you care about more than all this. People who care about you?"

"Why do you believe that so strongly?" Pangaea is unsettled by the sincere curiosity in Persephone's face. "Why do you think there's this premium on who we are to other people? Is there anyone who matters to you, who doesn't in some way serve a purpose to you? Is there any motive at all behind having a relationship with someone other than what they can do for you?"

Pangaea says aloud to Lena, "No. there are some people we're simply bound to. We have to be." Then, as an afterthought, "*They* have to be."

Persephone studies Pan for a moment. "I think we'll come to see that as an antiquated idea as we evolve. And that's what Wonderland is—evolution. An evolution of human experience."

"So, what're you saying? That it's all right to leave people behind once they mean nothing to you? That the love they may feel for you means nothing?"

"Would that really be love? If it only goes one way."

Do you want to have this baby?

I don't even bother asking myself that, honestly. If I had a choice, then I'd wonder. But I don't. So why waste the time thinking about it? Once I'm his mother, I'll be his mother.

"Then you think what my mother did was justified, don't you? You think it was fine for her to leave." She waits for Persephone to meet her gaze.

"No. I wouldn't say that."

"Then you do think there are some people we're bound to."

"No. You didn't let me finish." Pan can't tear her gaze away from her reflection in the eye. "I would say that woman was never your mother at all."

ON DEAF EARS

"**I** can't hear you at all, Pan!" Devorah shouts. "Let's go back there."

They walk away from the stage, where Alvin and the band are playing, and settle at a picnic table in the rear of the outdoor bar. "That's better." She sighs. "You know," looking down at her belly, "I certainly want him to be musical, but even his little ears need a break."

"Mine too." Pan's taken aback to see Devorah pull out a joint.

Devorah notices her skeptical glance. "What? It's not booze."

"I'm pretty sure you're not supposed to smoke at this point either."

"Cigarettes, sure. I haven't touched one since I first took the piss test in April. Weed is fine. It's from the earth and all that." As she takes a hit, Pan envisions the fetus coughing within her. She looks back at Lunar Grove. They're playing an acoustic song, Alvin sitting behind his drums, idly staring at the snare and lightly air drumming atop the cymbals. *When did this become so miserable?*

Why look for anything from anyone at all? If all they can do is fail you.

She tries to forget the projection of Alvin's face, but now she's back in Ellis's basement, staring at herself in the headset. *It's not real, Pan. It's not really you,* she hears him plead.

"You already finished that?" she asks Dev incredulously, seeing the nub of a roach.

"Fuck off. You're not my mother."

"Maybe not, but eventually you're gonna have to start being one."

"Where's this fucking coming from? All the sudden you're my life coach? It's not your baby, it's mine. I know what to do." She waves off the waiter-drone, whose screen displays a continuously changing collage of photos of attractive, ageless, bleach-toothed smiling faces toasting the various beers on tap.

"Do you? I mean, you're due, when, November? December? August is almost over, Dev, and you still don't seem to get that there's a little life in you now. That's literally in your hands."

"Fuck you!"

A few people nearby look over as Devorah shouts.

She lowers her voice. "I'm gonna be a great mom. Easy for you to talk right now, still living with daddy and trimming roses for a living."

Lena: *What's really on your mind, Pan?*

"Shut up," Pan says aloud to Lena.

"Fuck you." Dev gets up to leave.

Why am I here? Do I need any of this? Pan reaches across the table and puts her hand on Dev's wrist. "Wait. I'm sorry. I'm just...I—" She lets go and sinks her head into her hands, massaging her temples. "I don't know what's bugging me."

Devorah sits back down. "Look, Pan. I'm here, but you can't be bitching me out about this baby. You may think you have an idea what it's like, and you may think you mean well, but you have no clue what this is. It's not just my life that's completely changed now; there's a whole new one I'm fucking responsible for. A whole 'nother life with all its headaches and pain and joys and agony that's now on my plate. And those aren't just words; it's what it is. So, lay off me, all right?"

The band is playing a loud one. Pan looks at them and doesn't realize the disdain painted across her face as she wishes, *Will you just shut up and let me hear my own thoughts?* She grimaces as the decibels climb, forgetting how she used to mosh and flail and jump around and scream throughout Alvin's shows. She doesn't let herself dwell on the question of how long it's been since she looked forward to one of these gigs.

"I'm sorry, Dev. Look, I—"

The drone returns.

"Hello there! You look like you could use a top off! Would you like—"

"I just told you *no* a second ago," Devorah snaps at it.

It hovers for a moment, the screen facing Devorah, before floating off to another table. Dev watches it drift away. "It just doesn't stop. Everyone—and I mean *everyone*—loves to remind me what I'm responsible for. Everyone loves to pile on the guilt. As if I've already killed the little shit." She affectionately rubs her stomach. "You know, I almost think people are holding their breath for me to kill him. I feel like that's what it is. That they expect me to steal the life from him before he even he has it."

"Don't say that. I don't think that. Ivan doesn't think that."

"Ivan might as well not be in the picture."

Pan grimaces again as the band's noise crawls into her ears.

"He's checked out. He treats me like I'm not *me* anymore but just the vehicle bringing about the end of his life. All he talks about now is all the things he won't be able to do now that he's gonna be a father. Like it's completely my fault. That's the idea in his head. That our child's life means the end of his. Well, I suppose the end of his life in everything but flesh and blood."

"Thank you," Marina says on the stage as the noise concludes in crescendo, "we're gonna take a ten-minute break and be right back!"

Alvin walks off the stage and looks around for Pan, expecting her to be near the front. He catches sight of her sitting near the back of the lawn and walks there, nonplussed.

"Hey!" He sits next to Pan, who gives Dev a to-be-continued look, then gives Alvin the wet kiss she knows he wants.

"Great set, Al," knowing the script she's to follow.

"How you doing, Dev? The little one kicking yet?"

"You know it. Everyone's already started making the soc-cer-ball jokes."

After some mindless banter, they sit in silence. Alvin looks around, people-watching and trying to gauge by the crowd's demeanor if they're enjoying the music, if they think Lunar Grove is too good to be playing at some small outdoor beer gar-den, which is what he hopes is in everyone's head. Devorah and Pangaea look at each other but don't speak, eye-telling each other that their conversation is to be had within the hearing of no other ears but theirs.

"All right, we're going back on," Alvin says. "Pan, will you help me pack up the kit at the end of the set?"

"I'm your number one roadie. Why else d'you keep me around?"

He bends down and kisses the top of her head and jogs back to the stage. She watches him run off, then turns back to Dev, about to resume the conversation but sees the drone approaching again.

"Hello there!"

"How many times do you have to fucking hear me say we're fine?" Devorah says.

But then she and Pan notice this is a different drone. Its screen flickers for a moment, and a nurse's face appears, the drone now live-streaming a video-conference call. Pan sees the color fade from Dev's face.

"Hi, Devorah. How nice to see you," the nurse says.

"Hi, it's nice to," she has to swallow to compensate for how dry her throat has become, "it's nice to see you too, Marie."

"Are we enjoying ourselves today? It's such a nice time of year here—when autumn begins. Isn't it?"

Dev looks at her fidgeting hands, not the screen.

"But, certainly I can trust that you're not having anything to drink today, are you? I surely hope not. For your sake and for the child you're carrying. The life you're holding."

Dev still can't look at the screen.

"I'll remind you, if it becomes necessary, you can always stay at one of our Maternity Centers for the remaining duration of your term. That option is always available to you. We know how difficult it can sometimes be, bringing life into this world."

Alvin and Pan are driving back to her house. She's been staring vacantly out the window, glancing at the trees lining 95 South.

"I mean, when we finally do get together to play, it's always great. It's just so fucking difficult to line up our schedules consistently." He's been ranting about the group's dysfunctionality, with Pan half-listening, paying only enough attention to know when she should say something to evince evidence that she's listening when, in fact... *Why am I here? Why am I here with him? Devorah needs all the help she can get to bring this thing to term, and this is the shit he worries about?*

"Don't you agree?"

Pangaea still looks out the window. "About what?"

"You haven't heard anything I just said, have you?"

Still staring at the trees. "No, Al. I haven't. Sorry. I just...I have a few other things on my mind. A bit more worried about Dev's situation than who you play music with. I can't hear you bitch about the band again today. Tomorrow, my ears are all yours."

"Right. When it's convenient for you, I can talk about my problems. Right."

"These aren't even real issues. You're talking about people you play music with, not the cure for cancer. If they annoy you, then, fuck it, play music with other people. I mean, come on. What the hell are we talking about here?" Now she does look at him. "What the hell are we talking about *ever*?"

"That's beside the point. The point is, you're only halfway present when it suits you, regardless of the issue. I'm there for you whenever you wanna bitch about something."

"No, Al. You're a backboard in your best moments."

The decibels begin to rise.

"Why don't you really say what's on your mind? Obviously, something is fucking bugging you."

Do you really want me to say it's you that's bugging me? That, for whatever reason, it's that I don't want to be with you? That I don't need to be with you?

"It's Devorah, it's me, it's, shit, I don't know." *It's you. Right now, that's what the problem is* "Alvin. I—Devorah is falling apart right in front of me, and you're here bitching about absolute nonsense."

"Of course. Who am I to feel upset about anything."

"Al, you have nothing to worry about. That's the situation you've given yourself. You choose to do absolutely nothing and take me along for the ride, and no one gets in the way of that choice." *And why the fuck have I gone along for the ride so long?*

They stare at the red light, unwilling to let their gazes even attempt to cross.

"You know what, all you're trying to do right now is pick a fight. That's it. You're just trying to inject a little pace into your day 'cause you're bored and don't have some acid or your flowers to twiddle around. You're just stuck with me, stuck with an actual person and not yourself."

"If I'm bored, it's only because I'm here in the car with you. Maybe that's all we are. Two people content to be bored with each other. You want me to tell you what's really bugging me? It's you. I have no clue how I've spent this long with you."

The light turns green.

"Yeah? I'll tell you. 'Cause no one else would be willing to put up with someone as lost as you are. You've spent so long with me because the only other person who could be with you, is *you*. If you didn't have me, then you'd be stuck alone with yourself. Your own mother didn't even want you." He puts his hands over his mouth once the words touch their ears. He doesn't realize he just blew through a red light until he hears the cars honking on his left.

They drive the rest of the way in silence. He pulls into Pangaea's driveway, and Lena says, *People fight, Pan. It happens. If anything, the people you love are the only people you can fight with.* But she chooses to ignore the voice as she opens the door.

"I'm sorry, Pan," Alvin stammers. "I think I just—"

And she chooses to ignore his as well.

HINENI

Mom,

I haven't written one of these in almost ten years. I just read the last one. I don't know if it's sad or funny how little has changed in my life since then. But, here I am.

I'm still at the shop with Dad. He misses you, which I'm sure you know. I wonder if that bothers you, wherever you are. Does the fact that someone else actually feels your absence weigh on your mind? It's strange to think about. A physical sensation in response to an empty space. It's like there's more meaning in the hole you occupy in our lives than your flesh and blood.

I've met someone. That's why I'm writing to you. His name's Alvin. A bit of a nebbish name, but he's cute. Does that make me shallow if that's what I care about? It's only been a month, but somehow it feels routine, like he's always been a piece of my life. Is that what love is? Someone who becomes a routine. I think I once wrote in one of these that love is a scar someone etches beneath the skin. Once it's there, it can't go away, only the person can. It's why, if I ever saw you, I would be okay saying, "I love you." It wouldn't be a compliment.

Do you understand that? It's almost the opposite. It's more like blame than anything. What I don't know is if I love the person you may have been, someone who looked at me and held me and never wanted to let go. Or if I love the phantom.

But you know what? All of that is bullshit. Because you've never been here. Now someone is. Now there's someone who I can look at and say I love you and know it's not some idea about scars and skin. It's just fucking words. Words that might as well be gibberish because what matters is I can look at Alvin, I can hear him, I can hold him. That all he and I need to say to each other is, "Here I am."

Pangaea

PART FOUR

AN ISLAND ENTIRE

SU'S FLOWERS

*I*t looks just like it, even the spots where mold can't be scrubbed away.

"You and your dad certainly have kept it up well." Lena stands alongside Pan as she walks through the aisles. The colors are slightly enhanced in the simulation, but *even in reality, flowers are where color finds a home on Earth.* She plays with a kaleidoscope bouquet of hyacinths that pulses with fluctuating shades.

Pan turns a corner and sees herself standing behind the counter, writing in the logbook. "It was a slow day, I remember that." She stares at the projection of herself, sizing herself up as if seeing another person. *But is it another person? Is my memory of myself, distilled into pixels, any more or less real than any idea of myself I may have in a given moment? Are we just living our lives in the third person when we see ourselves in memory? But how is it different from seeing ourself in a screen?* She looks at the door as Alvin walks into the shop; Pan tries to imagine the present-tense experience of the projection of herself within this simulation but can only recall the memory:

"Hi there," I said as I saw him walk in. I didn't think much of him; he looked a bit boyish and elfishly harmless. Though, later he'd tell me he was more Hobbit than elf.

"Hey," he mumbled, staring for an extra second longer than he would've looked at most people once he noticed my purple hair.

I nodded and looked back at the logbook. "Let me know if I can help." He didn't look like the sort of guy who normally bought flowers.

Now in the simulation, Pangaea walks behind him as he ambles through the aisles, pretending to know what he's looking at. Pangaea looks at the simulation of herself and sees herself look up intermittently from the logbook, breaking eye contact with him whenever their eyes meet, since he, too, is intermittently looking back at her.

Lena: "It's like watching two schoolkids."

"More than anything, I was just curious about him. I was trying to guess who he might've been buying flowers for." Pan watches Alvin pause; from where he stands, the projection of Pangaea can't see him. She watches him now, though, as he closes his eyes and inhales, exhales slowly. Then he walks toward the register as Pan is no longer watching the projection of herself in the third person; she's back behind the counter, looking at him:

"Actually, I could use some help."

"No worries. Most guys do. First things first: who are the flowers for?"

"My mom."

"Trying to play the good-son part, I get it. All right, let's get mom some flowers." I walk around the counter and lead him down the aisles to arrange a bouquet. "Is it her birthday or something?"

He doesn't respond.

I stop walking and look at him. "Dude, *tell* me you didn't forget her birthday and are just now getting these."

He laughs, and it's wonderful to see he takes care of his teeth.

"No, no. Her birthday's in October and—"

"Hey, mine too!"

I continue to get flowers, and he walks beside me.

"Right. So, uh, no, these aren't birthday flowers. Though, I'll have to remember to come back when that time comes."

"Just don't forget her birthday. Moms don't like that. But, what's the occasion? You just buying these out of the blue?"

Again, he doesn't respond at first, and now I'm wondering if I'm prying.

"No...," he finally says, though I can hear he's deliberating if he should go on. "She's coming back from Chicago today. She's been there for a few weeks."

"Oh, cool. For work or something?"

"Not exactly."

And, luckily, he's behind me and can't see me wince after I ask, without thinking, "Someone die?"

"No. She, um. Hmmm."

I turn around. "I'm not trying to be a snoop. Sorry. I'll just help you get the flowers."

"It's all right." As he looks at me, his irises begin to liquefy, like he's found something, "It's just family. My uncle—her brother—he gets suicidal. Years ago, he really tried to, well, end it. So, whenever this happens, we have to take it seriously. He lives alone, though, and it just, it just all falls on my mom when this happens. So, she's been with my uncle the last two weeks helping him out, taking him to his appointments and, I dunno the word, she's just been taking care of him, and I know it's exhausting. So, useless as it may be, I figure I should get her some flowers to see when she comes back home."

"I didn't know how to reply," Pangaea tells Lena, now observing in the third person. Alvin and the projection of herself stand with each other. "I think my guts wished I knew him well enough

to hold him right there, but I just stood there. A bit stunned someone could be so transparent with anyone, let alone a stranger."

"Sorry to hear that," Pangea tells Alvin. "I don't know much,
but I think it's a safe bet that she'll like the flowers."

"Yeah, I think so too. Or hope, at least. I'm sort of wondering
if I'm doing this, though, just to feel like a good son."

"I don't know. Usually, going through the motions of being
decent is what makes decency just that."

"How about you? What would you do if it was your mom?"

"Uh, well, that's tricky. I don't have one."

"Oh, fuck, I'm sorry. Now I'm the one who shouldn't pry."

"No worries. She ditched me and my dad when I was little.
Wherever she is, she's not much of a mom, so…"

Alvin, after allowing a pause, not knowing how to reply, says,
"I'm Alvin, by the way."

Pangaea shakes his hand, unperturbed by the clamminess.
"Pangaea."

Alvin, after laughing at his own joke, then sharing it, says,
"That's gotta be a heavy burden. Being the world before it split."

Pangaea smirks, more at his self-gratuitous grin than the
quip itself. "Eh, or the world that couldn't keep itself together.
Depends how you look at it. But, all right, this should do for a
bouquet. We do have some designer pottery in the back from local
craftsfolk. *If* you wanna go above and beyond for your mom, that
is. I can pot these in there with some dirt."

"Were you trying to keep him around?" Lena asks. "Or just
being a shrewd salesman?"

"Be quiet." Pan keeps her eyes on herself and Alvin, trying to
relive this day through her own eyes, not the distant perspective
of an outside voyeur. *What was it I fell in love with?* she wonders,
watching them:

"Sure." His gaze lingers on me, since maybe he can see I'm inviting him to do just that.

I start walking back toward the greenhouse where we keep the pots. "You can come with." I gesture to him, noticing he's unsure if he should stand where he is or come back with me. "I'm not gonna chop you up and feed you to the Venus flytrap. Already fed her today."

Thank God he laughs. "Um, okay, cool. That's what I was afraid of. Last flower shop I visited I had to crawl out of one." I can't help but laugh as he staggers at the humidity once we walk in. "Fuck." He dabs at the sweat jeweling his lip and eyebrows.

"Yeah, gets pretty thick here in the summer. Spring too. You get used to it, though. Pick your poison." I show him the cabinet where we keep the pots. He looks at them, and I can see he's actually curious about the designs, not just grazing over them.

"This one's nice." He points to one whose circumference is engraved with whorls and swirls, no trace of linearity.

"That's one of my favorites, actually." And why am I relieved to know I'm being honest? "The lady who gave us that one said she wanted it to be like *Starry Night*. It's a good one; your mom'll love it. Gimme a sec to pot the flowers." I take it out of the cabinet and start clumping the dirt.

"No rush. You know, I walk past this shop every day on my way to the Blue Line. Just never gotten around to coming in."

"Well," I don't know what to say, but it sounds like he doesn't either, "I like to think this shop makes the commute a little brighter for everyone, if nothing else. Literally." I think we just want to hear each other's voices. "Can I ask," I can feel his gaze on me from behind, and for whatever reason, it's warm, "what happens next, you know, with your uncle? Like, does your mom have to keep going back and forth to check on him?"

"Honestly, it's one of those things where it's day-to-day. Two summer ago, this happened, and my uncle came and lived with us for six months. I think that drove my dad crazier than my mom. Her name's Susan, by the way. Um, but anyway. It's always sort of up in the air. This has happened a few times. My uncle will be responsible the first few months after something like this happens, but inevitably, he just, I don't know, stops caring that much, stops going to his appointments, stops taking medicine, then it comes to a head, and my mom has to pack up again and start the whole process over, and it takes so much out of her, but she's not just going to leave her brother and who else is there to do it, and there's not really anything I can do to help, so I just watch the whole thing unfold, and my dad can't help because he has to work, so we can only watch her drain herself, and even when we tell her she needs to think about herself too, that it's not selfish for her to try to keep her own sanity, her own fucking health, inevitably we open a can of worms, and then the three of us end up shouting and—"

I turn around; he's forgetting to breathe.

"Hey, Alvin. Are *you* all right?" I stop potting the flowers.

Pangaea observes the next moments from a distance: she sees herself and Alvin leaning against the counters opposite each other, separated by only a few feet. The dense flora surrounds them, and the moisture in the air is visible, like the whisper of fog. The sunlight seems so distant, the way the plants steal most of the light and leave only scraps for Pangaea and Alvin. Yet, perhaps because of the inevitable sweat beading their faces, or perhaps because of the mutual quickening of their hearts' pulses, the vibrancy of life within them illuminates the two in a glow brighter than anything the sun can muster.

"I'm fine, it's just, I want to do right, but I don't know how.

And, whenever I actually *can* be helpful—like, if it's even just going to the grocery store or doing dishes or walking the fucking dog—just to give her a break, in those moments, I get so selfish and just want to do whatever it is I'm doing. Which," he laughs one of those sigh-laughs that are full of nothing but self-loathing, "is usually nothing. Do you know what I mean?" He looks at her. "Do you ever want to be someone that you can't will yourself to be? Like feeling stuck in the person you are but seeing someone better so close in the distance?"

She sees Alvin in the first person now, standing in front of her. She wants to reach out and hold him or, rather, wants him to try to find comfort in her arms. Instead, though, the colors of the flowers around her begin to flicker, and the shapes of the wall distort; the projection of Alvin rapidly begins to lose shape until what Pan sees in front of her is the flesh of a human face with only shade and indentation where features would be. Then, all is black, and Pangaea wakes out of the simulation.

"Pangaea?" Persephone asks. "Pangaea, are you awake?"

She drinks all the water in the glass next to her. "Yeah, I'm here."

"Take a minute to collect yourself. Then we can begin."

"Can I ask you something?" Her eyes are still closed as she ruffles her hair in swirls, trying to squeeze the fogginess out of her mind. "Do you have a family?" She looks at Persephone and, still unaccustomed to the effect of it, glances uneasily at her own reflection trapped in the glass eye. Persephone's expression reveals only a hint of amused surprise.

"No, I don't. Now, are you ready to begin the interview?"

"Do you want one?"

"Pangaea," her expression still inscrutable, "we're not here to ask me questions. We're here for me to ask *you* questions."

"I'm just trying to talk to you like a person."

"I understand that. And maybe, under different circumstances, we could talk more candidly. But," she opens her laptop to begin typing notes, "we must maintain the professional nature of our relationship. So, let's begin the interview. Tell me about your simulation."

"Have you ever tried to have a family? Or even just a partner?"

Now her face shows hints of frustration. "Let's be serious here."

"It's a simple question. You know so much about me now, and I know nothing about you. I think I have a right to know even just the slightest bit."

"Where is this coming from? Did something happen in there?"

"I don't know. Why don't you or your analysts go review the readings you got while I was in there and tell *me* what my experience was? Since all of this is synthetic anyway."

Persephone studies Pangaea for a moment, then closes her laptop and scooches her seat closer. "No, I don't have a family. I was almost part of one once, but that might as well have been a different life."

"What happened?"

"My life. Now, can we move on?"

Something instinctive prompts Pangaea to ask: "Did you have any children?"

"Was this simulation also about your mother?"

"You didn't answer the question."

Persephone seems to intentionally let Pan stare at herself in her eye in discomforted silence. "You didn't either."

She's not gonna budge. And even if she did, what's the point?
"Yes, my mom was in this one but just sort of in the background. This was actually a memory I wanted to revisit. When my—"

Well, what is he right now? "When my boyfriend and I met. Or ex-boyfriend. I don't know yet."

"Was it accurate to the memory? Or at least, to the design you specified for the programmers?"

"For the most part. It all seemed consistent with my memory. The only thing is," she wonders the thought to herself before vocalizing it, "I can't be sure how accurate my memory is to the actual event. I mean, do you think," she hears herself and Alvin shout at each other in the car, their voices somehow louder in her head now than they were the other day, "our memory has a will of its own? That changes to conform to the event we *wish* happened, rather than the events that actually did? That we remember people as they need to be in our heads, not who they really are?"

Which means I don't need to see Al for him to mean something. I don't need to hold him. I can just remember him however I need to. Since that's all Lena is too.

"All I can tell you is that here, there's only the experience you choose to have. The program can't deviate from anything in its design; the only variable is you. So, let me ask you—how did you want this simulation to go?"

Pangaea doesn't hear the question. She mutes out everything but memory:

Alvin looked at me and asked, "Do you ever want to become someone that you can't will yourself to be? Like feeling stuck in the person you are but seeing someone better so close in the distance?"

I leaned back against the counter, looking at him and wondering where this sense of familiarity stemmed from. *I don't think we've met before. And yet, it's like we know each other. Somehow.*

"I don't know." I was unsure where my thoughts would lead but trusted that I could follow their trail with him, that he wouldn't care what I said, as long as I said it to him. "I can tell you that when I wake up, I'm not always thrilled to be me. I'm not always happy that I know my day will unfold the same as the day before and most likely the next. And that that's what I'm looking at for the rest of my life. But, I guess I feel at peace with the motion of moments that bring me wherever I am. That of all the trillions of different collections of particles there are in the universe, the collection of atoms that comprises me, moving through the universe and glued together by the will that *is* me, that all of that is Pangaea Green—I'm at peace with that most days. But, sure, I think I know what you mean. About seeing—"

He surprised me, not by finishing my sentence for me but by the tone with which he said, looking right at me, "Seeing someone better so close in the distance."

Pangaea looks at Persephone, who repeats her question: "How would you have liked this simulation to go?"

"Exactly how I remember it."

HOUSEKEEPING

Pangaea watches Devorah's mom throw garbage with one hand into the trash bag she's holding in the other. "I don't understand how you could have let it get like this, Devorah, I really don't." Pan's oblivious to Nancy's words, hearing only her own. *Is it so wrong of me to just want Alvin as I need him to be? Tolerating anything else is just a lie to both of us. Both of us acting the part of caring for the other when, really, we just fill some longing. No relationship can last when most of the time you're pretending to see someone who isn't there.*

Lena: *I'm still here with you, aren't I?*

Pangaea sits at the kitchen table, sifting through a folder that Dev's mother stuffed with papers that were scattered around the apartment. Dev sits on a chair pulled in front of the refrigerator, sniffing food items and fluids to determine if they're to be placed back in the fridge or deposited in the garbage. "I can't even begin to imagine what it looked like when Ivan was still here."

"Mom...please, don't," Devorah says in a distant, defeated tone. "I fucked up. I know. I feel bad enough. Let's just leave the whole Ivan thing alone, okay?"

Devorah's mom looks up from the trash bag: "Oh, no. I'm sure you wish you could leave it be, but you can't. And that's the bed you made for yourself. Baby or no baby, the police are going to come talk to you, and so are the lawyers. You think they're not going to want to talk to the girl the drug dealer's been living with? Just count your blessings there were no drugs here when they ransacked the place."

Devorah called Pan's house a week ago:

"Pan! They arrested him! They found…they found him with—" The rest was indiscernible.

"What? Hold on. Slow down. Why're you calling the house?"

"You haven't responded to me in, like, a week, and your cell just goes to voicemail. Ivan just called. They arrested him for possession of heroin. He's in jail. Pan! What am I gonna do?"

Devorah's mother, Nancy, came to Dev's apartment that night and helped her and Pan eradicate the presence of every drug on the premises. She remained silent, but after they stuffed everything into a bag and Pan drove to the dumpster behind the Shaw's a mile away to toss it, Nancy locked herself in Devorah's bathroom for the night. She's slept every night since then in the bedroom with her daughter.

"I don't get it," Nancy continues, "did he not think about the baby? Has he ever? I just don't get it. How have you let it get to this point with him? Your dad and I have always known he was bad news. And now look: he's going to jail, you're due with his child, and there's gonna be a trial. I mean, sweetie, you know we've been warning you about this for years. And—"

"Mom!" Devorah turns her tear-stained face to her mother. "I know! I know, okay?! You can say it all: you can say I'm selfish, you can say I'm a brat, you can say I need to grow up, you can say it all! But you're my mom, and I need you right now." She begins to choke over her words. "I need you."

Nancy pauses her movements, as if trying to resist a temptation, puts the bag down, and goes to Dev. She bends down to hug her, letting one arm curve its way atop the baby bump.

"I'm here." She tries to wipe away Devorah's tears, but this only hastens their fall. "And," she says in a brighter tone of voice, altering her tactics, "You have your guardian angel too." She turns to Pangaea and gives her a wink mixed with some other combination of gratitude's face algebra.

Pan resumes sifting through the folder as Nancy returns to her garbage collection. She glances intermittently between Devorah and Nancy, seeing the same face on both heads. *Will the baby be another one of them too?* She imagines Devorah having a girl, the rapid growth of the infant's face into the same one Nancy and Devorah wear. *Are we only reiterations? Is every child simply the next effort of a generation? Just codes of DNA duplicated like any other program.* Pangaea is about to toss away the next piece of paper but begins to scrutinize it once she sees a few words:

Dear Devorah Gordon,

Congratulations! We know you are expecting a child this December, and it's been such a joy getting to know you these past few months! What an exciting time this is for you and your loved ones. I am writing this letter to inform you of the voluntary option to finish the remainder of your term at the residence of our Maternity Center here in East Boston. Each Maternity Center in the nation is a federally funded facility that you and other taxpayers support. Our mission is to provide you with the best experience possible for the duration of your (and other expecting mothers') term. This service is available to you, voluntarily, at no cost to you. Here, we provide you with housing, food, and emotional and medical support for you and the life budding within you. Should you elect to join us, please call the number provided.

As a reminder, this notice is to inform you of your option to voluntarily finish the remainder of your term with us at our caring Maternity Center; however, we have received multiple notices suggesting that your circumstances might be such that our professional service is necessary for the health and safety of the life you are carrying. Should we receive further notification about these circumstances, one of our representatives will, in coordination with local authorities, contact you in person about the opportunity to finish the duration of your term at our facility. As always, our mission is to ensure the human life you are carrying can safely enter our beautiful world.

I look forward to hearing from you. And, of course, we will see you soon for your next checkup.

Once again, congratulations.
—Maternity Center No. 618

Pangaea remembers listening to Nancy read this aloud to Devorah two days ago, when she unearthed it from among the pile of rubble in the living room:

"Devorah, did you see this?" Nancy said.

"See what?"

Nancy proceeded to read the letter.

"I'm not staying in one of those, Mom. It's bad enough I have to go there every week for checkups."

"You might not have a choice."

"According to the letter, I still do. I'm not going to one of those."

"Dev, this might be exactly what you need. What your child needs."

"You know what those places are like. You've heard the stories. You'd have me go to one of those? They monitor you twenty-four seven. They force you to eat their, like, laboratory-packed cat food. Girls get strapped to their beds and sedated. They're prisons. That's what they are. They don't even treat the women there like humans. It's like they're just the package the baby is stuck in until it finds its way out. That's how they'd look at me in there. Some box with a gift inside."

"Sweetie, you're exaggerating. But even so...you have the baby to think of. Think of what's best for the baby."

"A baby I wouldn't be having if I had the choice."

Her child will be no different in her eyes than what I am in yours.

Lena: *No, in my eyes you're not even my child, Pan.*

"I know," Nancy says. "But you're having it. It can't be helped."

In the kitchen, Pangaea sees Devorah get up and put her hands over her stomach. "He's kicking." Nancy's eyes perk; she goes to her daughter and puts her hands on the bump.

"How about you take a break. Go lie down."

Devorah doesn't argue and goes to her room, leaving Pangaea in the kitchen with Nancy.

Lena: *Just like Alvin isn't his true self in your eyes either. With Wonderland, people are only what you need them to be. Is it so hard to call that evolution?*

"I really don't know how to say thank you for all this, Pan." Nancy sniffs a milk carton; her nose wrinkles, and she pours the chunked fluid down the sink before sitting down at the table. To Pan's surprise, Nancy takes out a pack of cigarettes and puts one in her mouth. She notices her expression and laughs. "Oh, no. I don't smoke them. Not anymore, at least. I just sometimes need to put one in my mouth when I get stressed. Old habits. Actually," her gaze grows distant, and Pan can see that Nancy is seeing memory, "I quit a little before I knew Devorah was coming. When Steve and I were trying to conceive. He never smoked, but he told me he'd stop drinking alcohol for as long as I stayed away from cigarettes. He thought that'd make it easier. My knowing that he was making sacrifices too. Thing was, I hated that he drank, but I just let it be. Funny how a child changes everything. That was close to thirty years ago, Pan. And here we are now. You just have to wonder why Dev—" She bites her lip as her voice quakes. Pangaea doesn't bother trying to think of something to say, most of Nancy's words evaporating before they can settle on her mind.

Maybe it is evolution. And Ellis, for all his problems, hasn't been wrong. Only the body can lead to problems like Dev's.

"And she shouldn't *want* to love this baby." Nancy's words now occupy Pan's attention. "She should just love it. And if she did, she wouldn't have put herself in this situation at all. When it's your turn, you'll know what I mean." *Maybe that's all bodies can do.* Pangaea realizes her face must show her thoughts because she sees Nancy grinning at her. "What? You don't want kids?"

"Of course not. I don't think a crueler thing can be done."

Nancy stares at her, the cigarette dropping a bit in her mouth.

"You don't think there's something miraculous about life? That there isn't anything beautiful to it?"

"It's hard to see it these days. I mean, I can't imagine Dev's gonna be much more of a mother than Lena."

It's only after she sees Nancy's face that Pan recognizes what she said.

"Oh my God." *Your own mother didn't want you.* "I'm sorry. I didn't mean—"

"You still wish you knew her, don't you? Your mother."

Why did I say that? That's not…that's not me. "My mom?" She blinks away the tightening sensation in her chest. "I've never met her so, in a sense, it's not like I've ever had a mother to miss."

Lena: *That's not the truth. I've been with you all these years. Better than I could have been in the flesh. I've been the mother you've needed. Just like you can create all the relationships you need with the press of a button, the quick slip of a needle.*

"I'll never know how she could have…" Nancy stops herself, watching Pan scratch the crook of her elbow.

"How she could have left?" Pangaea finishes for her.

Lena: *Don't be ashamed of what you believe to be true.*

"Beats me. It really does. But, she did. And here I am. All things considered, I suppose I could've come out worse, but," Pangaea looks up and sees that Nancy isn't sharing in the levity of her tone, "I try not to feel too sorry for myself. Healthy or not, that's how I deal with it."

"You and your dad both, Pan. It's like you both're happy to pretend she was never there."

Lena: *Why don't you tell her it's the other way around?*

"As far as I'm concerned, Nancy…"

Lena: *I'm still here.*

"My dad and I have made it fine without her. He's always let me try to explain the world to myself and offer a helping hand when I need one. Sometimes, yeah, I think it would've been great to have a mom." *You told me Mom would always be in me.* Isaac's face on the tracks all those years ago flashes before her. "But, if nothing else, the blessing of living today is that there's nothing I can't ask Google to answer for me. There's nothing some screen can't solve. I can shop around for a thousand different moms." Only later will Pangaea wonder what prompts her to say, "I remember my first period. What girl doesn't, you know? Even then, I knew I couldn't go to Isaac. So, you know what I did? I Googled, 'My first period.'" She laughs emptily again, swallowing the sting of dryness in her throat. "Why would I need a mom when I could get hundreds, maybe thousands of motherly solutions? You know? I could shop for the answer I needed. The mom I needed. And wouldn't even have to wonder if it was the right product since I could just find another one. I'd just know when something on the screen gave me a solution. But if I had my mom, I would've had to settle for whoever she was, whatever she told me. I would have only had her. So, sure: I've never had a mom in my life. But—" *Wait, what?* Pangaea surprises herself when she notices a tear in her eye. *Stop that. You're fine.* She continues to talk, her throat tightening in an effort to stay composed. "In a sense, it's a blessing that I've never known her. Since she's never been there to disappoint me." She's interrupted by the voice of her own memory. *As I got older, if I look in the mirror, I might see you looking back.* "Instead I've been able to be my own mother and to imagine what I need to hear and feel and hold and think and believe, and I can invent her, and she's everything I think I need, and she's not even there so she's really just me and..." She continues on, trying to suppress the thrusting arms of memories reaching from the grave, but the words are suddenly stolen from her by the sight of Nancy, who's begun to dab her eyes.

So then, you do think there are some people we're bound to.

And one of those corpses breaks free from the trampled dirt of moments Pan has buried before they're cold.

"Pan." Her words remain stolen as Nancy goes to her and puts her arms around her, unable to mute another zombie's whisper in the boneyard of remembrance:

Your own mother didn't even want you.

As Nancy holds her, Pangaea holds her too.

BLOOD PERCUSSION

L ena held her. It was just them in the kitchen. With the only light above the sink, the room was little more than shadow. Her and Pangaea's silhouettes against the wall coalesced into one: the hunching figure of Lena staring at the infant in her arms.

"This doesn't mean I don't love you," she told her daughter. "If anything, maybe what I'm doing is because I love you. Now. In this moment. I can leave you in love." Pangaea opened and closed her fists, eyes scrunched shut. A clean diaper too. Lena bent her head down to kiss Pangaea's forehead and closed her eyes. Simply feeling the body in her arms. Only feeling it.

Isaac snored upstairs.

When Lena opened her eyes, she was greeted with the open eyes of her daughter. The milk-cloudy gloss still dewing Pangaea's irises as she calmly awoke.

The mother and daughter stare at each other. Past and yet once and therefore eternally present in the way that anything that's ever timed into existence always is.

"Mom," Lena hears Pangaea say without speaking.

"Pan."

She begins to gurgle and squeal. Lena brings her closer to her chest, and Pan nestles against her breasts. Lena doesn't know if the pulse she feels is her own heart beating or her daughter's. Synchronized to the rhythm of blood's percussion. And in the kitchen that's mostly shadow, Lena tells her daughter something she knows she can't understand.

"This is the last time you'll see me, Pan. And the last I'll see you. And if there is a God, I know He'll torment me with this memory forever, and if there is a God, I pray you have no memory of me at all. I pray I won't even be an idea." She closes her eyes again, and when they open there are tears. "Maybe that's my curse. That I can only ever let you be an idea. An idea of life. Something I've created synthetically with flesh and blood and the shell of love but not the body of it. Only the surface. So as long as I'm in your life, you'll only ever be the surface of a child, the surface of a girl. The surface of a woman. Trapped in my perspective. Don't you see? I have to leave you. I have to. Otherwise, you'll never be anything but my idea. Your life would only be the fleshed development of an idea in my head."

The infant in Lena's arms said nothing. Only breathed. Breathed and moved with the minor motion of Lena's inhalation exhale. The way bodies can speak with silence. With her sleeping child in her arms, Lena asks God:

"How can you do this?"

"What is it I've done?"

"Curse a child to have a mother like me."

The way silence can speak without sound.

"Or is it me you've cursed?"

The way nothing can speak with silence.

"So, that's it. You've cursed me to carry a burden I'm not meant to. To live with that shame. To live knowing I can give the gift of life but choose not to. You've cursed me with the choice to hand life down as a punishment."

"No. I've blessed you with that choice. It's for you to decide. Whether you can give life as a gift or as a burden."

Silence.

"Do you not wonder at the burden I carry? Do you not look at what's in your arms and wonder what I hold in mine? Do you not wonder what it is to give life only to know you have to take it as well?"

"Then you should carry that burden alone. Not put it on us."

"What makes you think I can carry it alone? Could you? That's why you're here. To carry it as well."

Silence.

"Do you know what the only difference between you and I is?"

Lena looks at Pangaea, peacefully asleep in her grasp.

"I can only create human life. I can't live it."

"Pangaea, are you all right?"

Pan keeps her eyes closed, unwilling to see herself in Persephone's eye.

"Are you all right?"

Pan grogilly opens her lids and sees the unrevealing gaze of Persephone, holding a nondescript cup of water.

"Do you believe in God, Persephone?"

Persephone's eyes flicker with surprise as Pangaea sluggishly reaches for the cup.

"No. I don't believe there's anyone or anything that makes choices for me."

"That's not what I asked you."

"Let's talk about your simulation, shall we?"

"But we are. I am. All of these simulations, what you're doing here, what I'm doing: we're playing God."

With a hint of condescension, "And why might that be?"

"You're trying to recreate life here. You're trying to recreate the image of human beings."

"Haven't you said yourself that what we're doing here is only in the mind?"

Pangaea sees herself in Persephone's eye. "What if that's all that's needed? Since, even living in the first person, we can only ever see our bodies in a reflection."

Persephone smirks. "You're starting to sound like me."

"I don't sound like you. I don't sound like you at all."

"What was it you said a few weeks ago? Do you remember? I have it recorded here." Persephone clicks away at her keyboard and emphatically presses the space bar, then looks back to Pan, who hears her own voice play through the laptop: "All of this is synthetic anyway."

Persephone stares at her a moment before resuming. "Pangaea, don't you understand what we're really trying to accomplish here? This is evolution. Look at your body. Look at any body. An amalgamation of proteins and lipids and calcium. Some congealed jelly in between the ears. Is this what life should be housed in?"

Pan thinks of Ellis. *I probably should check on him. It's been weeks.*

"Is the fate of intelligent life to stay within the same confines that exist in an animal? We're merging the experience of life into something that can truly foster it. The epitomized experience of it, not the thin shell. Not the fragile shell of a human body. Is that really the only thing that makes you alive? Now, if you want to call that playing God, I won't stop you, but tell me this: is it any more noble to recreate a human body to just recreate a body to trap life in? Is a mother anything more than someone else pretending to be God? A God who fails to preserve life and only knows how to let it die in a body?"

"You're wrong. You have to be." She wants to keep speaking but doesn't know what to say. *I can't believe she's right. I can't let myself believe that.*

Lena: *But you do. It's not even a matter of belief. It's something you hold as true.*

"Pangaea, it's the future. The future is one where life is not our bodies' unique privilege."

"You talk like life is some entity that exists separate from us. Like it's this tangible thing you can just pluck out of a body and transplant. Do you have any idea how nuts that is?" It's not Ellis Pan sees in her head anymore but Devorah.

"Ones and zeroes. Electrical signals. Silicon chips and a bit of plastic. The experience of life can be recreated in these. So, yes, to answer your question: I do think life is some tangible thing. I don't think there's any more nobility in the clumsy anatomy of procreation than there is the systematic interpretation of data."

"What you're talking about isn't real. What you're talking about isn't freedom. Creating the image of life isn't the same as living it."

"I'll ask you the same question I've asked you before. What's more important, being at home in the world around us or the one within us?"

"But what about..." *What about what? What is it you want so badly to defend?* "But you're not thinking about other human beings. That we need other people. What you're talking about is the experience of a mind alone. A solitary life of delusion. You're forgetting what it is to connect to another human being."

Then why is it I believe I don't need Alvin?

"It's interesting to hear you say that. Considering everything you've told me about your simulations so far. Everything you've done here seems to be in pursuit of designing just that."

Because what if she's right? Wait, what did she just— "What?"

"Every simulation you've created has had other people in it. People from your life. You've been recreating your experience with other human beings. Your experience of relationships. Only, here what you've done is create them on your own terms. So, again, the question comes back: is there anything, truly, more valuable in the relationships you have with other people out there in the world?" *Alvin.* But there's no feeling; she feels nothing for the name, the idea within the name. "Than those you have here, exactly how you want them."

She sees Devorah's face and Ellis's face and Isaac's, all their faces in memory. *How is it I feel nothing for any of them?*

"And let me ask you," Persephone begins.

Pangaea thinks there's malice in her stare, but this vanishes, and there's just *the same stare. The same empty gaze as always.*

"Your mother—a woman you've never met—has been in most, if not all, your simulations. A woman who has been nothing more to you than an idea in your head. Tell me, is what you feel for her in there," she gestures to the Human Connection, "any less real than what you feel for anyone else? Or is it the same? Is all that matters," Pangaea tries to conjure a memory of Alvin's face, tries to think of anything to shield her from the reality that she just might agree, "the idea in your head?"

But she can't see him. All she sees is herself in Persephone's eye.

PHANTOMS

She writhes, her eyes closed.

"It always starts with suffocating, that's the first thing." Pan looks around the forest. It's night, but there are no stars. "There never are. Without fail. That never changes." She walks without direction, the space between trees foggy, her voice the only sound. *There's no one here but you, remember that. It's always only—* "What was that?" She twists around after hearing the snap of branches.

"Breathe. Remember, it isn't real. It's just a dream." Aware that she's lucid dreaming, Pan reminds herself, "I can't control it. All I can do is follow its pace and remember." When she tries to inhale, the suffocation returns, gripping her throat and chest. "It's just in my head."

Pan jogs ahead, all black around her, save the bark of trees and leaves. The snapping of branches pops behind her and surrounds her. She increases her pace, trying to drown the sound of alien footsteps with the crunch of her own on the dirt.

Then falls.

"Fuck." She looks at her palms to find they're coated in gore, the flesh torn away, leaving only bone. Cartoonish the layers of skin, muscle, bone. The pain slithers down her wrist, and a budding sense of nausea percolates in her throat. *It's never like this. I never actually get hurt.* She places her palms back down atop the forest and to calm herself picks up a leaf, staring. She notices how the thin, uncolored veins that artery the flesh of the leaf's green resemble a tree. She begins to get up, and there is someone standing in front of her.

The shock blinds her for a moment, and her shriek is so loud it burns her ears. She's unable to close her eyes, and all she sees is the outline of a person, the face empty of feature, save for the hollow eye sockets that allow her to peer through at—

"Wait." The fear subsides to curiosity. "It's back. There it is." The hazy shimmer that has plagued her simulations spreads through the sockets and obscures the body. As she's about to reach out and touch it, the haze dissipates, leaving only the forest in daylight. The trees are bare of all leaves, only their branches remain.

"*Claws,*" she reminds herself, trying to stay lucid. "I've always remembered them as claws, not branches, reaching up." She looks up to read the clouds, but there are none. Only a blue sky she can't be certain isn't the ocean. Pan turns back around, anticipating the footsteps. "This is where they always start to rush me." But hears nothing. Just an expanse of trees aligned in lattice. She picks a direction and moves along, waiting for the sensation of being watched to settle itself.

The sky begins to change. Lightning flashes, the white sears streaking the sky like valleys in the moon.

"There's the cliff." Pan notices the familiar terrain that marks the impending end of the dream. She doesn't need to walk ahead; the forest seamlessly becomes the cliff upon whose edge she now stands, looking down at the waves. The whitecaps crashing against the rocks. When she turns around, the forest is gone. She stands alone, surrounded only by water whose percussive swell rises in clamor like applause. The anticipated clench of dread yawns in her chest, and the feeling of suffocating returns. *It'll be here in a moment. It always is. Only now, I can look at it and say what it is. Now I can look at my—*

She loses her thoughts as the ocean rises around her. An alien deviation from the dream she knows like kin. Pan watches in impotent despair as the water shoots up toward the sky, herself in the center of a halo reaching for stars that aren't there. Her gaze follows the supernova blast so far that she can't see where the water meets the sky. But as it begins to crash down, Neptune thunder reverberating the air, it's not water that falls atop Pan.

"What is that?"

Pan watches in awe as a face begins to fall from above, a bust carved out of cloud and ocean spray, plummeting toward her, and as she begins to discern its features... "Is that...it looks like—"

Pan awakes, reaching her right hand for Lena, like she always does after the dream, but there's no hand, real or phantom, to hold her own. Just her phone buzzing.

"Who the hell is calling this early?" But when she grabs her phone, Pan is almost as shocked to see it's nearly noon as she is to see who's calling.

I still don't know if I can talk to him. She lets it go to voicemail, knowing Ellis won't leave one.

Next door, Ellis puts his phone down and looks at his computer. *Just give it up. She doesn't want to hear from you. She wants nothing more than to forget you exist.*

Pangaea lies down in her bed, eyes closed, hoping sleep will kidnap her. *Why bother with any of it? Devorah, Al...now him.* She's annoyed and shocked to hear her phone vibrate again.

She's your only friend, Ellis tells himself, resolved to keep trying.

Pan continues to let it ring, looking out her window at the scattered snowflakes. She locks onto one and tries to follow its ebbing trajectory as it descends, bringing her gaze and memory down with it back to sixth grade:

It's recess. The last Friday before Christmas break, and even the teachers are as happy to be outside as the kids. How they huddle with their thermoses. All the boys are running around the soccer field, throwing snowballs. Half the girls huddle around the swing sets, casting glances at the boys and trying to look away before any meet their gaze. The girls with phones have a gravitational effect, sucking into orbit the girls without phones to loom over their shoulders at whatever's on the screen. The other half of the girls totter around the playground in various groups, discussing nonsense with the utmost degree of gravitas. Faces severe as monks in prayer.

Pangaea walks over to Ellis.

"Hey, what're you watching?" she asks, sitting next to him on the bench.

He wipes his nose with his mitten'd hand and answers, without taking his eyes off the screen: "I'm playing a game."

"What're you playing?"

With his eyes still on the screen: "It's just a game. You wouldn't like it. It's for boys."

"Then how come none of the other boys are playing it right now? How come all the boys, except you, are throwing snowballs at each other?"

He wipes his nose again.

"Why're you always so quiet? Even when your mom and dad do barbecues with me and my dad on Sundays. It's not nice."

He sniffles and leans a bit closer to the screen.

"My dad says that's how kids go blind. Looking at screens too close. You're gonna go blind if you keep looking at that."

"Being blind wouldn't be so bad."

"I don't think anything'd be scarier."

He looks at her now. "Why don't you leave me alone? You don't need to pretend to be nice to me here just 'cause we're neighbors."

"My mom tells me I should be nice to you."

"You don't have a mom." Even his child's mind knew he'd said something wrong. "I'm sorry. I just—"

"I hate being alone. It always feels like everyone is gone and that I can't get them back. Just like Mom. How come you like it?"

"I don't." He looked down at his feet. "I can't stand it either."

"But you always keep to yourself. You never try to do things with anyone. You're always alone, Ellis."

"No, I'm not." He looks at the screen, as if this gesture speaks.

The snowflake leaves Pan's sight. *He has no one.* She reaches for her phone, which has stopped ringing. *But is that my problem? So what if he wants to stay alone forever? So what if he should?* But, as if on autopilot, she begins to call him.

Next door, the last five minutes:

Do you know how pathetic you are? His head bowed in defeat. *She doesn't want to talk to you. You're worthless. Could you even muster the balls to apologize, or are you that afraid of her? That afraid of what she thinks of you. Count it as a blessing she hasn't picked up. It'd just make you see yourself through her eyes, hearing her voice. There's nothing that frightens you more. The danger of seeing yourself.*

He looks at the screen with its multiple windows, each one offering a different rabbit hole of distraction from the current agony, each hole equally infinite in depth behind the centime-ter-thick screen.

It's not even her you're afraid of. It's you. It's the reality of how she sees you. That's what you're afraid of. Of knowing how repulsive you are to her. To the one human being who's ever tried to be decent to you. You pathetic waste of a human.

It's not relief that floods him when he sees she's FaceTiming him. *Ignore it. You don't deserve to hear her voice.* It's nausea.

"Hey." He's unaware that he's invisible on Pan's screen, his body enshrouded in the darkness of his room.

"Ellis? You there?"

He increases the brightness of his computer screen, and in its glow, Pangaea can see him. *Oh, God.* She sees the depth and darkness of the bags beneath his eyes.

"How've you been?"

"I'm all right. Anything new with you?"

"Eh. Alvin and I might've broken up. I don't know."

"Oy. What happened?"

Both content, for the moment, to pretend nothing has happened. To pretend it hasn't been an entire season since they've spoken.

"Just one too many little fights or something. I don't know. I just know I need a break from him. And..." *Why not say the truth? Why not finally say it aloud?* "Actually, I know exactly what the problem is. The piece of my life Al has been these past few years isn't part of who I am anymore. When he and I are together, it's like...I'm trying to think of the words...it's like—"

"The reality of each other gets in the way. Seeing each other in person can never live up to the fantasy in your head."

That's exactly it. But wait. She chews her lips. *It's not the same as how he lives.* She looks at his screen but can only see his outline. *I'm not the same as him.*

"Ellis....we can't pretend what happened didn't."

Next door, he feels the anchor drop in his stomach, the light-headedness that arrives once a future most dreaded becomes the present. He looks at Pan on his screen, no different now than she appears in the countless programs in which he's designed her likeness.

Just pretend you're talking to one of those Pangaeas. It's not like you plan on ever seeing her in the flesh again. She's only as real as you let yourself think she is.

Stop. Please, stop.

You don't deserve her friendship.

Why can't you shut up?

I'm only you. You can't shut up because you know it's true. Look at her. Look. The woman on the other end of that screen means nothing to you. All that matters is the image of her in these pixels. That you can contort and twist to say and do whatever you want. That's all that means anything to you. The idea of what her body can be.

"Do you remember when I first met Alvin? At the shop a few summers back?"

"Don't blow off the subject, Ellis."

"I'm not. Please. I'm trying to... Just, do you remember?"

"I guess so, yeah. You came to the shop one afternoon, and he was there."

As Ellis slips back into memory, he finds it easier to speak, since it's not to Pan he's addressing his words, not even the image of her on his screen, but the phantom face he sees in memory.

"You and your dad were just about to open up for a flower show. It was July Fourth weekend, and the exhibit was going to run all through the month. You and Isaac had spent the entire spring preparing for it, ordering the most exotic flowers you could find and trimming all these hedges and bushes. It was like a maze in there. You called me up and asked if I wanted to the see shop a day before you opened to the public. You didn't say it, but I knew you wanted to let me see it privately, not with a mob of strangers."

On the other side of the screen, Pan remembers *He came. He took the Blue Line from Wonderland and actually came. I didn't tell him Al would be there. I can't even remember why. Did I think he'd be jealous? No, I think it was something else. I think I was afraid it would hurt him to see something he could never have.*

"So I got there. Al greeted me before you. I didn't know who he was. He stuck his hand out to shake mine, and when he saw my hesitation just called for you. We stood there for a few seconds, not looking at each other, as you wound your way through the maze. The first thing I noticed when I saw you was how sweaty your orange bandana was."

"Real flattering."

"You came right up to me and hugged me before I could protest and introduced me to him. Then you started guiding me through the shop, showing me…"

He was so at ease, Pan remembers, half-listening to Ellis as she recalls her memory of the same moment, seen through her own eyes. *He was so comfortable around Alvin. I thought he'd squirm. And the flowers too. He bent down and sniffed the most pungent freesias. He twirled around the Himalayan honeysuckle. Usually he'd never touch them, afraid of the dirt. The worms and bugs he thought were there.*

"I had to swallow my vomit on the train back," she hears him say, snapping her out of the memory reel.

"What?"

"I felt so sick that I had to swallow my vomit. I could only hold it in for so long."

"What? No, you were so happy. You got along with Alvin so well. I'd never seen you so at ease that far from your house."

"That's what I'm trying to tell you. It's funny how much our bodies can contradict what's really going on inside. How our body defines nothing about who we are. I felt sick the whole time I was there, Pan. From the moment I got on the fucking train to the second I stepped into that shop. The second Al was in front of me, so close I could see the beads of sweat on his face. And then you came, hair matted to your temples, pores clogging with debris. The goddamn fucking stench in that shop of all those flowers. I couldn't believe it then, and I still can't understand now how you can stand it."

She listens to him, not staring at the pale ghost on the other end of her screen but the boy she sat next to at recess, ruddy-cheeked and shy. The next-door neighbor she'd play hide-and-seek with in their backyards. The high school friend she'd talk to every night, asking if it gets any better. The past faces of the man talking to her all superimposed upon each other, different somehow each second of breathing life, yet the same sum total being who was born and eventually dies.

"This isn't you, Ellis. Why are you saying this?"

"Don't lie to yourself. You're not lying to me because I know who I am. But don't lie to yourself. This is exactly me. I'm the loser who lives next to you and imagines fucking you on a screen. I'm the guy who stares at photos of women and imagines what he'd do. The guy who sits behind his screen and talks to girls just to see how much I can frighten them. I'm not the brother who drives his sister to and from school. I'm not the son who has dinner with his parents every night. I'm not the gym junky who trains like a triathlete. That's all surface. That's just my body. The truth is, everything about me exists under the skin. So, please. Don't waste your time trying to be nice to the guy you see on your screen. I don't need the person I see on the other end of mine."

VIRUS

"W here are you going?"

"Out. Maybe the shop."

"Pan, it's snowing. The shop's closed." Isaac looks up from the cutting board, and if Pan could see his gaze, maybe she'd stop.

"I don't care. I feel couped up. I'm heading out."

"I thought we could have dinner. I was making—" But his daughter shuts the door. He looks at it for a moment, not expecting her to walk back in but he stares as if somehow her shadow is still there, like the space she occupied might still be imprinted with her body. He resumes cutting celery.

"She's been acting strange, honey. Any ideas?"

"She's a woman, Isaac. That's what we do."

"Maybe. It's like she's been a ghost of late. Whenever she's home, she's up in her room, and at the shop, it's like her mind is somewhere else. I haven't seen Alvin here in weeks, come to think of it."

Lena puts her hand on Isaac's, and he stops cutting, not looking up at her face but only her hand resting on his.

"People change. You can stare at the same woman you saw yesterday, and today the world behind her eyes may be alien to all you thought familiar. You look at her and see the infant you held in your arms. She smiles at you, and you see the teenager with her tongue stuck to her cheek, mulching flowers. You see her walk out the door and you see—"

"I see you," Isaac tells the empty space next to him.

After driving aimlessly until bedtime hours, Pan gets on the Blue Line, heading into Bowdoin.

If that's how he wants to leave it, then so it goes. The ghoulish outline of Ellis on her screen earlier that day is still in the front of Pan's memory. *Ellis, when you're ready to talk to me*, she'd said, not knowing what else to do, *I'll be here. Please know that. I'll be here.* She couldn't be sure when he had hung up or if he had heard her say anything at all.

Lena: *Why try? Why hold on to your friendship if he doesn't want it and all it is is work?*

Because I'm not like you. But she can't convince herself of the sentiment. She looks out the bus window at the sky, the sparse stars speckled wide and far, visible only in their afterlife, light-years beyond the molten plasma of their living core.

She gets off at the stop and walks through Government Center Plaza, empty of all people at this hour of the night. She waits for the buildings to kvetch their habitual Yiddish complaints but only hears silence. She waits for Yetta or Yoni to accumulate beside her, but again, there's only silence. Then she goes into the shop.

The blue light of night sits atop the flowers and spaces in between. Their colors aren't visible, only sketches of stems and petals greet Pan's sight. Even they don't speak with her, preferring to dissertate among themselves the quiet mysteries of the Calvin cycle.

"What am I even doing?" she asks, as if her echo can be her company. She's surprised by the movement of her hand, reaching into her pocket with a will of its own to take out her phone and dial.

What can I even say to him?

After two rings, "Pan?" She can hear the chap of Alvin's lips part as he opens his mouth, a nose breather even in sleep. "Pan, are you all right? Is everything okay?" And she can even hear him sit up in mild alarm.

"I'm fine, Al."

Then, connected by nothing but satellitic photons, neither say a word for a minute. Maybe they can hear the other's breathing, but that's all.

Say something, she prays. *Say something that I can hear and feel under my skin that lets me know we mean something. Say something that lets me know there are words you can tell me that I can't tell myself.*

"Where are you? It's, like, midnight. You sure everything's all right? I can come to you, just tell me where."

"I was talking to Ellis earlier. First time in a couple months."

"So you're home? Listen, let me come over. I feel like we haven't talked in so long. If I can see you and—"

"He told me he doesn't need me. That's what he said before hanging up."

Alvin has no reply.

"And now, I'm here in the shop wondering—"

"You're at the shop? Pan, it's like twenty degrees outside. I'll get in—"

"Wondering if he's right."

"What do you mean, *right*?"

"Do we need each other? That's what I'm asking you."

"Pan...please. Let me come over. If you want to talk like this, let's at least be together. Let's not just hear each other's voice."

"What difference would that make? If you have an answer, you have an answer. With or without me in your sight."

"Of course we need each other. I need you. I love you, Pan. And I still believe you need me. I still believe you love me."

"Al, you're not saying anything I haven't heard myself say, trying to convince me that there's something between us that's more real than our individual selves. Do you get that? It's like *we* never say anything. We trace the vacant shell of a relationship but don't put any of ourselves in it."

"That's not true. I let you see everything I am. The parts I'm proud of and the parts I wish I could change. I try to be better because of you, not even just for you. I—"

"No, do you hear yourself? You see me as a part of you. Someone for you to sap bits and pieces from. Like I'm some element to complete the larger chemical formula of you. I don't know if you've ever, once, actually cared about me as *me*. And," *no, no, don't finish it,* "I don't know if I've ever cared about you as *you* either." She waits for him to respond and is surprised by the duration of silence on the other end. *Alvin, wait. I didn't mean to—*

But before the thought even discovers itself, he speaks. "I don't know who's talking to me right now. All I hear are the words of a stranger who's infected your body. It's why I can hear your words and not even cry."

Then he hangs up.

When she's back in her room, Pan goes to her desk, rummaging through a drawer until she finds the envelope she knows is in there. She pulls it out and goes back to her bed. Pan takes out the stapled pages, greased at the edges from her fingerprints superimposed upon each other in the dozens of dozen times she's read this and begins to read it once again, hearing Alvin's voice:

Dead skin cells pebble their way over my clammy palm as it rests atop the mouse, which itself has dead skin caked into the grooves of the scroll wheel; the nooks and valleys of the cheap plastic's curvature. I've been staring at the same page on this computer screen for five minutes, my attention devoted instead to this bootleg Led Zeppelin concert from 1971 in Japan. It's impossible to decide between the 9/23 show and the 9/29. But even if my eyes were to focus at this screen, I would only see last night's dream.

It wasn't actually her. There's nothing to feel guilty over.

Of course there is. She had no say in it. What would she actually say if she knew what was in my head?

I'm snapped out of my self-deprecation by the Outlook icon going orange with a new meaningless email.

"Hi Alvin. Can you send me a list of all my cases set for trial in October? Thanks."

Just check the fucking case list. I update it every goddamned hour. "Sure thing. I'll send it over now."

Why don't you ever just tell him to do this shit himself?

Because it's my job to do the jobs he doesn't want to.

If that were really the case, then you'd be doing his job.

Funny.

True. And funny.

My fingers click their way to the spreadsheet while my thoughts shift lanes, and I end up back on the face of Violet.

You're allowed to think what you want. You're allowed to have whatever fantasies your heart desires.

No. There has to be a limit to those too.

Why? That's restraint: keeping your ideas within your body. If you deny yourself your own thoughts, then what do you have left?

But even my thoughts shouldn't cross a line.

Why?

And now I can't get the imagined sensation of my skin rubbing against her out of my head. *How can a dream be so real?* The absence of smell, which itself was pungent, a null space of fragrant dimension. I close my eyes and am back in the dream with her.

Why call it illusion? Feelings are feelings. You have a memory in your mind. There really was a body to share it with. What wasn't real enough?

No, it wasn't actually her.

In the flesh. No. You're right. It wasn't "that" her. But it was what she is to you. So, again, where's the illusion? The only part that isn't real is the painful part, that she doesn't look at you the way you look at her.

That's the only important part.

My phone rings, and I need to blink to be sure I'm not hallucinating: Violet.

Pick it up, you dolt.

"Hey, Violet."

"Hey, Alvin. How's it going?"

"Oh, you know. Just another day." *Really? And you wonder why you still eat at home with your parents.*

"So, what's up?"

"Very serious subject here. Are you gonna be at the verdict party Friday?"

My stomach melts with the cadenced intonation of her voice.

"Don't you think you're getting a bit excited there, boychik? She's just asking a question." Yoni assembles into being next to me. I can smell latkes and gefilte fish; something pickled too.

"Of course, I'll be there. Nothing better than going to an office party where you don't have to worry about being the drunkest one there since you work with lawyers." *A bit too much?* I wait two and a half painful seconds before she laughs.

"Yeah, I suppose that's one way of looking at it."

"I assume you'll be there too?"

"Oh, you know it. Of all the uncomfortable office parties we have, these celebrations take the cake. Remember last year how Robert got cut off by the bartender, and Lawrence had to remind him that they were our client?"

At hearing the words "last year," I reflect upon the fact that it's been two years since I started here, and it's been two years since I wanted to leave.

"She's going to hang up if you don't think of something to keep her on the line, boychik. Ask her out to dinner. Don't be a putz. Be a mensch," Yoni says.

"How could I forget? He almost grabbed the guy by his collar. Never thought I'd see him that feisty outside a courtroom."

Yoni slaps his forehead in disappointment.

"Five thousand years of heritage, and that's what you muster for this shiksa? Aye, aye, aye."

The conversation soon ends after some more banter that's painful to all but the participants, but usually them as well.

"All right, well, I guess I'll talk to you later."

"See ya, Violet."

Of course, the first image that paints itself across my mind now that I've hung up the phone is her face as it was in my dream. No, not past tense. Appears. How her face somehow finds its way in all my dreams. The ghost I love to haunt me.

I see the bed and imagine Violet and me interlocked atop it.

"You see," a Hebraic devil perches atop my left shoulder and prods Yoni away with a fanged menorah, twisting his sidelocks, "what difference does it make if it's really her?" I see myself squeeze my arms around her as tightly as I can and sees her legs clamp around mine, and for an instant, I try to imagine what it'd feel like to melt into another person, not just cum into her but fully disintegrate away in the comfort of her whole body. To be so fully close to another person that I could forget I am one.

Shit. My erection is now about three-quarters of the way complete, and *I might have to take care of it in the bathroom.*

I've only recently begun to indulge this habit (having become emboldened after reading *Sabbath's Theater*); I don't think I've masturbated in the office bathroom more than ten or so times.

"Go ahead, Onan," the devil says before blowing the candles out of the menorah, adjusting his yarmulke, and coughing in the aftermath.

I put the computer to sleep and get up. Once in the bathroom, I find myself confronting a new variable I had, somehow, not foreseen: both stalls are occupied. *Fuck. Goddamnit.* I stand stupefied for a moment, then notice the invisibly thick, clouded stench that only white-collar men can produce after about six cups of coffee. Two men, at that. *Fuck. Can't masturbate at the urinal, obviously. And even if you wait, then you'll have to contend with the aftermath of whatever these guys are bombing the toilets with. Fuck.*

I exit the bathroom. Once back at my desk, I find my cock still engorged, but when I shake the mouse, I see Outlook is invaded with three new emails, and that flaccidly solves that.

I pass the rest of the day away in much the same way as everyone else in the office, the office's building, the building's city, and the whole world, while we're at it, in much the same way as they all do: a whole world of people doing everything they can to forget the impatience of time while somehow hoping to slow its escape. A whole world of people who inherit the burden of the past simply by coming after it, and a whole world of people shirking the responsibility of the future since we never can, despite our best efforts, keep a leash on the rabid spasm of time.

I respond to my emails and bill my feigned work and dream of Violet all the while, unsure whether it's really her I want or if she's just a convenient stand-in for something deeper within me, some hope or desire buried so far within myself that's not even mine, probably never was to begin with; but, like the past, something universally bequeathed from parent to child, and maybe the longing I feel, the perennial yearning for *something*, is the only limb of time our bodies are granted a share in, and maybe that's why we never possess it. Because maybe time is trying to forget its solitude too.

Goodnight, Violet. I pretend she's next to me as I get up from the desk to head home.

I love you, I hear her say, and hear her say again with each step I take toward the Blue Line. Where it'll take me to Wonderland like it always has.

Pangaea puts down the pages.

This was his apology. She recalls their first fight. Not even what it was about, only how it was the first time they both faced the possibility of anger, fury, pain at the other. With the other. The first time they both recognized that something had happened, something they could never prepare for but eventually know— that they mattered to each other. That they'd infected each other with the virus of love and could now claw at each other's hearts.

She remembers how he had mailed it to her without notice. The sticky note atop the first page: *If I didn't have you, I would only have these fantasies I write myself.*

And as she stares at the stapled story in her hands, Pan wonders, *But is that all we are to each other, Alvin?* She puts the letter back in the envelope and kisses it before putting it back in the desk. *Are we just deluding ourselves with the fantasy of Us?*

A BAND-AID WON'T SUFFICE

"**H**ey, uh, Pan?"

Pangaea is staring at Devorah's TV: slippers, sweatpants, and one of those hockey sweatshirts with the neck strings pulled out. It once belonged to Ivan. The clock of her phone blinks 10:17, and the lamplit streets blind starlight.

"What's up?"

Can you please pick up your fucking phone, Dev texted her earlier that afternoon. Pan hadn't responded to her in over a week.

Hey was the sum total of textual energy she could muster to quell Dev.

Dev texted back: *my mom went back home for the night, which is totally fine, but I need company. please.*

Which brought Pan here.

"I'm bleeding," Dev says.

"I think you have Band-Aids in the bathroom, below the sink. Did you check in there?"

"No, I'm not bleeding like that. I just peed, and there was blood. Like, a lot."

Pangaea looks away from the TV now. "Oh. Um. Shit."

"Yeah."

"Okay, uh…fuck, well, uh," leaning forward and moving her feet from the classic resting-the-feet-on-the-coffee-table position to the poised-and-ready-to-spring-into-action position, "does it hurt anywhere?"

Devorah's not sure if her body hurts, but now that she's thinking about it, and now that she sees Pangaea's freaking out a little, cheeks reddening, she does start to hurt, and so, "Yeah, yeah, my stomach kinda hurts."

And now the infant panic in their minds starts to sprout.

"Okay, okay, well let's, uh, let's Google this first, right? I mean, you'd probably be in a lot more pain if—" She stops herself before saying it outright. "If something real bad was happening. I mean, can you feel it, like, kicking or anything?"

Devorah's hands have been resting over the baby bump this whole time. Now, she starts circling her hands over the area, tilting her head like a doctor with a stethoscope.

And, for a moment, Devorah's eyes change their hue or shape or maybe something else. Maybe there's a flicker in the eyes when they see through the three into some other dimension of connection not possible, and so the world before her eyes vanishes in this immeasurable instant as she listens, feels, and *sees* the infant breathing in her body, as she sees the connection that isn't even in her body but just proxies the blood-liquid grip, and she knows, for certain in this moment, that there's an impossibility of life struggling to elude the jealous grip of Nothing, and so she can say, for certain, "No, no the baby's not angry right now, but we gotta go, something's going on."

Fast-forward five minutes.

Pangaea, looking in the rearview mirror: "All set back there?"

Devorah, lying stretched out on her back across the Subaru's back seat: "Yeah, yeah."

"All right. I'll try to avoid the potholes, but you know Boston."

"You're the best."

The odyssey proceeds:

A rocket ejects from the world in three blinks, surfing the void. Empty wind scratches at the windows, and ghouls with hollow eye sockets grope as it propels forward, squinting in the distance with the sounds of suns bursting, and here and there there's a cosmic cry, a supernova shout, a quasar cackle as the universe tries to blow its speakers.

"Hey." Devorah's voice quavers. "Pan..."

Pangaea, still staring ahead at the road, easing on the pedal to stop at the yellow-turned-red light: "What's up?"

"What if it's...what if I'm having..."

Pan, now looking into the rearview, anticipating what she's about to say: "Don't even say it. Don't even think it. It's nothing, just an upset stomach."

But one of those ghouls has melted through the glass into the rocket.

"What if I'm having a miscarriage?" And now the ghoul has condensated into tears, tears crawling their way down Devorah's cheeks, and she's heaving, and for a few seconds Pangaea's just as scared and maybe even more so, the way an audience sees death before the victim but knows to keep to looking.

Pangaea reaches her right hand into the back seat and wiggles her fingers in a gesture commanding, gently but without the possibly of refusal, Devorah to put her hand in hers, which she does. And then Pan squeezes. Hard.

"Devorah, you're gonna be fine, all right? That beautiful, little fucker that's hijacking your normally adorable, little belly, and who's been jacking all your food, that beautiful, little fucker and you are gonna be just fine, and you're gonna live beautiful, wonderful lives as mommy and little-baby, okay?" Emphatic pause. "All right?"

Devorah closes her eyes and breathes deeply, proceeds to nod in the affirmative: "Yeah, you're right, you're right. It's gonna be okay." And then she does some more deep breathing as the guy in the car behind them blasts his horn because the light's been green for seconds.

The rocket moves forward, not even trying to dodge the incoming asteroids, comets, whirlwind saucers, or nebulas, just smashing through and staying ahead of that grip, that jealous grasp of nothing which tries so desperately to spread its shroud and engulf the expanse of Everything That Is into That Which Isn't. And the only way to stay ahead is to Here yourself into position in the same way that—

"We're here, Devorah. We're at the hospital."

She's parked the car, and now Pangaea's holding Dev's hand as they walk to the ER, through the autosliding doors.

The receptionist's nails clickety-clack against the keyboard, while she stares at the duo, asking, "What's your emergency?" The gum in her mouth is green.

Pangaea says, "My friend, Devorah, is about eight months pregnant, and she's bleeding. Where do we go?"

The receptionist stares at them, mewing her gum like a cow with cud. "I'm gonna need you to fill out some forms."

Fast-forward here.

Pangaea sits in the room, staring at her shoes. Restless-leg syndrome and chewing her nails. She's never had the habit before.

Devorah lies on the table, the crinkling white rollout paper bubbling in various corpuscles with the slightest iota of movement, and she stares at the looks-like-an-adorable-rabble-of-children-painted-this-here wall painting of a bunch of smiling stick figures holding hands in a chain of other smiling stick figures with a great-big, orange-yellow sun staring down at them. But Devorah stares at this and sees something else: Dracula in a midnight-black cloak with glue-white skin and red eyes staring at the little cherubs sprawled along browned-out dead grass, waiting to straw the thinning blood out of their nostrils, navels, spaces between eye and socket, and any orifice possible because Devorah right now isn't sure if the baby she's responsible for bringing to life is dead inside her.

And here comes the resident who begins introductions, but Dev is too busy with the mob between her ears:

Oh my God, oh my God, oh my God. I killed him. Her. We don't even know. Oh my God, whatamIgonnatell Mom? WhatamIgonnatell Dad? WhatamIgonnatell Ivan? Fuck. Ivan. How do I even call him? He should be here for this, oh my God. Fuck. Fuck! I'm a horrible person. Shit, how'd this even happen? I haven't had a goddamned sip of alcohol in months. I mean, what the fuck could be doing this? I mean, maybe it's the, oh shit. She doesn't let herself dwell on the reality of her habits; she knows her conscience will force its way into her focus soon enough. *Maybe it's the McDonald's. But, no, that's like...twice a week...not even. I mean, fuck, can't I even have that? This baby, you...you better be okay in there, you hear me? You better be okay in there, and you better be a bundle of fucking joy, you little.... fuck, fuck...fuck! Listen to me, whatamIsaying? Jesus, I can't have a baby. I can't raise a kid. What do I know about anything? OhmyGodohmyGodohmyGod.*

Now she's hyperventilating and going through her memory reel at warp speed, distorting the colors and sound. Pangaea sees the distress but doesn't know what to do.

Maybe I should have listened to Ivan and just had the abortion. But…but there's so much risk there. Why am I even thinking about that asshole? This is his fault, and he's not even here. He doesn't even know half as much. He doesn't know what responsibility is. He doesn't know what it is to make a real decision. Holy shit, what am I doing?! She clenches her teeth and lets out one of those incredibly loud, almost deafening, whisper-shrieks that are far more frightening than decibel-bursting yelps, and what's even more frightening is that there are no tears. *All right, Devorah, get a grip. Just try to calm down and wait for the doctor. Just breathe.*

Which she does. She breathes. She remembers telling Nancy:

Mom. It was a phone call.

Hey, sweetie. Everything all right?

Her hesitation said it all.

Yeah, Mom, I'm fine. It's just…I have some news…

And if Dev could have seen her mom on the other end of the line, if she could have seen how quickly Nancy's jaw slacked and how her eyes glossed over; if she could have seen that, Devorah would have been the one to reach for a seat first.

Devorah, what is it? What's wrong? Do I need to jump in the car?

No, Mom. Just let me talk, all right? I'm fine, I just have… some news. Some pretty big news. All good, though. Good news. I'm kind of, well, I'm kind of, and at least she realized then that it was best to treat it like ripping off a Band-Aid: *I'm pregnant.*

At the time, Devorah wasn't sure how she would have characterized the noise she heard through the phone: if it was a yelp or a shriek, a cry or shout, or just some mutation of a sigh. Whatever it was, Devorah wasn't braced for the volume of it.

Devorah! Oh my God. W-when did this happen? When'd you get the news? You have to come home right away, or I'm driving to you. I mean, I...I... And then it dissolved into just noise and babble, cuing Devorah to speak again.

Well, Ivan and I just went to the doctor yesterday to confirm, but I did the pee test last week so, I don't know, I guess April?

And, despite the chemical reactions going on in her brain and stomach, her mom gathered the poise to play her role: *Devorah, are you keeping it? I know it's risky, but...are you?*

Devorah, though bracing herself for that question in the minutes, hours, days and eternities leading up to the call, was not ready for the reality of the sound of those words, for the reality inhabiting them, the way words are just clothes for something so real we can never say, touch, smell it, hold it, or Is it into reality, we can only say it: *Am I keeping it?* she asked herself, again, for the infinite time already by then.

Pangaea watches Devorah.

Pangaea: *What if it's dead? What happens then?*

Lena: *Are you so sure you can even consider it alive now? How can something die before it's alive?*

Pangaea: *Is that what you wish had happened to me? That I never would've cursed you with my life? Either way, you got your wish because wherever you are, my life isn't part of yours.*

Yes, I'm keeping it, Mom. Dev had said, hearing it aloud for the first time. *I'm keeping the baby.*

Right on cue, here comes the resident.

"Hi, Devorah. I'm Dr. Moreland."

"Hi there."

"Hi," Pangaea says, sheepishly, unsure if she should still be in the room.

"So, what's going on?" Devorah asks before Moreland can settle in.

"Well," he props open his laptop and punches away, maybe just recording the conversation, since what the hell else could he be typing already by now? "We can't do a cervical exam because of your trimester stage. We could risk doing some damage to the baby."

"But, I mean, she's bleeding right now. Like...what if there's already damage done?" Pan looks over to Devorah because she's afraid she's said something wrong. Devorah's eyes are scrunched closed, her hands resting over her stomach. Pangaea prays the doctor will speak.

Pangaea: *You know what? In a sense, I am your abortion. I'm the child you never had. Since you made the choice not to be a mother.*

Lena: *If you can convince yourself that, then you can free yourself from being bound to anyone.*

The doctor nods, staring kindly at them, almost frustratingly kindly, not like false kindness but sincere, which makes the whole matter worse, overspraying the room in a perfume of tenderness. "Look. We're gonna take an ultrasound, and that'll give us a clear image of your baby. If there's something wrong, then we'll see it on the ultrasound, all right? So let's take a peek."

Dev and Pan watch him disinfect as if seeing it through a screen, somehow happening in a world separate from theirs, even as he lifts Devorah's shirt and applies the jelly with one hand and adjusts the screen with the other. Even as he starts to probe the belly, UV'ing vision through the skin.

While all this happens, Ivan is asleep in jail, miles away. In the morning, he'll wake up and get a call from Devorah. He'll begin to cry and start speaking, but she'll hang up on him and hug her mother, who sits with her through the conversation. But in Devorah's mind, she pretends he's with her now, pretends he's been with her the whole night, even back in that rocket:

"What if I'm having a miscarriage, Pan?" And, yes, now the ghoul has condensated into tears, crawling their way down

Devorah's cheeks, and she's heaving, and for a few seconds Pangaea's just as scared and maybe even more so, the way an audience sees death before the victim but knows to keep to looking.

Ivan speaks before Pan can reach her hand back. He says, "Dev, you're gonna be fine. Look at me: it's going to be okay." Her head is in his lap as she's laying down across the back seat. Both of her hands squeeze his, and the four hands sit atop her stomach, inches separating their fingers from what's within. "We're gonna go to the hospital, they're gonna do some scans, maybe take some blood, and they're gonna tell us everything's okay. We're gonna laugh about it afterward, and whenever she's born, whenever—"

"Or he," Devorah interjects, thankfully, almost divinely, with a bit of a laugh, "or *he*, Ivan."

And after squeezing her hand, continuing, "Or he, Dev. After our baby crawls out that cunt of yours I love so much," giving a mischievous grin to Pangaea, who meets his eyes in the rearview, "we'll let him know how much of a pain in the ass he was from the get-go, and we'll let him know we wouldn't have had it any other way, all right? And when we're watching cartoons with him every minute of every day, and he's giggling his chubby, little cheeks away, you and I'll think back to tonight and say, 'Remember how it started? Remember that?'"

She nods and brings up their hands, the division between her flesh and his blurry, brings their hands to her lips and kisses the grip as Pangaea blows through a red light.

This is the world. And as Ivan leans down to give Devorah a quick one, not some long, drawn-out, dark-and-mysterious kiss but one of those quick let's-melt-for-a-moment kisses that leave him loving her so much because now he and she can feel the lip-glue that they never want to let dry. Now, they can feel the sensation of Us-ing themselves together, and so, in this moment of their lips' collision, Ivan and Devorah liquify into one and now slowly evaporate, leaving a pulse of purple-red in the center of where they were. And now even the rocket crumbles apart, as the pulse soars through empty space propelling through cosmic debris until there's only the empty, black void of no-Time and this pulsing nebula of proof: proof that We exists in this world and maybe only in this world. Maybe we can only exist in This world.

But Ivan is asleep in jail, and this is what Dr. Moreland sees in the ultrasound:

The screen is bluish-black, a lot of circles. Looks like everything is some jelly-like liquid, gooey. But there it is. In the middle. A collection of curves and something magnetic that focuses all gaze upon itself.

Pangaea sees it first, something fluttering, a flicker of what looks like lightening inside this undulating mass of flesh discovering itself inside Devorah. She asks, "What's that?" pointing at the screen, the fluttering, "it looks like, I don't know, like, a, well—"

"It looks like a butterfly flapping its wings," says Devorah, a bit hoarsely.

Moreland smiles, sort of like a teacher would after a student queries the question he's set up for the asking. "That," pausing theatrically...

Pangaea: *But why? How come once my life became part of yours, you had to be rid of it? Rid of me?*

"Is the heartbeat."

Lena: *Because your life was just a piece of my body, and once you left it, you were nothing.*

Pangaea folds first, bending her head down and bringing up her hands to meet her clenched eyes, halfway in the descent as she's sobbing, saliva everywhere and drool and she's sobbing. Devorah's mouth hangs open as she stares at the screen; Moreland leaves the room with a feeling of accomplishment, and now Devorah's sobbing too, open-eyed and staring at the screen, looking a bit frantic but not feeling like that. Not feeling anything.

The two sit there letting their tear ducts free everything that refuses to be imprisoned within the words of thought. They simply sit there and allow the Here of this moment to Is its way into their lives, the way Devorah's life and Pangaea's life and Ivan's life are just the vessels for Here to be. The way the life inside Devorah is fleshing itself in unison for its chance to be a moment of here and forever in this world too.

PART FIVE

HERE

BY ITS RIGHT NAME

"You know," Persephone says as the anesthetic begins to fog Pan's mind, "I'm going to miss these little conversations of ours."

The sky is some mixture of night, illuminated in a purple glow like a floating ocean of mauve. Planets sprinkle the sky next to pink and red clouds. Almost too many stars to see where one begins and another ends. Evergreens and weeping willows sweep the ground, old wistaria draping pink blinds in full bloom. Mountains curve the sky in the distance.

Pangaea walks under a wistaria, caressing the leaves. They curl around her hand at the instance of touch. Her feet are bare, the dirt warm beneath her skin, the blue grass soft. Fireflies emit green light and mosey through the air. Somewhere, seemingly everywhere, there's a waterfall, pulsing a trickling whisper through the world.

"Where are we?" Lena asks as they amble through the trees.

"Nowhere. We're just here, exactly where I want to be."

They walk into an open space encircled by trees to find flowers of every color, each radiating a glow that diminishes the closer they get, almost retreating.

"Why does this place feel familiar?"

Pan ignores her and grabs one of the flowers, each petal a different color. She plucks it up without resistance, and a new plant grows from the root of the stem. The petals burst into stardust, coalescing into a spheric rainbow that sits in her palm. She stares at it as she tells Lena, "It should look familiar. This is where you live. This is the haunted house you've carved out in me." Lena looks around, and as her gaze circumferences the world, it changes, losing its color and becoming the forest familiar to Pan's nightmare, dense and green, only blackness above. "Where nearly every night now, your ghost chases me off the cliff of my dreams. But here," the world's colors return as Pan faces her, "I can look right at you and say you're no more a mother to me in my head than you are out wherever you are in the world. That you're only as real as I let myself believe you are. And, in here, so is everyone."

Then Lena's gone. Pan walks ahead, the grass becoming taller around her. Soon, she feels a foreign hand find its way into hers.

"Hey, Al." She faces him, his simulated eyes one-dimensional and flat. "Here we are."

He kisses her, and they make their way to the cliff, the water pink with green sand visible below. The stars are closer now as Pan and Al are level with nebulas and moons. The galactic light nestles itself into their hair like glitter.

"It's like we're angels," he says, "better here than we can be anywhere else. Almost like this is the only place we can be that better person so close in the distance."

No, she looks closer at his eyes, their pixelated shimmer, *this isn't him. He's still—*

"It is me, though," he vocalizes her thought, "better in your eyes now than I can be someplace else. Since, even if you were to hold me in the flesh," he brings her closer to his body, "your feelings are only your own. All you feel is only within you."

"But what about you? You say all this about what I feel and see, but what about you?" She backs away, startled as his body fades, disintegrating pixel by pixel like sandcastles falling.

She sees rustling in the woods as someone approaches, but before fear can settle itself within her, *I'm not dreaming now. It's no ghost.*

"Lena," she begins, "you're not supposed to be here anymore." But she continues to approach. "Mom, there's no place for you here. Don't you understand that?" *Shouldn't she fade away?*

"If I weren't here, neither would you be."

Pan startles backward to the edge of the cliff as she hears her own voice say this, walking toward her. She looks back at the precipice, the distance below her seemingly infinite as the ocean is gone, leaving only stars twinkling with hushed light. She looks ahead again and sees, standing inches away from her, herself. The purple hair the only thing with color, skin somehow translucent, drained of vitality, her eyes too, pixelated attempts at green that reflect nothing.

"No, no, this isn't how it goes. It's always Lena who haunts this nightmare. It's always the sight of her that wakes me up."

"How can you see someone you've never met? When you tell her she's a ghost, you're telling yourself—" She steps closer, and Pan backs away, falling off the cliff. She tries to shout, not merely from fear but to block the sound of her voice, but she can't. There's only silence as Pan falls. She stares down at the stars where the ocean should be and suddenly finds her bearings. She looks down at where she stands, seemingly atop a floor of stars, minute and twinkling beneath her feet, but when she looks up it's not starlight above, nor below. It's snow.

Confused, Pan looks around. "Where am I?" The snow falls atop and in front of her, and in the distance there's a festival of colors, lights blinking synthetic and electric. *I know this place, but where is it? This isn't what I designed.* Trees sprout through the snow around her, dead and bare of all branches. She hugs herself for warmth.

"That's..." The lights become clearer as she sees the caricature of a face, painted cheap white and chipped, a tongue sticking out. "This is the carnival." She walks under the arch and sees, illuminated brighter than any of the other lights, a shimmering glow in the center. "There it is again." She walks toward it, and it remains still, letting her approach.

She halts, putting her arm ahead to feel it. *It's just light.* She pulls back her hand and inspects it for marks, but there are none. *I can finally see it for what it is.* Then she walks through it.

The shimmer clarifies, and Pan discerns it's the light from a flashlight glaring in her eyes. She stares closer *Is that...wait, is that...*and then covers her mouth in shock. Pan sees herself holding a flashlight pointed at her. She turns away from the sight, only to see herself again. She turns around once more and there she is. She looks back to leave through the door she came through, but there's no door, only Pangaea standing.

"Wake up," she tells herself. "Wake up, and look at Persephone, who's sitting next to me right now in a room." She closes her eyes, willing them to open awake, but she hasn't moved. She looks at herself, not seeing a projection with hazy eyes and saturated hair but herself in full body. Pan steps to the left and sees herself do this, and when she looks around the room there are infinite iterations doing the same.

"This is..." Pan steps closer, the flashlight dimming down to a haze, "the house of mirrors." Then Pan looks at herself in the mirror. She puts her other hand forward like she did as a child to feel the glass but feels flesh press back against her palm.

"I thought maybe it'd be a way I could hold your hand."

She recoils as she sees her reflection speak and hears the voice of herself as a child, echoing all around.

"Maybe I wondered if I could forget you're just a reflection." Pan staggers backward and bumps against another mirror as her myriad reflections begin speaking, all in her own voice.

"Your own mother didn't even want you." She watches her motion trapped in the mirrors like an endless wall of dominos. "Let me out," she says, trying to look away from the mirrors. "Persephone." She looks up as if she'll see her there but only sees more reflections. "Persephone! Wake me up!" And suddenly she hears her own voice shouting back in a repeating chorus. "Wake me up!" She presses her hands against her ears but hears her voice within her head. "Please..." She can only muster a whisper, hearing a cascade of her own voice echo, "Let me out."

Then she looks up, staring at herself in the mirrors as she hears Lena say, "If I look in the mirror," *but it's not her voice, it'll only ever been mine*, "I might see you looking back." *In here, it's only me.*

For a moment, Pan wonders if she's still in the simulation, the funhouse mirrors simply replaced by Persephone's eye, but glances at the pulsing red of the Human Connection and knows she's awake.

"Before we begin, I'd just like to thank you for all you've offered us. Your truthful responses have helped us tailor the product in more ways than you can imagine. So, thank you. Now, let's get started. How was your final simulation?"

It's only me, she thinks, Persephone's words not registering. *This place, it's only another way to trick myself that I'm living my life when, really, I'm running away from it.*

"Pangaea?"

She looks at Persephone, so distracted it's as if she's never seen her. *If it weren't for that eye, she might almost look kind*, suddenly appraising her like a stranger.

"I don't know what I can say. What you've built here, this technology, it's perfect. You can't make anything feel more real."

Confusion clouds Persephone's face. "What do you mean *feel* real? It is real. All of this. Everything you've seen and heard and said and felt when you're connected, when you're in these simulations: that's all really happening. I thought by now you'd understand that."

"No, it isn't. It's nothing more than a fantasy I'm playing in my head." *It's only me in the mirror. No matter what this place may convince me of otherwise.* "It's just, it's a delusion." *No different from you.* She thinks of Lena.

"Pangaea," Persephone closes her laptop, "I'd have thought that, by now, you would have seen enough to understand it's only what's in your head that matters. It's only who or what something is to *you* that makes it alive. Is the fact that I can reach out my hand and," she jabs at Pan, who's startled by the sudden contact, *she's never touched me before*, "you can feel it. Is *that* really what makes anything more real? The nerves of your flesh and blood?"

Nine months, and we've never even shaken hands. Pan puzzles over the oddity of this, scrutinizing Persephone with new eyes.

"It's more than that. It's not simply that my skin can recognize someone else's touch. There's more to the world than how we conceive it in our head. We live in it and, for better or worse, our bodies are the only things that let us do just that. They're the only things that lets us know we're part of something, not alone." *Alvin*, she thinks upon hearing her own words.

"Pangaea!" Persephone shouts, catching Pan off guard. "My work has been lost on you if you can still think like that. Here in Wonderland, you can experience any and everything you want. The freedom to go somewhere beyond the world you're given, somewhere *more*. Beyond the people you're given too."

"But there are people who mean something to me and who..." *Who I mean something to. Alvin*, she thinks again, *I do still love you. I do.* "People who we mean something to."

Persephone stares at Pan, almost like she, too, is seeing a stranger. In the quiet, Pan's gaze roves to Persephone's natural eye, not seeing her own reflection but the iris of another person.

"Why should you feel any commitment to them?" Persephone asks. "Why should you tie your own life—your *only* life—to someone else? To anyone? This whole time, I've been trying to get you to understand that. In fact, your whole damn life I've been trying to get you to understand that."

She looks at Persephone closer than she ever has, not at the glass eye, the glass eye that draws all attention away from every other aspect of her face and body toward its own empty orbit. Pan sees for the first time that Persephone has green eyes—eye—just like hers. Pangaea pales, but Persephone holds her gaze. Pan tries to speak the word she wants to but can't.

"Say it, Pangaea. Go ahead," she leans closer, and Pan sees what might as well be her own eye looking at her, "and say it."

IN HER PLACE

"I'm excited to start working with you."

"Likewise! On behalf of everyone here at Human Solutions, we're excited to have you onboard. You enjoy the weekend, and we'll see you back here Monday."

She got up and shook his hand once more, but before turning to leave, "Oh, and one more thing?"

"Of course."

"I'd prefer, if you don't mind, if you all call me by the name I brand my code with."

Once back in her hotel room, Lena showered and got into bed in her towel. She turned on the TV for the white noise. Lena closed her eyes and leaned back against the pillow, thinking *Nine years. It's taken nine years to get here. The startups and solo projects. My name on all of it. Just mine.* She recalls the first few years back on the road, how easy it was to slip back into her itinerant habits, the years of hitchhiking and traveling without destination, all for the sake of movement. *As long as you stay running, you'll never be stuck. And if everyone falls behind, then*—try as she might not to finish the thought, sometimes it would catch up.

Lena opened her eyes in the hotel room and got up to retrieve her bag, her movements deliberate, a disciplined routine, not a desire. As if her body was acting on its own accord. She went back to the bed with her laptop. The blue light illuminated her face in a ghoulish glow, making her appear not a corporeal body but rather some hologram transmitted through the screen. Her fingers of their own unconscious volition typed away as her eyes gazed at the screen.

There you are. She scrolled through Isaac's Facebook page, though it was only his in name, since the contents were nearly all of—

Lena had never let herself think of the word *daughter* since she had departed. She felt an urge to touch the screen, as if she might feel Pangaea's hair, but before her arm even began to move, Lena suppressed the urge. Instead, she continued to look at the girl and father in the photos, scrolling through them quickly enough that during the stray moments when she recognized her own face in Pangaea, she could move on. *It's just strands of DNA. That's all. Just a human algorithm. No different from the algorithm that puts these pixels on this screen, since that's all these are. Pixels on a screen.*

She paused on a photo, taken from behind Isaac's and Pangaea's backs. They're on the summit of a mountain trail. Isaac is crouched, level with Pan, his right arm hanging over her shoulder as his left points outward. Pangaea's head is tilted in the direction of his arm, trying to see what he's pointing at. But even in the photo, Lena could see what Isaac was pointing at. *The future. He's pointing at her future. That's what he used to always say. Chasing the future is what makes us alive.* And suddenly Lena found herself injected into the photo; in the screen with Pangaea and Isaac, there at the summit with her child. And as Isaac points into the distance, Lena leans down and kisses the top of Pangaea's head and tells her, "That's your life. That's what it looks like. It's the promise that you can always look forward. That you can leave everything behind. That you only need *you*."

But Lena was not, in fact, in the screen because she was not in the photo because she was never there with Pangaea. She never said these words to her daughter, only to herself. And, as she stares at the screen, writing code that brings movement to these photos as if they have thoughts and will, hearts of their own, she'll stare at Pangaea's face on the screen for years and continue to say *just strands of DNA. A human code. No more than pixels on a screen* until—

Pan looks at Persephone closer than she ever has, not at the glass eye, the glass eye that draws all attention away from every other aspect of her face and body toward its own empty orbit. Pan sees for the first time that Persephone has green eyes—eye—just like hers. Pangaea pales, but Persephone holds her gaze. Pan tries to speak the word she wants to but can't.

"Say it, Pangaea. Go ahead," she leans closer, and Pan sees what might as well be her own eye looking at her, "and say it."

"...Mom?"

She leans back. "No. I'm not your mother. Even if I'm the woman you came from. Even if you can call me Lena."

Pangaea scooches back from her. "But..." She has no doubt that Persephone is indeed her mother. The omniscience of blood. "But why?" Not how.

"Why what? Why am I your mother? Why did I select you to be part of this? If you have a question, then ask me." What shocks Pangaea is that Persephone can't guess her question.

"Why did you leave me?"

Lena nods, as if this is expected. "I wasn't ready to be a mother. I wasn't ready, and I didn't want to be. I thought I did, at one point. Your father and I certainly discussed it. You weren't a surprise. But then I started feeling you in my body. You were something foreign, something that felt like it had invaded me. You never felt like part of me, and then once you actually arrived, once you were in fact here, I realized that you couldn't be my child. I knew I wasn't a mother just because biology told me I was. Surely you'd agree that's not motherhood at all. And so, leaving was the only choice. To do anything else would only be living a lie."

Pangaea doesn't realize how tightly she's clenching her jaw as she watches Lena speak. "You keep saying, 'it,' but how about," she leans closer to her, her voice quaking, "how about you actually say what *it* is."

"Motherhood," she says, as if it's obvious.

"No!" Pangaea shouts, "Me! I wasn't what you wanted! I wasn't what you were ready for! Not motherhood. Not some idea. But me!" She picks up the pillow and screams into it with all the decibels she can, tasting the salt of her tears.

Persephone sits still, watching Pan's movements.

"Me! I'm real and I'm yours and you left me! How can you fucking sit there? How can you have sat there across from me all these fucking months? For all my goddamn life! How on Earth can you be as fucking cold and cruel and *lifeless* as this? How..." She has to catch her breath. "How can I be *yours*?"

Persephone's expression doesn't change as she watches this.

"How can I be yours?"

"You're mine only in body. Nothing more. I left before there *could* be anything more between us. And for that," Persephone waits for Pangaea's tearstained eyes to meet hers, "you can thank me."

What happens next surprises her. She scooches away from Pangaea, as if she's contagious.

Because what's happened is that Pangaea can't stop laughing.

"You want me to thank you? You want me to say *thank you* because you left before you and I could have some connection?" She looks up at her. "Am I right? Is that what you just said?"

Persephone looks at Pan with something almost like revulsion.

"You want me to sit here and listen to you say you left me because you weren't ready to be a mother, and then you want me to say thank you because, not only did you leave me, but you left before I could even know you? To say thank you because I didn't lose a mother; I never had one?"

"Pangaea. What you need to understand is—"

"No." The shock in her nervous system surges adrenaline. "I asked you a question. You told me to ask you questions. So, answer it. Yes or no?"

Persephone maintains a collected gaze. "Yes."

"Yes," Pangaea repeats, as if tasting the word to see if that'll help her make sense of it. "How about this, Lena." She gets off the bed and down on her knees, takes Persephone's hands in hers. The first time they've mutually touched. She leans her head down and glides her right cheek over Persephone's hands, allowing the two skins to meet. *Cold. They're so cold.* Persephone is frozen, immobile. "How about you look at me," Pangaea lets go, "and say to yourself, 'I made the right choice.' How about you go ahead and do that."

Persephone swallows and looks at her but doesn't see the body of the young woman in front of her eyes. She sees the infant she once held. She sees the little bundle of pudge she stayed up all night with, every night for weeks, as Pangaea cried and fussed and shat and cooed. She sees the two luminous eyes that looked up at her; the twin set of eyes that belonged to her own head. Lena sees this little infant look up at her and reach her hands out to hold her and feel her flesh, the validation of knowing, if nothing else—*if nothing else, at least she's in the world.* Since what more can an infant recognize beside the fact she's not alone? Persephone sees her infant daughter in this moment and experiences something whose last occurrence she can't recall. She feels tears collect in her right eye and the burning sensation in her left; the nerves that used to connect to her ducts now simply leaking electrical signals into the synthetic eye.

"I did what I felt was right, Pangaea. Right by me and...and you. Even right by Isaac. I would've only failed you if I'd stayed. I would've only failed to be what you needed me to be. And the longer I would've stayed, the worse it would've been. I have to believe this...you understand?" She waits for Pangaea to look at her before asking again, "Do you understand?"

Pan's back in Dev's kitchen, hearing her tell Nancy, *You're my mom, and I need you.* "You would've been my mother," seeing Nancy hug her daughter, "that's all you would've been if you'd stayed. It would have been better to have any you than have no you at all, M—" She swallows the word. *Who else could've needed a love so strong that people can only feel it in belief?* Pan feels Yetta beside her, phantom and home in her heart. *The choice to love Him only if you can believe He's there. Without any assurance He can love you back.*

They sit there looking at each other. To see them from afar, it would appear Pangaea was holding Persephone prisoner with her eyes. She looks at this woman and tries to see the canopy of Lena's faces she's pretended to know over the years; she tries to see them superimposed upon the flesh of the woman who sits inches in front of her.

Persephone tries to see Pangaea in this moment, tries to see her truly for the first time, but what she sees instead is the amalgamation of photographs she's looked at over the years, the photos she's told herself are Pangaea and are just as real as actually seeing her in the flesh. And so, it's with a gasp that in this moment Persephone recognizes she knows nothing of what has connected the infant she once saw with the reality of the woman whose face is her own and only inches away from her. For a moment, Persephone feels as much a stranger to herself as she is to the daughter she had without love.

"What happens now?" Persephone asks.

Pangaea wipes away a few tears and stands up. She's puzzled for a moment, wondering, *How is it I'm not angry?*

"What happens now, Pan?" Persephone asks again.

But Pangaea isn't interested in this woman's questions.

"All you had to do was take the risk of loving me like I was part of you." Persephone can't look away from her. "And believe I'd love you in return."

She continues to sit immobile, staring at the Human Connection as Pangaea walks out the door.

FARFEL

Pangaea calls Alvin once the key is in the ignition. *And she's been here, all this time, talking to me. Looking at me. Being with me. My own—but what do I call her?* She pauses, realizing she's waiting to hear Lena's voice. *No. She's not there. There's only me.*

Alvin answers, but she doesn't hear anything. "Alvin? You there?"

He sniffles and takes a long breath. "Hey, Pan. I was actually gonna call you in a bit."

"I beat you to it, I guess. Listen, I...wait, what's wrong, Al?"

"It's Farfel. We have to put him down. We're taking him to the vet tomorrow."

"Oh...Jesus, Alvin. I'm—oy gevalt. I'm on my way."

The thought doesn't enter her mind whether she needs to ask if he wants to see her. Or if she needs to ask to see him.

"Pan." Susan sees her when she walks in the door. Mark is sitting on the opposite end of the kitchen table; he looks up and nods through red-rimmed eyes. Susan gets up from the table to hug Pan and squeezes. She's surprised to feel how tightly Pangaea squeezes back.

Pan reluctantly breaks the embrace. "So, is Farfel still…is he…I mean, Alvin told me tomorrow you're going to…"

Susan's eyes flick back and forth between Pan's as she tries to read her and say whatever her gaze can. "He's upstairs with Alvin. I'm sure he'll be happy you came to see him one last time." She holds Pan's gaze before she can go upstairs, her eyes speaking something that can't be translated. Then Pan walks upstairs and hesitates before opening his door.

I would've only failed you, Pan. If I'd stayed. I would've only failed to be what you needed me to be.

All you had to do was take the risk of loving me like I was part of you.

She opens it and is confused at first; she doesn't see anyone. "Al?" Then she sees Alvin poke his head above the bed on the other side of the room.

And believe I'd love you in return.

"Hey. We're over here." She walks around the bed to find him sitting on the floor, leaning against the mattress, Farfel's head in his lap as they look at Polaroids.

"Pan, pleasure as always, bubeleh," Farfel says, turning his matted head in her direction. "Alvin and I are just doing a bit of time travel."

She sits down next to Al, who slowly shifts Farfel into her lap.

"Oh, yeah?" She nuzzles her nose atop the dog's head. "And where were you two just visiting? Or, 'when,' I guess, is the question."

Alvin hands her a Polaroid.

"This was when I was ten or so. Farfel had broken one of his legs that winter and had to walk around in a cast for months." She looks at the photo: Alvin is waving at the camera, absurdly bundled in red snow pants, brown fleece, a puffy purple jacket, and a Russian dog-ear flappy hat, holding Farfel's leash. Farfel stares at the camera with impatient disgust, the blue cast on his leg riddled with Sharpie signatures.

"Farfel! Look at this. You were famous! But, seriously, who all signed that cast?"

Alvin takes back the photo. "Random people. We still have that thing up in the attic. Pretty much, whenever my mom or I took him for a walk, other dog walkers or passersby would ask to sign his cast. They felt so bad for him."

"I didn't need their pity. A lot of good those signatures did," Farfel says, then begins to wheeze.

Pangaea looks up at Alvin in mild alarm.

He shakes his head. "That's just how it is. It's why we're taking him tomorrow."

"About time," Farfel mutters.

Pangaea shifts him back to Alvin.

"Almost eighteen years, you two. Don't even ask me how old that is in your human time. But it's long enough for me. Oh, stop that, you." He barks at Alvin, who's begun to cry. "That's enough. That's enough. Dayeinu! If you must cry, at least wait until you have my ash box and sit shiva. Lotta good those stale treats will do me then, eh?"

"Farfel!" Alvin says, "don't say that."

"Why not? I've had a good run. At this point, my days are just stooling—wherever I happen to be when my bowels decide to vacate—chewing absolute slop with my five remaining teeth, waiting for Susan to put whatever suppositories she must up my rump, and sleeping—which, mind you, I can barely even do anymore. Enough is enough, boychik. When you get to this point, you can feel your will yearning to leave the flesh and find The One On High. Greener pastures, Baruch Hashem."

"Amen." Yoni says as he kneels—grunting, sighing, and steadying his yarmulke—to pet Farfel.

"It's been a while, Yoni." Pan takes the moment to stare at his Tevya garb. *Of all the iterations of himself he could have chosen to be in heaven, he chose hunched, old man.* She looks at Alvin, who's staring at Farfel and rubbing behind his ears. *What will he look like?* She tries to see the time-lapse of Alvin's features into the geriatric. She looks at Yoni, who's petting Farfel's back, muttering a prayer. She sees his face and sees Alvin's and recognizes *there is no difference. Not just between them but between all the family they're from and will create. Because all family is is spreading life from one body to another. Which means the only part of my mother that matters is in me and always will be: life.*

"Don't worry about him, Alvin," Yoni says, "we'll take good care of him. He'll have all the salmon and Shabbos chicken he could ask for. And," he smirks at Farfel, "your bowels won't begrudge you the treat."

Farfel licks his phantom hands.

Alvin laughs through the tears. "So, what? You're stealing him from me, is that what you're saying? And you, Farfel, huh? You're asking to get traded?"

Yoni takes the bundle of photos from Alvin and stares at them, pausing on one and handing it back. Pangaea leans over to look at it, her hair falling on Alvin's shoulder. It's a candid of Alvin and Farfel on the couch. Alvin leans back with Farfel lying across his chest. He's reading, propping the book up against the dog.

"But you'll still be with him." Yoni begins to say. "Just like you're with me, and I'm with you. That's time. It's the thread that connects us, and even if our bodies can't hang on forever, the memory of our life can. And with love, it does. That's why we never truly die, boychik. Every birth is just another breath of all your family that's lived before you. Your body is a tattoo of the past, a way of painting time with proof that you're here. That's why family is all there is. We keep time alive. And we're given the choice of who we continue the painting with. *That* is the blessing. To choose who you want to share life with. To choose it."

Then he's gone, leaving Pan and Al with only his memory.

"I miss you," Alvin says. "Even if shitty circumstances are why you're here, I'm glad you are."

"I miss you too. Listen, I—"

Farfel interrupts. "Al, bring me back to Su, eh? I can feel the river of a bowel coming, and it looks like you're in the middle of something. You'll see me in the morning. I promise you one more night."

Alvin leaves, tenderly cradling Farfel.

Pan watches them leave, how closely Alvin holds Farfel to him, as if it's not a dog he's holding but something sacred to be touched.

No, she thinks as he passes out of sight, *what brings them together is something beyond touch, something that touch only hints at. It's their hearts that ties them. In a way Lena's never was to mine. And so she isn't my mother but just the shell. Only the body of the person my mother could have been. And if she chose to be nothing more, then why would I choose to let even the idea of her be anything more either?*

Alvin returns a minute later and sits next to Pan. She scooches closer to him and lets her right foot rest against his left.

"Hi."

He leans over and hugs her. She feels electricity swim within her as her neurons recognize his squeeze.

"I miss you, Pan. I really do. And I...I don't know what went wrong. Like, sure, we fight. We bicker. But, that happens. It's not like I'm..." He blushes and fidgets his hands. "It's not like I'm seeing someone else or even want to. Who would have me, you know?" He tries to laugh, but she can hear the despair.

"I know, Al. It's not really something you did. Or even something I did. It's more been...I don't know how to phrase it. It's more just been me not knowing what I want or—"

"Or who?"

"Or *who*, yes. But, not even in a personal sense, if that makes any sense. What I mean, is that I'm not sure if I even want a *who*, for total lack of a better word, or if what I get out of a relationship is even something I need. And, yes, I know, that's selfish of me. Not only selfish but cruel. I know that you're the other half of this, I get that. I think these past few months I've...I don't know...I've just—"

"You've thought everything you need is within you."

Pan stares at him, unable to break away from the gravity of his gaze. "That if you can have gone this long without your mom, then you can make it without anyone."

"No...it's not that simple. I..." *Should I tell him about Persephone? About Lena?* She notices the absence of emotion as these names enter her mind, purely stuck in the sterility of logic, untainted by the mess of unlogic where everything in the heart lives; since belief precedes knowledge and succeeds it too. "Al, I just wonder if people—anyone—are really worth it. I mean, sometimes all we ever are is a burden to everyone in our life. Sometimes, yes, you are a burden. And I know—believe me, I know—I am too."

"So what's your solution? To leave? If people are such a burden, the only choice is to leave them?"

You never felt like part of me...leaving was the only choice. To do anything else would only be living a lie.

She looks at him, staring internally, aghast at herself, at what a mirror could never show. *I would only be her. I'd be no different from her.*

"Pan," he begins, "you talk about love like it's this burden. Like all it is is holding someone's life in your hands. But," for a moment, she's back in the house of mirrors, trapped in her own reflection, saying *I'd be no different from her*, "it's the farthest thing from that. Because holding the weight of someone's heart is just half of love."

"Then what's the other half?"

But she's not in the house of mirrors, she sees only Alvin.

"Giving the weight of your heart to someone else."

Then Pan sees nothing at all as she kisses him until they both lose their breath.

CALLER ID

Pangaea is in the shop, trimming potted wistaria. She feels her phone vibrate and looks at the caller ID, rolling her eyes. *Oy, what could she want now?*

"Pan." She's surprised to hear Nancy's voice instead of Devorah's.

"Oh, hi, Nancy. Figured you'd be Dev. Is something—" *Oh, no. Wait.* "Oh my God. What happened?"

She hears Nancy sigh but doesn't know if it's relief. "He's here, Pan. Dev went into labor last night. The baby's here."

THE ULTIMATE HUMAN EXPERIENCE

Ellis lets the car warm up before pulling out of the driveway. He waits, staring out the window at snow dandruffing down from the clouds.

It's cleaner than the mess of actually trying to be with someone else.

He booked an appointment after seeing an ad online.

I don't need the person I see on the other end of mine.

Driving down the Lynnway, he tries to remember the last time he took himself along this road. *Maybe going to Fenway; that would've been ten years ago.* He keeps digging into memory. *Maybe it was taking Lauren to Children's Hospital, but no; Dad drove.* He stops thinking at a red light. *Just look at the light.* He feels the stare of the driver in the car next to him (who isn't, in fact, looking at him). *They're not looking at you, they're not looking at you…*

He sighs with relief once the light turns green. Soon enough, he sees the sign: *Wonderland.* It's the same one that's been there since the dog track was open, only now refurbished, the words "greyhound park" replaced with: *The Ultimate Human Experience.* Even through the snowfall, he can read the neon letters clearly. He pulls into the lot, parking near the large

Christmas tree, and feels his stomach turn when he sees how full the lot is. *They're just people. Just like you. They're only people.*

But they're not like you. No one is like you. You're alone.

He closes his eyes and breathes meditatively, trying to recall his YouTube-learned lessons. He gets out of the car and walks to the entrance, keeping his gaze focused upon the graying snow on the ground so that he won't see any passerby. He takes a deep breath and opens the door.

"Hi, there! Do you have an appointment?"

"Um, uh, yeah. Yes. I have an appointment for one thirty. I, uh…" Unsure if he should lean closer and whisper, be discrete, he says, "I sent the programmers my, um, preliminary design a few days ago through your portal."

"Of course! Let me just have your name please, and I'll check you in. You're a bit early so I'll just ask you to wait over here." She gestures to a lounge room.

He hesitates upon entrance. There are six other people waiting in the lounge room, none of them watching either of the TVs on the wall but rather leaning back in their chairs, MyAIs perched atop their faces.

Ellis tries to innocuously apply the hand sanitizer, but inevitably the guy sitting across from him glances at him as he rubs his hands together. He blushes and takes out his phone once his hands are dry. He wants to have someone to text or someone's texts to read, but the most recent conversations are just grocery questions exchanged with his parents. Instead, he digs back to:

Pangaea: *Happy eighth night, Ellis! Let me know when I come over.*

That was two days ago. Pan's tradition has always been to go to his house for the last night of Chanukkah. This year, though:

Ellis: *Thanks. We're just keeping it small this year. Lauren's a bit under the weather, and I wouldn't want you getting sick.*

He waited, eyes stuck to his screen, for her reply, since even though he was still afraid to see her in person, he thought, *Maybe she still wants to see me.* But all she said was: *Okay. Hope she feels better.*

And now, in Wonderland, he stares at his phone, donning the appearance of being engrossed by something demanding his focus, since he wants the people around him, whom he assumes are staring at him, to think he has something, perhaps even someone, to occupy his thoughts. Instead, he simply stares at the screen until his name is called.

"This way, please." The woman from reception leads him down a hall into the control room. "It'll be a moment before your technician is in," she says with a smile before leaving him.

Ellis sits on the edge of the bed, unsure if he should lie down, feeling like he's at a checkup. Eventually, the technician walks in.

The last thing he notices before the anesthetic drapes his mind is his own reflection in her glass eye.

A FUNNY WORD

Do they change them every day? Pangaea can't shift her focus from the angular sanitation of the white sheets. *And those pillows? Can she sleep on them?* The linearity of the edges. How it contradicts the ruddy bundle of curves swathed in cloth in Devorah's arms.

"Oh, I think he just—" Dev leans toward the bundle and sniffs, then looks at Nancy. "He just shit again."

"They tend to that. Here, give him to me."

Devorah slowly passes Page to her mother, shaking minutely in fear of dropping him. Visible relief once he's no longer in her hands.

"Hello, you, you beautiful bundle of pudge. Let's change that diaper." Nancy continues to mutter incoherent babel to the infant in her arms as Devorah and Pan watch in silence. Pan stares with an unconscious smile, curious, more than anything, at the thing in Nancy's arms. Dev watches with mouth agape, confused, more than anything, at what she's supposed to do, think, feel for the thing in Nancy's arms that came from her body.

"How'd I do it, Pan?" She keeps her eyes on the child that's lived within her for nine months. "How is he here?"

"He crawled out the tunnel of your vagina, is how, Dev," Alvin says from the peanut gallery. Pan punches his arm.

"Alvin, don't be a shit. Why don't you make yourself useful and buy something from a vending machine."

He kisses the top of her head on his way out, then begrudgingly holds the door open for the maternity ward waiting to walk in.

"Hello, mommy!" she says with hyperbolized joy to Devorah, rubbing her hands together with disinfectant.

Dev nods, her eyes on the infant in her mother's arms. Nancy doesn't look up from Page.

"And how are we doing today? Any successful feedings?"

"Well, he, um, latched but…" Dev looks at her mom, waiting for her to supply the words.

"One sec." Nancy bends over Page as she finishes wrapping his diaper. "Right." She looks at the woman from the maternity center. "He latched and fed but spit it up about a minute later. He's just not keeping anything down."

The ward nods. "Well, that happens. Seen it before. For now, you'll have to start consistently using the bottle and formula until he can begin to gain weight. It's nothing unusual, it's just—"

"Well, it's a bit early to make that decision," Nancy says. "For the time being, we're going to keep trying to have him feed from Dev. We're going to keep trying to have him feed from his mother. Instead of something synthetic in a bottle that comes from one of your centers."

Again, the ward nods as if this is all expected. "I understand, I do. But," she looks at Devorah, "we have to think of what's best for your child, now, don't we?"

Dev looks down at her hands, fidgeting with the sheets. She nods.

The ward sits down. "Once you're discharged, we'll begin our weekly check-ins at the maternity center, and our staff will give you a call daily. That said, we also…"

Pan registers none of this as she spectates. Instead:

Lena looks at Pangaea in her arms as the nurse asks her, "Did either of you at least get any sleep last night? I know she's a fussy one." She smiles at Pangaea, swathed in cloth.

Isaac rubs his eyes at the word *sleep*, and Lena laughs, though there's no smile.

"Yeah, right. I don't think this one's gonna let either of us get that anytime soon."

The nurse, beaming at Lena: "Well, you'll look at back at these days a few years from now with nothing but love. Everyone does."

Pangaea gurgles infant noises, which don't fail to get a laugh from the nurse and Isaac.

"Just remember: she's yours. She's your gift to the world."

Only silence from Lena.

"And at your centers, this 'staff,'" Nancy says, air-quoting the word, "do you have doctors on call there? Nurses? You're telling me that when my daughter comes to these 'check-ins,' she's meeting with licensed medical professionals who can help her take care of her baby?"

The ward's smile doesn't falter. "Why, what else would we be?"

Nancy's face doesn't change either. "People acting like you want to take care of her baby."

The ward clicks the pen in her hand a few times. "I can assure you, Mrs. Gordon, that your daughter and her child will receive the best care possible with us. That's our mission. To ensure that every child, every newborn life, gets the best possible treatment. Since life, wherever it is, is a blessing. It's why we do what we do."

The two women stare at each other, testing whose silence is louder.

Eventually, the ward turns to Dev. "I know this all seems so new right now, and I understand it will for some time, but eventually you *will* get used to being a mother. I promise you. It's impossible not to. I mean, after all, you *are* now a mother, aren't you?" She supplies her own laugh to deafen the quietude of the room. "But our studies have determined there are various stages to maternity. Right now, you're in the first one: acceptance. Acceptance of the responsibility you've inherited. Though, admittedly, I prefer the word *blessing*, but it's no doubt a responsibility too. Which is why I'm here on behalf of the maternity center, to help you with this newfound responsibility."

Meanwhile:

Lena: "Gift. That's a funny word."

Isaac: "Oh, hush, you. We both know our little Pan here is a gift."

Lena: "I'm not saying otherwise. I'm just saying, it's a funny word."

Isaac: "Well, call it what you will. But just look at her. Look. She's real. She's here. Can you believe it?"

"But I can still," Devorah starts to ask the ward, looking at her mom, "I can still, like, do my own thing...right? Like, if one night I wanted to just go see, I dunno, if I wanted to see my friends, I can still..." She notices how her mom closes her eyes and sighs, bringing Page closer to her chest.

"Well...yes," the ward begins, "every now and then you can get a little reprieve, Devorah. But...you're a mother now. You have the life of your child to think of before your own. Most of your life is now dedicated to taking care of his."

Lena: "You know..." She looks at the infant. *So you're really here, huh. You're really here and alive. And you're from me.* "I don't know if I can, Isaac."

Isaac laughs: "Well, I guess that's why they call it a miracle. It's just that hard to believe."

Lena: "A miracle…" *But now that you're not part of me any-more, what are you? You're just…you. You're your own life. Which also means my life is now just mine again too. And maybe that's all birth is. Separating one life into two. Just because I chose to share my body with you for all these months, why should I choose to share my life with you forever?*

"But I didn't…" Devorah stops, looking at her child. "I didn't ask for any of this. I thought once he was here, once he was out of me, this would all just…"

The ward says, "I don't know how you can say that. How you can look at your child and even think that? The simple sight of his life should be enough for you to—"

"That's enough," Nancy says, the weight of her tone knocking the words out of the ward. She looks at her daughter. "Dev, we'll get through this. Okay? You and Page are going to be fine. And," she looks at the infant, asleep in her arms, "you will love each other. You will. And I'm going to help you every step of the way. Do you know why?"

Devorah can't answer for a moment. The blush radiating her face mutes her.

"Because I'm your daughter…," she mumbles to the sheets.

"Because I love you."

Lena: "Maybe she is a miracle, Isaac."

She lets him scoop Pangaea out of her arms; he nestles his nose against the squishy top of her head and bobs her in steady rhythm, muttering, "I love you," in varying, silly intonations of iteration *but not for me. Maybe for you. Maybe even her. But to me, her life bears no connection to mine anymore. Our connection was just in body. Maybe that's all we'll ever have shared: a moment when one life was trying to share two bodies.*

"No, just wait for me in the lobby, Al." Pan hangs up and reluctantly gets into the elevator with the maternity ward.

"You know, your friend may not like it, but we're the best thing she has going for her and her child. If it weren't for our centers, she wouldn't know what to do."

"Well," Pangaea watches the numbers of different floors momentarily illumine as the elevator descends, "she wouldn't even have had the baby in the first place, if it weren't for your maternity centers. If it weren't for your Pact."

The ward smiles. "I sort of figured you might think that. We're not evil, you know. I've never understood that. How people thought, when we were first pushing the legislation, that we were all such terrible people, such awful arbiters of oppression. All we are, are people who cherish life. And who want to protect it. I mean, is that so bad? Is that such a bad thing to commit to?"

"Who are you to meddle in the lives of others?"

The ward shakes her head. "Anyone who wants to take life away from a person because they're too selfish to nurture it *should* be meddled with. Imagine if your mother didn't want to have you. Wouldn't you want someone to stop her? Wouldn't you want someone to protect your life?"

Pangaea laughs.

"And why's that funny to you?"

"Because—the woman you call my mother left me after I was born. To her, my life means nothing at all."

The ward is momentarily silent.

"Well...I'm sorry to hear that. I, obviously, didn't realize--"

"It's quite all right. I'm at peace with it."

For the first time since she's been in Pan's presence, the ward sounds sincere. "How can you say that?"

271

The door opens to the lobby, and Pan sees Alvin standing near the exit. "Because," he waves to her, unaware how much of a jackass he looks doing it, "I only want to share my life with people who want to share theirs with me."

HERE

When they're back, Pangaea and Alvin lie in her bed. His nose is runny, as it tends to be when he first acclimates to her room, which looks like this:

There are potted flowers hanging from hooks on the ceiling. Each pot has a large bowl dangling an inch or so below it, attached by string, to catch and collect the water, which she drains daily. The room smells like damp earth, the breath of flora and fauna. The walls are hand-painted in the spectrum of color and beyond. There are areas of nonsensical whirls and swoops and circles on the walls; a fictional solar system with a purple sun and orange planets and floating smiley faces and little green Martians swimming in space. Photos casually glued onto the walls, surrounded by concentric circles of varying colors.

It's an impossible room, in other words. Where Pangaea lives. And Alvin's here with her.

"This one's cute." He takes a Polaroid from her, in which are trapped two-dimensional depictions of she and Devorah in their high school graduation gowns with unlit cigars in their mouths (which they proceeded to toss in the garbage).

"Ah, young Pan." She takes the photo and muses over it. "If only I could go back to then and talk to her."

"What would you say?"

"To do everything that brought me here."

She leans her head against his.

After a few moments of letting their bodies say hello, Alvin resumes the topic they've been discussing as they look through photos. "I still think you should tell your dad. I kind of think you owe it to him."

"Why? What possible reason could there be for me to owe it to him?"

"It's his fucking wife. Like, legally, even, there are ramifications for her ditching you two. And now, you're saying she's here. Like, she's legit here, pretending to be someone else. And you don't think you should let him know?"

Pangaea told Alvin about Persephone two weeks ago.

"That woman isn't my mother. I've already explained that to you. And, technically, they were never married. They just lived together and they—or, at least, he—thought of it as marriage."

"Pan, let's get real. She *is* your mother. Like, legitimately, actually. And was fucking looking at you on a weekly basis for months without saying anything. That's gotta be illegal or something."

"Alvin, honestly. I don't know if this is something you can understand, I really don't. I feel nothing for that woman. In fact, maybe the closest thing I feel is pity. If anything at all."

"That's fucking crazy. You're fucking crazy."

"Maybe so. And yet," she leans closer to him and whispers into his ear, "here you are. Next to crazy."

They interlock fingers and squeeze.

"Here I am."

They continue to distractedly look through photos, all of which they've seen countless times before. Alvin does pause on one, though, a photo of he and Pangaea: she's pressing an ice cream cone into his nose, and his eyes are scrunched up, trying, but failing, to contain his unrestrained laughter, saccharine bliss. A laughter that eats his whole face.

"Remember this one?" He hands her the photo.

"Of course. That's from Canobie Lake Park. What was that, like, our—"

"That was our 'second anniversary.'"

"Right. Do *you* remember how that day started?"

"No," Alvin lies with a smile that he knows she can read, "how about you refresh my memory."

"Certainly." They're close enough to appear Siamese'd together. "I woke up and texted you: *Hey, let's do something today*. And you said…"

"I said, *What's the occasion?*"

"And I said, *Let's call it an anniversary*."

"And so we went to Canobie Lake Park."

"Indeed. Only, you were such a wuss. You wouldn't even go on the elevator ride with me. The most intense ride we went on was that—oy, what do you even call it?"

"Zero Gravity. Where you're pinned against the wall, and the floor drops from under you. Pan, you may not have known it, but I almost vomited getting the nerve up to even do that one."

"And you may not have known it, Al, dear, but if I knew that, I probably would've just ditched you then."

"Well, lucky for me, you didn't know it."

"Lucky for you."

"But, you know…"

Pan can see he's trying to map out his words, that he's still along for the ride of his own thoughts as they gallop ahead of him, not slowing for him to catch up but forcing him to stick with their pace.

"You have to wonder, are we still there? Are we still in that moment? Maybe memory isn't just in our head but something physical. A limb that grows across time, not our bodies, and so you and I will be there forever in just as much a way as we're right here."

He tries to get closer to her but can't. There's no space between them, so all he does is friction warmth into their touch.

"But that means all Here is, all Now is, is just the fleeting sensation of our bodies touching time."

"Alvin, dear," she kisses his nose, "you're talking nonsense."

"Of course. And I know you understand it."

Then they leave the room. The world, for that matter. It's not their bodies that leave, remaining still in the room, in the bed as they do strip and unite their skin and close their eyes and somehow see each other more clearly than they could if they were to stare at each other, unblinking, from an asymptotically close distance. They see each other more clearly than ever in the singularity of their embrace because where they truly are is here:

At the cliff—the edge of the horizon where the blue of the sky and water melds together, the division blurred. To their left is a sunset, to their right the sunrise. The sky above a roseate marriage of orange and pink. Behind, the world is draped in the silver light of the moon where all the shadows sprint; the silhouette of their unity stretches over the mountains, and as they roll off the edge, plummeting toward the water, they know what's real is their belief that if they hold each other, then the memory of their Us will be infinite and—

They open their eyes and see each other.

"Alvin, don't ever let me forget."

"Forget what?"

And themselves reflected in the other's eyes.

"We aren't a fantasy."

He's so close that the motion of his lips moves hers, as if she's speaking with him. "Pan, we're here in plain sight."